# After Our Castle

THE CHRONICLES OF ALICE AND IVY, BOOK 6

# After Our Castle

by

KELLYN ROTH

Published by Kellyn Roth, Author
Wild Blue Wonder Press

ISBN: 978-1-7341685-7-0

Scripture quotations are taken from the King James Version (KJV).

Cover design by Carpe Librum Book Design
Line edits by Grace A. Johnson
Copyedits by Andrea Cox

Kellyn Roth, Author
Wild Blue Wonder Press
3680 Browns Creek Road
The Dalles, OR, 97058

contact@kellynrothauthor.com

www.kellynrothauthor.com

To Aimee, who wrote more of this book than I did—or at least, made me write more of it than I would have.

After all, what's a villain without their origin story?

# CHARACTER LIST

## IN KEEFMORE

Ivy Knight McAllen — our fair heroine.

Dr. George "Jordy" McAllen — our hero, sort of.

Mrs. Daphne Wright — also known as "Aunt Daphne," Violet's eccentric, widowed aunt, and a somewhat new citizen of Keefmore, a village in Scotland.

Agnes Graham — a girl who works for Aunt Daphne.

Duncan Graham — Agnes's illegitimate son.

Ena Owen — a widow with two small children still living and a dear friend of Ivy.

Bridget and Alistair Owen — Ena's children.

Wallace Lennox — a farmer, a widower, and a friend of Ena's late husband who has returned to Keefmore after a long absence.

Willie Lennox — Wallace's only son.

Mr. and Mrs. McAllen — Jordy's parents.

Tristan and Edith Kendrick — Jordy's sister and her husband.

David George Kendrick — Jordy's nephew.

Benjamin "Ben," Michael "Mick," William "Liam," and Thomas McAllen — Jordy's younger brothers.

Mrs. Abernathy — the pastor's wife.

Mrs. Grear and Mrs. McDermid — women of Keefmore.

## AT MCCALE HOUSE

Violet Angel — perhaps the villainess, perhaps another heroine. A former student of McCale House and Ivy and Jordy's dear friend.

Dr. and Mrs. McCale — owners and founders of McCale House, a school for children who are "different."

Felix Merrill — former student, current visitor.

## VISITORS TO KEEFMORE

Peter and Alice Strauss — Ivy's brother-in-law and sister who live in America.

Claire Knight — Ivy's mother.

## NEW ARRIVALS

Hamish — a baby.

Keith — a baby.

Molly — a baby.

Letty — a baby.

# SCOTS TRANSLATION GUIDE

Ach = "oh" or "ah;" sometimes used to express frustration or disagreement, as in "ugh"
Are no' = are not
A'right = all right
Aye = yes
Bairn = child
Blether = babble, talk nonsense
Bonnie = pretty
Braw = fine, good, nice-looking
Burn = stream, brook
Canna = cannot
Canny = clever; can also mean pleasant or nice
Changeling = a fairy or other inhuman creature who was swapped at birth with a human child
Chitter = chatter; to shiver
Clipin' = tattling
Coos = cows
Couldna = could not
Coulda = could have
Crabbit = crabby
Da = dad, father
Dafty = silly, foolish
Didna = did not
Dinna = do not/don't
Doesna = does not
Dreich = dull or gloomy, often referring to bad weather
Drookit = extremely wet, absolutely drenched
Eve = evening
Fash = to fret, get upset, or be angry
Faye = fairy, fairies
Flichterin' = fluttering
Glaikit = foolish, thoughtless

Gowk = from "gawk," meaning to stare vacantly; a fool
Hadna = had not/hadn't
Hasna = hasn't
Havena = haven't
Havering = to talk foolishly, to chatter
Intae = into
Isna = isn't
Is't = is it
Ken = know
Ken't = knew
Kirk = church
Lad/Laddie = boy, young boy
Lass/Lassie = girl, young girl
Loch = lake
Me = my
Minna = minute
Morn = morning
Nae = no
Needna = need not
No' = not
Noo = now
O' = of
Ontae = onto
Oot = out
Peely-wally = pale and ill-looking
Sae = so
Shouldna = shouldn't, should not
Tae = to, too
Tha' = that
'Tis = it is
'Tisn't = it isn't
'Til = until
'Twill = it will
'Twould = it would
Up tae high doh = to be in a state of nervous excitement
Verra = very
Wasna = was not/wasn't
Wean = literally "wee one;" a young child or baby
Wee = small/little

Wee Folk = small, imaginary beings; elves, fairies, or leprechauns
Weel = well
Werena = were not/weren't
Wha' = what
Wi' = with
Wi'oot = without
Willna = will not/won't
Wouldna = wouldn't
Woulda = would have/would've
Ye = you
Ye'd = you would; you had
Yer = your
Ye're = you're
Yers = yours
Yerself = yourself

"Cause me to hear Thy lovingkindness in the morning; for in Thee do I trust: cause me to know the way wherein I should walk; for I lift up my soul unto Thee."

~Psalm 143:8~

# CHAPTER ONE

*January 1, 1884*
*Keefmore, Scotland*

H appy birthday, Vee." Jordy McAllen propped himself up on his elbow and grinned into the dark, though as his eyes adjusted to the dim light, he could make out the pale form of his wife beside him. "Wha' will we do today tae calebrate?"

"Happy birthday, Vee." Jordy McAllen propped himself up on his elbow and grinned into the dark, though as his eyes adjusted to the dim light, he could make out the pale form of his wife beside him. "Wha' will we do today tae celebrate?"

Ivy stirred, her back arching off the bed. She shuddered. "What time is it?"

One thing that Jordy had discovered was that Ivy was a morning person ... after she got out of bed. That took a bit of time. Before then, she was positively incoherent. It was delightful. "Close tae six."

"Insanity. Go back to sleep." Yet she scooted over and cuddled against his chest like the wee kitten she was and sighed. "I thought you said seven today, to catch up for sleep lost."

"I did say tha', didna I?" His wife also hated getting up before whatever time she'd been told the previous night that they'd be rising. "But I'm up noo. Break yer fast in bed, maybe? I can arrange tha'."

She managed a soft laugh. "I thought you said that was an island benefit, too."

"Ach, I can do it one more day, love, even though we're home." They'd been celebrating the first year of their marriage, albeit a few weeks late, on a small island off the coast, and Jordy had done his best to make that time special.

However, for Ivy's sake, he'd had to clarify that this was not a new aspect of their relationship but rather an anniversary trip kind of thing. He hadn't had the heart to tell her that he couldn't afford to take a trip with her every year. He'd done it this time because she'd been drooping in the last months, and though she'd put on a brave face, he thought the long, cold days alone inside the cottage were responsible.

The trip had definitely raised their spirits, made their relationship feel fresher and newer. He breathed a sigh of relief for a crisis averted. They could still do this—the honeymoon stage, the excitement, and even, in little ways, the newness.

At least, that was the idea.

She stirred again, wrapping her arms around him and drawing closer. "Stay a bit longer, then go."

"Ach, an' now she's tellin' me wha' tae do again?" He tsked. "This is it, as th' lads always told me. She gains a small advantage an' canna let it lie. *Women.* Wha' will I do with ye?"

She shook her head with a somewhat despairing sigh, but her fingers stroked the small of his back. "Jordy ..."

"Sorry." The teasing wasn't easy for her, either. Ivy never quite understood it, and even when she did, it hurt, somehow, in ways Jordy didn't understand. He got the idea that there wasn't much teasing in the Knight family, whereas in Jordy's family, joking was just talking. It was how they communicated affection.

Small differences in expression told the teased party when it was more frustration, but to Jordy, that was all the same. When he committed to a relationship, any kind of relationship, both affection and frustration were a must. He couldn't have one without the other.

But Ivy hated to be frustrated, and she'd probably give up and die if she felt she had caused any negative feelings in the people she loved.

Her fingers traced his spine and slid lower. He shifted.

"Do ye ken ...?"

Again, her hand was wandering. Yes, the trip had been an excellent idea, especially if the benefits were still being reaped the day after their late-night arrival back at their home in Keefmore. As apparently they were.

Summoning all the brain cells he possessed at that present moment, he whispered, "Vee, do ye ken wha' ye're doin' tae me?"

"Mm-hmm ..."

"Then can we—?"

She sat up abruptly. "What about that breakfast?" Her tone was light, tinged with playfulness.

He flopped onto his back and moaned, then began to laugh.

"What is it?" she asked.

"I didna think ye could be ... Oh, never ye mind." He took her arm and pulled her on top of him. "We'll worry about tha' later."

Sometime later, Ivy still hadn't managed to get out of bed except for a brief moment half an hour or so ago when she had washed, found her nightgown, and slipped back under the covers. She hadn't asked again, but she had an idea it was nearing seven now.

Jordy stuck his head through the bedroom door. "I decided I'd best run up tae th' office, but I've left toast an' tea. Ye might want tae check tha' th' tea's done right."

"Oh, you're leaving?" A sad note, a confused note—hesitant with a bit of *tremolo*—played.

"Aye, I'd best. Try tae get oot o' bed before th' day's half gone." He winked and stood looking at her for a long moment, then he turned and left.

Ivy fell back on the pillow and bit her lip.

It hadn't worked.

Of course, it was unreasonable and emotional, the things she expected of her man. Though it wasn't, she supposed, that she expected them. Just that she *enjoyed* them. She held Jordy McAllen up to a standard that no human being could hope to reach, and her disappointments were, therefore, kept to herself. When only God Himself could hit the mark Ivy was aiming for, it was necessary that she shut her mouth when Jordy's humanity seemed, to her, irritating. Better to encourage him, to build his self-esteem, to tell him he was her hero—and dare him to keep it up.

He could've stayed another half an hour and eaten with her, though.

"Lord, I am growing bitter again," she whispered. At least, she termed it as bitterness. All of Jordy's attention was not hers, and it hadn't been for several months, and she missed that. Just thinking about it made her stomach hurt.

Jordy was devoted. She believed that, if only because she said it to herself every day. It wasn't Jordy's fault. It was *Ivy's*. It was her fault that she wasn't happy with the innumerous blessings God had given her.

Jordy adored her. She believed that, if only because she said it to herself every day. It wasn't Jordy's fault. It was *Ivy's*.

Over and over again, she repeated these words to herself, for if they weren't true, she didn't want to know. She'd rather die than not have those words—life-giving or veneer-maintaining, whichever they were—be true.

Perhaps Ivy was equating the wrong things to health. That could be because they hadn't been wed long—a year wasn't much in the grand scheme of things, she'd found—and there was so much to learn. Never before had she engaged in something so challenging, but apparently marriage was a lifelong education. Since she was learning, it was easy to look for markers that weren't the most sustainable for relational health.

Yes, that was it. She was confused. What else was new? She sighed and stood, made her way to the kitchen, and washed her face and tied back her hair. She ought to sweep the house and make the bed and get dressed.

Yet she lingered in front of the stove, stoked by her *thoughtful—* she must remember that—husband, enjoying the heat and daydreaming. The spring and summer had been so much easier. They'd been what she could only begin to describe as madly in love. There had been adjustments during those first three months, but good adjustments, and then the summer had been utterly delightful.

But now where were they? For the winter had come again, and Ivy doubted. She doubted she was qualified for this position she'd thrust herself into. She doubted Jordy had quite understood what he was getting into.

Ivy was no fool. Jordy had taken her on the trip because he'd seen how she was drooping. There had been no mention of a planned journey on either of the days when they might've chosen to celebrate their anniversary. He'd come up with it last minute, and granted, it had been delightfully romantic, and she'd enjoyed it thoroughly. She relished his company.

When she got his company.

That was the problem. There was never enough Jordy for Ivy. Yet even when Jordy could cut a corner and spend more time with her this winter, he didn't seem to want to. He always went to his parents' or to see Tris or to participate in some town event or to be with friends, and yes, he took her along with him, but that wasn't the same.

It was to be expected. Jordy worked long hours, and when he wasn't working, it was hard for him to fit into his family, his friends, and the community, which, in Keefmore, was as good as saying 'his church.' He was always out of the house before dawn and late for dinner, and sometimes sick people would take him away at any hour. In her company, this made him nervous, ever-listening for a knock at the door. He claimed it didn't wear at him, but of course it must.

It certainly wore at Ivy.

She took a deep breath in and out, walked into her bedroom, and began making the bed. The bitterness would get her absolutely nowhere.

She flipped the blankets back a bit more aggressively than need be, with enough force that she almost apologized to the quilt before realizing that, even when alone, that was insane.

Then she laughed at herself. She could laugh at herself, couldn't she? She just had to make herself do so more often. It was so good to laugh at oneself, Ivy felt—absolutely necessary to growth as a human.

"Lord, I want to grow," she murmured aloud. "I want to grow and flourish as a woman, as a wife ..." There was no third category to place herself in. Unless she wanted to say daughter, sister, daughter-in-law, friend. All perfectly fine categories. "*Stop it*," she mumbled. "You need to stop it. The boundary was placed; it is firm. Respect it."

Yes, she'd respect that boundary, set so irrevocably by her husband, who certainly knew best, and leave that third, unspoken category alone for now. Jordy was a doctor—both of medicine and the mind, though he always said he wasn't educated enough to claim the second title. She trusted him, and what he said she couldn't take ... well, she believed him. He always celebrated her triumphs; therefore, she was safe to trust in his judgments of her abilities.

But in the meantime, what did she do? For she needed *something* to do.

She glanced around the bedroom. Every morning, she made the bed, she straightened the room, and she picked up Jordy's nightshirt and placed it back in the drawer. Then she walked back into the kitchen. There, she would sweep, she would wash any dishes, she would cook small meals, and perhaps she would spend time reading the notes Nettie had sent her off with—though by now she'd memorized them.

She'd clean the windows three or four times a week. During the summer, she had experimented with gardening, but she wasn't Aunt Daphne. She wasn't going to weed in the snow. Though Aunt Daphne had the best soil in Keefmore, so perhaps there was something to raking over frozen ground again and again. Of course, there was always her cat Heather to play with, but Heather seemed to get fatter and lazier with every day.

There was also an empty room which contained odds and ends, mostly Ivy's trunks and some extra clothes. She never went to that part of the cottage unless she needed to get something out of storage.

There wasn't much cleaning or cooking to do. There wasn't *anything* to do.

Jordy thought she liked it that way. He'd come home and 'take care o' things.' He fixed anything broken, he helped clean, he helped cook, he helped and *helped*, and then Ivy had nothing to do for those long stretches when he wasn't home.

No, when she thought about it, she wasn't angry at Jordy. She was angry at herself for not finding anything better to occupy her time. Yes, she'd walk up to the church some days. Play the piano. She'd visit Ena, Aunt Daphne, other women. There were the weekly meetings for tea with the women of Keefmore, there was church, there were other activities about the village. None of it helped.

"Lord, what is this?" She felt empty, and she was angry that she felt empty. This was supposed to be her dream—her calling, even. This was supposed to be her 'happily ever after.'

How dare she be discontent? There was no point in it. God had called her to fulfillment as surely as He had to anything else.

"I can be happy," she whispered. "I can find ways to make myself happy with the blessings I have been given and not wish for more, endlessly more." Ivy knew enough of human nature, even if she hadn't experienced it herself until now, to know that nothing would ever be enough. There was no such thing as arriving. What was that quote? 'Know one's own happiness' or something like that.

Ivy's joy must come from God, her contentment from His love and blessings. She wouldn't find it elsewhere. She couldn't. Human nature would not allow her to do so.

"Lord, what am I going to do?" she asked. "Jordy knows that I'm not happy. I can tell he knows ... Oh, *that trip!*" She almost wished he'd never taken her, for having Jordy's complete attention had left her even more frustrated with the life she'd been given.

"Jordy has a daily purpose. He works hard as a doctor, he comes home, and he serves me." She dropped her face in her hands. "I have Jordy for those brief hours, and I can serve him. Then I have this house to clean ... but there's not much to clean. Then I have meals to cook ... but that doesn't take me long anymore. So what then?"

A great deal of Jordy's purpose came outside the home, but Ivy had always been led to believe, and this had been further driven into her mind from watching the women of Keefmore, that a woman's place was to create a home, not to go out into the world like a man.

Of course, with the exception of Aunt Daphne, they all had ...

"Children," she whispered. But she never let herself linger overlong on that thought. Even now, she pressed it down deep inside her, to a place where, if there was despair, it was too dark to be thoroughly examined.

There was no use in hoping or dreaming of what could never be. At least not in the foreseeable future. She sighed, and she went on with her life, and pretended that all was well.

There was a great deal more pretending in Ivy's marriage than she'd expected there to be.

Once she was dressed and most of her morning tasks completed, she picked up a book that she had read over and over again and opened it. It was the first time she'd read *Emma* since the spring, and she gasped as two crushed daisies fell out from between the pages.

Oh, she'd forgotten she'd been experimenting with pressing flowers.

Ivy knelt to collect them and the petals fell off in her hands. For some reason, this made her laugh, and the sound startled her. She'd been alone too long. She went to the door and threw the dismembered petals out into the snowy yard, watched them flutter down onto her icy garden.

*He loves me, he loves me not, he loves me, he loves me not ...*

Yes, she'd definitely been alone for too long.

She donned her warmest coat and a hat and a muffler and walked over the hill to the village. She tried not to do that too often on the coldest days, for Jordy had expressed a concern that she would slip and fall and he wouldn't come back until dark. Ivy was never one to ignore a concern. However, today it couldn't be helped. Sitting alone in that cottage all day, no matter how much she usually liked it, just wasn't to be borne.

She couldn't do it. Not again. It was the first day back, and she ought to be stronger, but she wasn't.

"I'm going to adjust," she said as she walked across the frozen moor, as she took in the sight of smoke rising from the village, the sunshine causing mist to swirl up from the ground. Her chest caught, but she forced herself to breathe, pushing out harsh huffs of icy mist. "I'm going to be so happy! And content, more than that. I'm going to give God permission to work through me because I won't sit and whine. I'm going to keep moving—keep moving somewhere, even if it isn't always forward."

She could do it. She could. What if she ... what if she asked for more to do with the church? Of course, everyone in Keefmore, especially the ones with children ... they needed help. The teacher might need help, too. She always seemed so worn out that perhaps she would welcome Ivy's assistance.

Tomorrow would be Wednesday, and she liked to go see her friend Ena on Wednesdays. Then after that, she would stop by the school and then in the evening, go out to see Edith, perhaps, and the other McAllens. Yes, that would be fine.

Today, of course, she'd go see Aunt Daphne. That was always a comfort. She dashed between two buildings and onto the main street of Keefmore. In the village, there was noise, there were people. She was glad of that, if of nothing else. Then it was a quick walk, her steps brisk, to Aunt Daphne's ridiculous little London townhouse dropped into the middle of the Scottish moors.

She let herself in, knowing that at this point in the morning it was unlikely Agnes wasn't in the kitchen and Aunt Daphne never listened for the door.

"Aunt Daphne?" she called as she shucked off her coat and the heavy boots she wore when it snowed. "Aunt Daphne, are you there?"

"Ivy?" Aunt Daphne's voice came from the room that was slowly being converted into a library. "Come help me with this."

Ivy hung up her coat and muffler and hurried through the open door. Mrs. Daphne Wright, aunt of Ivy's dearest friend and British transplant to Scotland, was struggling to lift a large wooden shelf into position. Ivy rushed forward and helped the middle-aged woman lower it to the ground.

"Ivy, I wanted it to go up, not down." She frowned as she regarded the wall skeptically. "Of course, I'm not sure how we'll manage it, but—"

"I think we should wait and let Jordy do it," Ivy panted out. "I can—"

"Nonsense. We can manage. I'll just call Agnes. She's taller than you."

Ivy knew better at this point than to even protest. Aunt Daphne would not be stopped once she had decided upon something. "Very well."

Agnes was brought in, and Ivy was given the charge of young Duncan, Agnes's son, while the servant helped Aunt Daphne hang the shelf. They only dropped it five times before they managed to get it hung, and it was only a little crooked. Ivy tried not to look at it, for she had a feeling she'd go a little insane if she overthought Aunt Daphne's shelves.

She wondered if Jordy would be willing to come in and redo the shelves while Aunt Daphne was away. It was going to bother Ivy until he did.

Ivy turned her attention back toward Duncan. He was a perfectly civilized three-year-old, but he was still a three-year-old. He had some carved blocks, which Jordy had made for him that Christmas at Ivy's suggestion, and they built three houses only for him to tumble each one over.

Which was exactly why Ivy avoided playing blocks with her brothers, but she was starting to get to a place where she could enjoy crashing over the blocks.

Then Duncan managed to knock over the blocks before he was ready to do so, leading to tears, and instantly he was changed from the most independent and boisterous child Ivy had ever met to a soft, cuddly creature who sobbed on her shoulder.

Agnes ignored him.

Ivy supposed, in some ways, her situation was good, as she wasn't quite sure she could ignore a crying child even if the child's reason for crying was irrational. After all, a lot of her own reasons for crying were irrational.

Ivy left without talking to Aunt Daphne, not sure how to begin. Back at home, she spent over an hour trying to light the stove again and cursing her own lack of experience.

# CHAPTER TWO

*February 5, 1884*
*McCale House*

Violet Angel paced the confines of her room, her body feeling tight and loose all at once. Her thoughts were bouncing about within the confines of the prison that was the self, and she rubbed her arms, pressed her hands to her stomach, and dragged her tingling fingers through her hair.

It wasn't a good day. It just wasn't. Yet she had gotten up and slipped out of her nightgown and into a day dress; she'd left her bedroom behind and made her way up to her attic chambers, lined with bookshelves and bad memories. She'd brushed her hair, though it had long tangled into knots again. She didn't want to bother combing it again. Not yet, at least. What did it matter how she appeared?

Yet if she was going to have one of these days, at least she was at McCale House. She swerved around a pile of books to the window, where she pulled back the edge of one of the heavy blackout curtains. Bars cast slants of harsh sunlight over her face, bright from the fresh-fallen snow on the ground three stories below. She sighed and dropped the curtain back in place, returning to navigate slowly through piles of books, cast-aside blankets, and childhood trinkets in this ghost of a room.

Her breath came in harsh pants as her chest tightened, the anxiety increasing. Her heart was thudding in her ears, and with every beat, another image flashed before her eyes. Spinning words, scenery, faces, ideas. She sat down at last on one of the two chairs before the fireplace and cradled her head in her hands.

"Violet?" A rap at the door. "Can I come in?"

She couldn't respond. Instead, she whimpered.

As she had known it would, for her privacy wasn't respected here or anywhere, the door opened. "Violet, what is it? Are you awake?" Mrs. McCale's soft voice held all the concern of a mother, but she wasn't a mother, and anyway, she was always asking questions.

Of course that must be asked even though Violet was plainly out of bed—out of her bedroom, even—and dressed, for she was prone to horrible nightmares. All the same, it irritated her enough that she managed a reply despite her difficulty remaining composed. "What does it look like? Am I known for sleep-dressing? That'd be a new development. Something new for the old case book."

Mrs. McCale sighed and crossed the room to perch on the edge of the chair opposite Violet. "You're having a difficult morning."

Violet rolled her eyes. "It's that obvious?"

"Aye." Mrs. McCale shifted, then half rose and removed a book from under her, setting it on the pile nearest to the chair. "On your first day back, too. What a shame. Will you stay here today? Or will you finally take my advice perhaps?"

Violet shuddered. Mrs. McCale always thought that moving onwards was Violet's best option on these shaky days. Violet wasn't sure if that was true, though sometimes it did help.

One thing she did know, though; it was usually easier riding out these periods at McCale House than anywhere else in the world. Well, relatively. She had rarely felt this way at Keefmore when she visited, but she tried to avoid visiting too much these days. Granted, she had last summer, but since then, she'd split her time between her parents' house—even though it was quite difficult—and McCale House.

She'd learned to visit Felix Merrill while she was in London, if only because it allowed her to be mean, but that was merely a slight relief. Felix was one of the few people she'd made friends with during her time at McCale House other than Jordy and Ivy—and even then, it wasn't so much a friendship as someone who she tolerated slightly more than other people.

Felix amused her, and he had something helpless and innocent about him, similar to Ivy. Actually, he was far more helpless than Ivy ever would be—and much more nervous, too. He seemed more grounded in reality, though, than her precious Trifle. Ivy never felt quite of this world. There was something faye-like about her.

"Violet?" Mrs. McCale called her back to the land of the living with a somewhat impatiently-cleared throat. "Why don't you come down and watch the children play in the garden for a while? The fresh air will be good for you."

Violet shuddered. "It's cold."

"All the better. It'll clear your head. Besides, we can walk together."

"I'd rather walk alone." Violet hoped this would lend a reaction in Mrs. McCale. She wanted to push her away. After all, she'd bother Violet constantly otherwise.

Yet Mrs. McCale barely reacted. She just nodded. "If that's what you prefer."

Violet didn't particularly prefer being alone, but it was also difficult being with people. In general, all states of existence, accompanied and unaccompanied, were alike in their level of disagreeableness.

"I'll go," she said, when Mrs. McCale made no move to rise. Violet stood, her legs shaking. "I just have to get my coat from my bedroom."

"I'll wait downstairs. I have to get one of the students to go out, too, I think." She left, and a few minutes later, after collecting herself, Violet slipped through the doorway, traversed the quiet, empty hall, and entered her bedroom. In this small area, that was no more her space than it was anyone else's, she collected her coat, gloves, and hat, and slipped on a pair of heavy winter boots. That ought to do, though she figured she'd still be cold.

She opened the drawer on the bureau near the bed and withdrew a journal. Perhaps she could attempt sketching again while she was outside. It had long been a goal of hers, but she had yet to feel even a basic competence in the art form. Her dogs looked like horses and vice versa.

As she lifted the journal, a slip of paper fluttered out. She sighed, bent, and plucked it up. Oh yes. Yet another of those stupid little notes, forever reminding her of her own stupidity.

She unfolded it and read the scraggly handwriting on the much-loved missive, the scrap of paper she had carried about like an idiot for several years before tucking it away.

The words were simple, yet the meaning to Violet was deeper than what they were meant to convey.

> *Dear Vi,*
>     *I didna catch ye this morn, but I've a mind to have a picnic at noon. I asked Dr. McCale, and he said nae. I ken if ye ask, we'll have a better chance at it. Do, and I'll be friends with ye for life.*
>     *Jordy*

The letter had been slipped under her door one spring morning, and she had at first disregarded it, then decided, a child of twelve though she'd been, that a lifelong friendship was worth pursuing.

Jordy McAllen didn't consider himself her friend anymore. She'd lost that position years ago, sadly. But that wasn't Violet's fault—at least, sometimes she pretended it wasn't.

In reality? Oh, it might be. There were factors involved, though, that *felt* beyond her control. Jordy was remarkably impatient, and he seemed to struggle to keep his promises.

Not that he remembered, probably, having made this one. Violet never forgot a promise, though, and breaking one always stole a little more of her humanity.

She tucked the note back into the journal. Time for fussing about that later. It was hardly worth a second thought.

Violet left her bedroom behind and took the side staircase down to the second level. In the hallway, she met Felix Merrill, who was similarly bundled to the gills in winter clothing.

"Mrs. McCale?" she murmured wryly.

"Mmph." His voice emerged from behind his muffler, which he had tucked up to the rims up his large spectacles. Felix was another student of McCale House who had since left. Only, he had left McCale House permanently, whereas Violet was an evergreen resident. Felix was only just coming back for a few days to visit. Even as he stood there in the hall, seeming unsure if he should walk with her, his hands fidgeted—some things couldn't change, even after years of whatever it was Dr. and Mrs. McCale were trying to do with their students. Sometimes Violet thought they were trying to help—other times, torment.

Felix felt quite helped; Violet did not, and yet there was not any way for her to be helped, so that was hardly surprising.

He gestured forward at last, his indecision perhaps breached by the uncomfortable silence. "Are you here on your way to Keefmore or just staying at McCale House?"

Why did everyone always assume she was on her way to Keefmore? She proceeded down the hall in front of Felix. "Yes and no. I'm not 'just' staying at McCale House; my stay may be somewhat extended. I'm not sure I shall go to Keefmore. Perhaps as it gets warmer ..." Though she rather doubted it. "These last few weeks have been difficult."

Felix nodded, not questioning her claim. That was one good thing about him. He understood difficult weeks and yet felt no need to pursue a further conversation on the subject. He was quick to learn, and one thing he had learned was that his empathy toward her was not often rewarded. She knew he had learned this because she had told him so on multiple occasions.

As they walked down the stairs, the odd vibrations that had been shaking her heart stilled. There was something calming about just making herself move, though usually it took much more for her to shake these types of moods. Hmm. Perhaps she was getting better.

"How are you feeling?" Felix asked. "I mean, presumably not well, but well enough?"

"Well enough." She didn't intend to expand upon it, though.

Again, silence fell between them. Based on Felix's constant shifting, he didn't care for it. They left the house behind and entered the snowy grounds.

"H-how are Ivy and Jordy?"

"Also well enough, I suppose." She wasn't going to give him further details. She didn't really feel like talking about them, either.

"No children yet?"

Violet couldn't help it; she winced. "No. At least, not as of Ivy's last letter." The words came out clipped.

Of course Felix noticed. And of course he turned sideways to face her. For some reason, instead of continuing down the path as she should've, ignoring his searching eyes tucked behind his large, thick-framed spectacles, she stopped in the path and faced him. "Please tell me that's not still going on, Violet. I thought surely ... I mean, you gave no signs of it at the wedding."

Violet practically growled in frustration. Why had she ever confided in Felix? She should've known better than to tell him anything about her personal thoughts or feelings, for he would always remember.

"You do care for him still!" Felix's eyes were wide. "Violet, what are you going to do?"

"Nothing! I don't care about him at all. I just care about Ivy." The lie she told herself every day had never been strong enough to actually equip her to push through, but still, she said it. She knew she was a liar; why would she believe herself? But Felix ... Felix sometimes believed in her still.

"I wonder if that's really true." He cast her a skeptical glance. "Or are you just saying that? Because I'd genuinely like to help. I worry for you. All alone ..."

"I'm not 'alone.'" She smirked. "There's always the voices in my head, telling me to do violent things."

"Don't joke about this."

She had to joke about it. If she didn't, it would become all too real. Violet cleared her throat. "You know, I think I'll finish my walk alone. I see one of the doctors over there—why don't you go talk to him?"

Felix hesitated, then nodded. "I suppose I did mean to speak with ... But do you—?"

Before he could finish the thought, Violet turned and scurried away. She wasn't in the mood for speaking on this subject—not that she was ever in the mood.

There was a lot to be said, but it could never be. Not to Felix, not to anyone. Her devotion to Ivy—and more than that, her commitment to Ivy's happiness—kept her lips sealed. No, she would never betray Ivy ... and neither would she say anything to her precious Trifle that caused her to doubt her marriage.

For Ivy would doubt. Her nature required it, and that she would try to find excuses for Violet. The last thing that Violet needed was excuses. She knew what she was, and she knew how she ought to behave, but her heart was stuck on an infatuation with a man who both hated her and was married to the woman who had been her salvation.

Perhaps it wasn't just an infatuation, though. She should give it a harsher word. She lusted for him—wanted him to give her something that he never would. A sense of self-worth, perhaps—yet that wasn't an accurate description, either. It was indefinable. Her desire for Jordy McAllen always had been.

So it went on and on, never quenched ... and it wouldn't be. What would it look like for the desire to be completely satisfied anyway? She wasn't sure. She'd never let her thoughts follow the path they were on to their natural conclusion. Perhaps there wasn't a conclusion.

She'd struck out around the mansion, following a slight footpath beaten in the snow by many students enjoying the few hours of sunlight on this February day. It was only natural that eventually she came on a group of such students.

Violet stood at a distance and watched them frolic in the snow, a group of boys and girls, perhaps ten of them, of various ages, all guarded by several McCale House teachers.

She'd never joined such groups, nor was she touched in the way other people seemed to be by the rowdy playing she observed. If it weren't for Jordy, she never would've made a single friend at McCale House—and if it weren't for Ivy, she never would've befriended a student.

As she walked away from the group of students, she came upon a familiar bench that brought back the memory of a warm March day. She smiled and brushed snow off the stone seat before lowering herself onto it.

What a day that had been, though she hadn't known it at the time.

*March 1874*
*McCale House*

*From the window of her room, through the bars, she'd seen the sun and the green grass, and though she was currently at her worst, she began to long for something more. Something in the form of fresh air and light beating on her head instead of the continual darkness.*

*So, while Miss Lang was down in the kitchens, she slipped from her chambers and made her way outside, to her bench.*

*After perhaps fifteen minutes of sitting there, a rustling was heard from her left, and she looked up, then stood. There was Ivy—only Violet hadn't known she was Ivy then. She'd just known she was a* small thing, fragile but with the beginnings of rosy cheeks, her blonde hair loose about her shoulders, her blue eyes wide with a mix of eagerness and fright.

Her Trifle had been beautiful even then, and she'd stood there, like the angelic, wee fairy she was, staring at Violet for several seconds, saying nothing.

Fidgeting with the sleeves of her dress, Violet at last felt compelled to say something. "I suppose I'll have to go now." Back to her room, since she'd been discovered, even though it was only by another student.

Her Trifle shuddered, her eyes blinking and winking as if she'd just woken up. "Why?" Even then, her voice had a soft maturity, though Ivy's voice had deepened with age—becoming more like her mother's, Violet had learned later.

"I don't particularly like the looks of you, and I don't want to talk. But Dr. McCale wouldn't like that." Dr. McCale wanted her to make friends more than anything. Something about her requiring a proper social life for emotional and mental development. "He'd like it if I said, 'Do sit down and talk with me.' So do. Why not? Isn't my life meant to be controlled by the whims of the masses?" With that, she sighed and sank back down on the bench.

So her Trifle approached the bench, as if compelled by Violet's very existence to politely engage with her, and sat down next to Violet. "I'm Ivy. I'm twelve." She'd extended her hand.

Violet hadn't known a thing about Ivy then, so of course she shifted away. "Violet. Fourteen. I don't care to shake hands—or to be touched at all—so don't." Touching wasn't Violet's favorite thing. Granted, she craved physical affection at times but mostly in inappropriate ways. Or she assumed they were inappropriate—at the time, she'd branded those off-shoot thoughts and feelings as evil. Now she wasn't sure. Perhaps there was a place, for some women at least, to wish with longing for the touch of a man—proof of their beauty, their desirability, of being wanted for something, when worth nothing in all other categories. Violet had grown into these thoughts. Were *they inappropriate, though? Yes, they still were that.*

*Her Trifle's hand dropped back onto her lap. "I shan't."*

*Violet half turned on the bench then to examine her new companion. "Do you intend to sit here for a long time?"*

*"No. Yes. I mean, do I?"*

*Violet shrugged. "I honestly don't care what you do." It made little difference to Violet how this small creature behaved.*

*"Oh."*

*"I suppose you're here because you're ... how does Dr. McCale put it? Mentally undeveloped?" She rolled her eyes.*

*Her Trifle folded her arms over her stomach. "I'm here to learn. I can play the piano now." Her words were repeated from an adult, obviously.*

*Violet raised her eyebrows. Something about the trust and innocence such statements suggested intrigued her, and she poked at the faerie more than she should've. "That's nothing. So can I. Anything else?"*

*The girl wiggled from side to side on the bench, eyes downcast, wringing her hands nervously. "I can read better. Dr. McCale says I can learn other things if I don't get overwhelmed, but I get overwhelmed a lot."*

*"Hmm. That's what he says about me, only I'm likely worse than you—unless you're running away, too." Might as well get the confession out of the way so the little princess could tattle on her. Violet did so hate anticipation.*

*"You ran away ... to the garden?" The Trifle looked around her.*

*Violet glanced over her shoulder. Silly, perhaps, to the outside observer, but everything made more sense from inside one's own skin. "Yes. I'm not to go outside unless someone's with me, but I don't like people, so why would I want someone to come with me?"*

*"I don't know. Maybe you should learn to like people? I don't mind them. Some of them anyway. But I don't have all the ones I don't mind anymore." Then the little girl dropped her eyes to her lap. She seemed close to tears.*

*How uncomfortable. Now Violet was the one who wanted to squirm. "Indeed. I'm sorry. That's how the world works, I'm afraid. I have no one. I imagine you have a family who loves you or else you wouldn't be here; I have a family who hates me, and so I am here. Though, I suppose they couldn't have known I'd rather have died in Bedlam than live at McCale House." This was naïve, a product of too many recently-attained adult feelings in a not-yet-adult body. Now Violet knew just how hard the human body worked to stay alive—and she knew that the path toward stopping that life was not easy.*

*The girl's eyes rose to Violet's face, wide and full of what she would learn was Ivy's token empathy. "I'm terribly sorry. I hope you'll leave sometime soon."*

*Violet forced herself to look forward at a distant point rather than at the emotional child beside her. "No. I'll spend the rest of my life here. I've heard them say so. I'm a hopeless case."*

*"But you seem all right. I don't know a lot about what people call normal, but you don't seem any different from the rest of them."*

*"That's because I'm calm today. I'm at my best. Tomorrow or next hour or next minute, I'll be back to what I normally am. I never know how long I can handle things." Maybe that would scare the little girl away from her. That would be nice.*

*"Handle things?"*

*"I've heard them talking about me. You'll probably hear them talking about you if you listen. But I don't care and neither should you." Violet stood, a sudden jerk of nerves causing an action to be necessary, then lowered herself back onto the bench, her fingers catching the edge and gripping it. The stone was rough and felt good under her twitching fingers. "I'm not here to be the way other people want me to be. I'm not even going to try. I don't think I could be normal if I wanted to be, which I don't."*

*"I'm going to try to be what they want me to be. But I don't think Dr. McCale wants us to be anything different than who we are at our best."*

*"Perhaps." Violet might have said more, but Jordy's voice was*

*heard coming down the path, and at that point, as deep in the grip of her affection for him as she was, nothing more could be said to Ivy.*

*Yet somehow the friendship had proceeded—in spite of Violet. Ivy really was a wonder.*

Violet at last left her little bench behind, her memories having made her at once morose and guilty. Ivy was a true friend to her, but Violet had not been anything like that to Ivy.

Granted, she'd had a few moments when she'd allowed selflessness to take hold, but they'd been precious few and far in between. She hated hurting Ivy, but rarely did she fail to do that at least once per visit.

Besides, with Jordy and Ivy now happily wed ...

But was staying away an act of selfishness, too?

As she walked back toward the house, now chilled enough to long for a roaring fire and a cup of tea, she contemplated her decision to stay away from Keefmore

Maybe it was time to go back.

# CHAPTER THREE

The sun had dipped below the horizon hours before Jordy made his way back to the tiny cottage to the north of Keefmore. He'd not expected to be kept so long, but there had been a number of pressing matters to attend to. That always seemed to be the case these days. But he refused to rest when his work was his only daily way of proving to Ivy that he was worthy of her.

His feet slid slightly in the slush, and he minded his steps. Oftentimes the first thaw was worse than the original snow and ice, and he wasn't about to set a broken bone of his own—again. Not only was it inconvenient, but it seemed like a responsible man wouldn't do such a thing. Ivy McAllen's husband had better be responsible.

At last he arrived at the cottage and opened the door ... only to be met with a sight that caused a twinge in his heart with more efficiency than any illness or injury he'd treated throughout his career ever would.

His wife was sitting at the small, round table, her head resting on her arms. As soon as he entered the room, her head jerked up and she hastily scrambled for a handkerchief.

"Vee, wha' is it?" He shut the door and hurried forward, reaching for her, but she jumped to her feet and mopped at her red, damp face with a dishrag she'd apparently had sitting on her lap.

"It's nothing!" She panted out the words, the remainder of the sobs that had been shaking her shoulders a moment ago making the words come out disjointed. "Nothing at all."

That was nonsense. Though his wife did tend to cry easily, there was usually a reason, and if pressed, she could at least give him an indication of what it was. "Tell me. Please, love." Again, he reached for her.

But again, she pulled away.

Now, that was unusual. Ivy always scurried to him for comfort whenever it was available. What could be wrong? He glanced around the room to look for anything obvious—a book with an emotional scene, a letter from a family member or friend, a broken dish—but nothing seemed wrong. All he saw was their simple kitchen, the two places set at the table—hers was pushed back as she'd likely intended to cry there for some time—and soup simmering on the stove. As it always was when he arrived home from work.

"Was it tha' I was late?" he asked. Though that happened often, and she'd never expressed any kind of concern, it might be that it was getting to her. When he'd mentioned at a family dinner a few weeks ago that he arrived home at irregular hours, his mother had commented that that would probably be hard on Ivy, as she would need to have dinner ready at any time. Ivy had never complained, so he'd thought perhaps his mother was wrong; however, Jordy was beginning to realize it was best not to leave any matter unaddressed.

"No, no. It was nothing like that. Nothing related to you." She managed to move around him to the stove without allowing him to touch her, which, again, was strange. No hug? No kiss? No greeting of any kind? Granted, he didn't expect anything when she was sad—*she* was the one who needed something at that point, not him—but ...? To refuse affection?

"I canna help but feel tha' it is. Come here. Please."

Then the strangest thing of all happened. For the first time in their marriage—for the first time, in fact, since they had begun to explore the possibility of a relationship—she didn't respond to this request. "I actually want to get your supper on the table. You must be starved."

That made his suspicions of his mother's observations being correct all the more founded. "Ye are frustrated tha' I've no' had regular work hours, are no' ye? Ye have tae keep supper for me, sometimes late, like this eve. An' tha' canna be easy. I'm sorry. Could I do better for ye? Perhaps we could have a few nights a week where I come home or send word, nae matter wha'." He couldn't promise every night in his line of work, but his marriage was more important than his job. Even if sometimes the two were so intertwined that prioritizing one was a necessary part of fulfilling his duties of the other.

"It's not that. I don't mind keeping supper late." She paused at the sink to wash her face, then dry it with a towel. "Sit down. I'll have this stew ready in a minute."

He sat, befuddled. What more could he do? He'd done his best for her, and he was no saint, but if they were married, she couldn't just decide one day that it was time to shut him out. A mix of indignation and frustration bumbled their way to the surface, causing his chest to tighten. "Vee, ye canna no' tell me. I ken ye remember all we've tae uphold in our marriage. So why are ye here?" If the words came out a bit more reproving and irritated and a bit less loving and patient than he'd wanted, was he really to blame?

Perhaps.

Ivy's reaction, however, was not what he'd expected. She was a mild woman, always gentle, apologetic, even when she had no right to be. So when she whirled to face him, ladle in hand, eyes flashing, he leaned back on his chair.

Yet as quickly as the spark of anger had arrived, it faded, and the hand bearing the ladle dropped to her side. "It's nothing. I just ... didn't finish my chores today." She shrugged.

Was that all? He could understand her not wanting to share the thought then. After all, it was ridiculous. Yet Jordy thought he'd made it clear that he didn't mind if she was ridiculous—only that she told him the *why* behind it. There was always a *why* with Ivy, even if he had to dig to find it.

"Wha' isna done?" he asked as gently as he could manage.

"The ..." She cast her eyes, wide as if suddenly unsure what wasn't done, around the cottage. Strange reaction indeed. "The floors. I didn't sweep today."

Right. Because she'd done so yesterday, and there wasn't much need to. But all the same, if it was bothering her, it was worth addressing. Jordy adhered to that mantra strictly.

He rose from his seat. "Ye finish tha' stew. I'll take care o' th' floors."

He'd expected relief to fill her big, blue eyes, or gratitude, or for her to get unexpectedly emotional again. In the past, similar offers had been met with protestations, if only, he thought, because she didn't want him to do something that she considered *her* job. It was sweet how well she'd taken to homemaking, but Jordy wanted to make her load as easy to bear as possible. He'd do anything to prevent unhappy tears.

Yet here they were again, pouring down her cheeks. He caught the glint of them and heard them in her breathing before she turned back to the stove. They weren't happy tears, either. They were at least frustrated, if not heartbroken.

He stepped toward her, then stopped himself. If she was overstimulated or overwhelmed in any way, physical affection wasn't going to help. He stood still, hands clenching and unclenching, frozen in indecision. *Why do I always have tae feel so lost wi' her ...*

He tried. He tried as much as he could. And it had been so easy in the first year. Yet as the winter months closed in on them, and he began focusing more on his work, Ivy had seemed to slip through his fingers, an errant will o' th' wisp always a step beyond his grasp. Yet nothing had changed, save time. Surely it was all in his head.

Had he proven too flighty for her after all? Was she tired of his bumbling ways, closing him out of her heart already? If so, of course he would work harder for her. But that hardly felt like enough.

"It canna just be th' sweepin'," he said at last.

Her hands stilled. "I'm ... on my monthly."

He cast his eyes toward Heaven. "An' noo she's lying tae me. Vee, I ken ye are, technically, but tha' is no' th' cause o' these tears. No' on th' fourth day."

"It could be!" Her defensive tone reminded him of how stubborn she could be at times. No sane man would call Ivy McAllen truly *stubborn*. She always put others before herself, and that usually meant giving in easily in any conflict. However, when it came to personal convictions, she could be impossible to shake. Perhaps she ought to be. But this wasn't a conviction exactly, so much as an unexplainable quirk that he couldn't seem to understand.

At last, he gave up and simply swept the floor without another word. Actions, he could do. Even if it felt difficult in the moment, he could keep his mind to a task when it really mattered. Oftentimes the action exhausted him so he had little time for anything else, but that didn't matter. He could live his life exhausted—he couldn't live without *her*.

They ate dinner in silence—Ivy only tried to start a conversation two times in a falsely chipper tone before she gave up and just ate.

When they'd finished, he helped her clean up, and then they sat again.

Sudden inspiration struck him. "Come tae th' office wi' me in th' morn. We can spend some time wi' each other." He suspected that, having borne the last several days cooped up in the cottage due to not feeling well enough to visit her friends, she was simply tired of being alone. Easily mended.

"Do you really want me?"

He raised his eyebrows at this question. Whatever could she mean? Though he didn't want her at the office exactly—she tended to get in the way more often than not these days, and he didn't know what he'd do with her when he was called away to someone's house or farm as he wouldn't want her to walk alone in this weather—it was still a ridiculous question. After all, she couldn't know he felt this way. She'd always helped him in the early days of their marriage, not to mention before they'd even been properly courting. He did appreciate her help. It was just that he wanted her to feel free to be a housewife—not a doctor's assistant.

Now he'd left her query unanswered for too long, however, and he hastened to correct his mistake. "Of course I want ye."

A few beats of silence, then Ivy shook her head. "No. Not tomorrow, at least. Thank you, though, Jordy." There was no real sincerity in her tone, though she tried to fake it. Badly.

He always knew what she was feeling. For once, he wished he could pretend he didn't. Something was making her unhappy. If only he had an idea what she was *thinking*, too.

Why didn't she want to spend time with him anymore? It defied all logic and all knowledge he had of Ivy.

At last, he rose and decided to just go to bed. If he wasn't going to understand tonight, he might as well not waste more thought on it. Perhaps she was telling the truth—perhaps it was just a passing feeling that he couldn't fix.

There was a mist hanging over Keefmore on this late-February morn, and Violet appreciated it. There was nothing quite like fog for leaving an eerie feeling to the most simple things, like a familiar Scots village with a few hundred well-meaning people whose mental capacity, in her opinion, failed to reach basic intelligence levels.

Ivy said Violet expected too much of people, expected everyone to be well-read and well-educated, and frankly, Violet *did* expect that. Was it so much to ask? At least they had a school for their children now, but Violet didn't believe school ever taught anyone enough to be human in this world.

Ivy would frown at Violet equating humanity to levels of knowledge, but sometimes it was necessary. How else was one to measure humanity? If Violet didn't measure it by levels of knowledge, she would measure it by levels of goodness. Goodness was hard to measure, but one thing Violet knew was that she had none, and that ... Well, it wasn't a path she wanted to traverse again.

The coach jerked to a stop—the drivers who came through Keefmore were always annoying. Violet stumbled out of the carriage. Her legs always got in the way of walking, which was counterintuitive of them. She straightened her skirts and turned to tell the driver to get her trunk down and place it in front of the inn. Eventually, one of the McAllens would see it and take it to her Aunt Daphne's house. For now, she would do with her carpetbag.

If the trunk got stolen, that'd definitely be a story. Especially in Keefmore. Violet would find it most amusing.

She carried her carpetbag down the street and ducked between buildings. There was Aunt Daphne's house, now ringed by a white picket fence with a garden entirely desecrated by her aunt's overactive gardening.

There was almost never a time, except for maybe a month in mid-spring and another month in autumn, when Aunt Daphne's garden actually looked decent. Even Violet didn't mention it to her. It was a useless waste of time, for no one was surer of themselves, more set in their ways, than Aunt Daphne.

Usually Violet resented people who were set in their ways. However, her aunt was set in the most unusual and ridiculous ways, and Violet enjoyed the chaos. Especially since it was clear that to Aunt Daphne, it wasn't chaos at all. It made an interesting case study.

She stepped gingerly around piles of dirt and sod and made her way to the front door, where she shook slush and mud off her shoes as best she could, then walked in.

"Aunt Daphne?" She dropped her carpetbag on the floor. "Agnes? Where are you two?"

"In the kitchen!" came a muffled voice.

Violet sighed and knelt to begin the process of yanking off her boots. Perhaps 'in the kitchen' meant that tea was underway. She hoped so. Once again, that coach ride had left her chilled to the bone.

She never should've undertaken it in the winter—it wasn't worth it.

But she'd been restless, and Ivy's call was never one to resist. Besides, her brain had been slowly unraveling from lack of use. Much as she at times resented the people of Keefmore, at least they were entertaining.

Then there was always ... Her mind tried not to linger on the things that hurt too much for words, that cut deeper than anything had before in her life. She tried not to think about it because there was nothing good about feeling betrayed and abandoned, nothing good about being the third wheel on a wobbly wagon, nothing good about the constant loneliness and anger.

Violet had just managed to remove her footwear when Aunt Daphne emerged. "There you are," she said. "I'd worried the coach would be late and it would get dark and you would be attacked or something."

Violet raised her eyebrows. "No one attacks anyone here."

"I have no idea where you got the idea that Scotsmen were entirely tamed."

Violet shrugged. "Observation. Tea?"

"Yes, I've had Agnes prepare some and set it up in the library—oh, but it'll be cold now. We both got distracted ... Duncan spilled an entire bag of flour all over the kitchen floor, and we were cleaning that up."

"Oh." She'd forgotten that Duncan was anything more than a baby now, though she supposed he must be. For Violet, time was no longer linear—or perhaps it was, but she was largely disconnected from it. Whatever the reason for the disconnect she felt between reality and her own consciousness, it was a difficult balance to have. It was hard to look, again and again, at her own life and realize that it was the same and then to look outwards, at her friends, and see such a separation. She wished that she could find a way to slow everyone else down, for she was unwilling to go any quicker herself.

"What you didn't mention in your letter, though, Violet dear," Aunt Daphne said as she paced into the parlor and began the process of testing the tea to see if it was truly undrinkable, "is exactly *what* you're doing here and *why* you're doing it. I was dreadfully surprised to hear that you were coming, as you usually don't come up until the spring ... and actually I had begun to doubt that you would ever honor my home with your presence again after ..." She cocked her head. "Actually, I think I can say it. After Ivy got married. I'm not the type to dance around a subject, as you well know, so I will make myself clear."

Violet raised her eyebrows again. "When have you ever not, Aunt Daphne?"

"Never yet, so I decided now was not the time to start. I hope you aren't going to cause trouble."

Violet innocently regarded Aunt Daphne, doing all she could possibly do to keep her face clear of all expression "Whatever do you mean?"

"Only that I know you, and I know that at times you tend to ... Well, Violet, you like to make everyone else as miserable as you are. Or perhaps you often are—miserable, I mean. I don't know how true it is, but I want to believe you. That said, I hope you aren't going to interfere with Ivy and Jordy. They've worked so hard for what they have now, and I think they're doing well. Ivy never says otherwise if they aren't, and they're affectionate enough in public to lend credit to her claims of intimacy in private. Which was why I thought you'd stayed away. Frankly, it was the strongest thing I've ever seen you do."

Deny herself torture? How was that strong? Violet slouched onto a chair opposite her aunt. "How's the tea?"

"Quite cold. I'll have to get Agnes to make more ... or perhaps I can." Her aunt played restlessly with the plate arrangements. She never could sit still to save her life. It was something Violet liked about her, the hints of humanity—or perhaps, more than humanity, the hints that her Aunt Daphne was very like other people Violet had known. People who society rejected and sent away.

Violet didn't say people like *herself.* That was too hard to say, too hard to talk herself into bearing. In fact, it was in all ways impossible for Violet to admit that she had a similarity to her aunt or to anyone. However, she always thought it. There was a difference between thinking something and saying something to oneself, and Violet believed that the impressions of the two acts, or at least the emotion left in one's soul from them, were quite different indeed.

"I didn't come to bother Ivy or Jordy," she mumbled. "You should know that much about me. I would never hurt either of them."

"Really, Violet?" Aunt Daphne stood and walked toward the door, then paused. "No, I can't leave, can I? We're still talking. Violet, Violet, I hope you know what you're doing here."

"Playing with fire? Oh yes, it's my favorite game. I'm quite good at it, too."

Aunt Daphne let out a small huff that could almost be counted as a laugh, but her face remained serious. "I know you think you're good at it, but no one is. I doubt even circus performers last long without getting burned. And you're no circus performer. At least, not to those who know you well."

Violet shrugged. She wasn't particularly interested in what Aunt Daphne thought about her. Well, in some ways she was. She cared about her aunt more than perhaps she was willing to admit. There was a small link in this particular aunt between family obligations and the reality of Violet's life.

Yet at the same time, Aunt Daphne's constant, well-meaning interference got old. Violet needed to be independent. In this last year, she'd come to appreciate being alone more than anything. The silence of her own thoughts had once been torture, but a quiet, if not entirely good, *something* had entered her soul, and it now allowed her to appreciate the lack of other people in her life in a way she never had before.

She'd call it adulthood or having found love and known the full weight of it. Yes, there was a weight to love, a heavy weight, and Violet struggled at times to hold her shoulders straight under it. Certainly, with the obligation of love on her, there was little hope for some of her dreams, though they were nothing more than daydreams that she never expected to find any intransient reality.

Of course, there was the fire. Still, in Violet's control, and when she was alone, the embers were soft and warm, and she stared at them, at times adding some kindling to watch a brief burst of flame— and then the steady orange glow again.

Being in Keefmore was like adding paper, adding wood, adding big logs that would burn all night. Yet Violet risked it, for she knew the fire. She knew its properties, knew how they reacted together. And she knew, more than anything, exactly how to keep the fire behind the grate.

Here she was getting poetic. She followed Aunt Daphne, who had apparently said her full piece, to the kitchen, where tea was brewed.

"When was the last time you've seen our little friend?" Violet asked in a way, a tone, that she hoped was casual.

"A few days is all. She's having a hard time thinking of something to do in the winter, so I suppose it's good you've come. If you behave yourself." Aunt Daphne sent Violet another exasperated look. "You will behave yourself, won't you, Violet?"

"Of course I will, Aunt Daphne. When have I ever not?"

A deep sigh was her only reply.

# CHAPTER FOUR

I vy had her sleeves rolled up to her elbows, her hair tied back in a scarf, and her arms sunk into soapy water when a knock was heard at the door. She called, "Come in!" without looking up, confident that anyone who would come to see her at this time of day was a friend.

Then, immediately, fear seized her as she realized she could've just told some sort of robber or, worse yet, a *stranger* to enter her home.

Hairs on the back of her neck rose, and she hunched her shoulders. "Who is it?" she asked even as the door of the cottage creaked open behind her.

"So domestic, Trifle."

Then Ivy's hands were out of the washing tub, and she ran, heedless of driplets and droplets, to Violet. In moments, she had managed a tight hug and three soft exclamations about unexpected arrivals and how glad she was about this and that, and Violet was pushing away and moaning about Ivy having gotten her all wet. "Can you at least dry your hands before you ambush me?"

Ivy stepped back and wiped her arms on her apron, though it was already soaked enough that it made little difference. "You didn't tell me you were coming! Aunt Daphne mentioned that you were talking about it but not that you'd absolutely decided to come. How long will you stay? What shall we do together? I suppose I could come up and stay with you tonight, couldn't I? Jordy wouldn't mind."

Violet raised her eyebrows. "Of course, Trifle. Abandon your husband. You know I'll support you no matter the reason. However, I will ask as to the cause, since I will then know how to properly—"

"Oh, Vi." At least Ivy had the immediate benefit of knowing her friend hadn't changed. "I suppose I ought to be mad at you."

Violet stepped back, and for a minute, a kind of hurt passed over her face. That was surprising. "What do you mean? Because of that little jab? I didn't even think it through, Trifle."

"No, I mean, you haven't come in so long! I missed you terribly. Why, everyone who cares about you most is here, except the McCales—and you went home to your parents?" Ivy clucked her tongue, but she smiled, unable to remain serious. "Vi, we've missed you terribly. Why, even Jordy has! Though he never says it."

Violet slouched onto a seat at the kitchen table. "Forgive me if I don't believe your womanly intuition. He's angry at me."

Ivy shrugged. This was true, though neither of them could tell her why. They'd been feuding ever since Ivy and Jordy got engaged, but when asked, both of them insisted it was their normal quarreling.

Nonsense. Ivy had watched Jordy and Violet 'fight' with each other for years. This was different. This was at times meanspirited and almost always in a tone from Jordy that indicated Violet was to back off. Ivy wanted to hurt him whenever he treated Violet badly, for in some ways, Violet was an extension of herself. Meanwhile, Violet had sadness in her eyes.

Yes, they'd both either said or done something that had majorly hurt the other, and Ivy wanted to knock some sense into both of their heads. However, she wasn't sure how well that would work since the stubbornness of both Violet and Jordy was a well-documented fact. Especially Jordy. Violet at times could give in, if she could do so in a way that saved her pride. Once Jordy dug his heels in, Ivy had learned to immediately stop tugging on the lead and walk away so he could decide on his own that he was being a grouchy donkey. Besides, she didn't like to tug. It felt wrong.

Violet, however? She'd tug and pull and yank, even when she knew it would do no good. Frankly, there was usually a way to tug that let Violet feel like she was doing Ivy a favor, at which point things would be resolved.

Until then, Ivy walked circles around both of her favorite people as they stood bogged down up to the ankles in mud, refusing help. She considered the exits and brought them up and tried to get them to stop hurting each other. Sometimes it worked, and sometimes it didn't.

"I wish you'd at least tell me why Jordy is so angry at you." He'd put his feelings aside for the wedding, yes, when Violet had served as Ivy's maid of honor. Right after, he'd dropped all pretenses. He'd even gone so far as to suggest that Violet wasn't a good influence on Ivy's life and she ought to reconsider their friendship. That had been one of their first serious fights, and Ivy had told him she would if it meant that much to him ... and then cried for three days. Violet would call that a manipulation tactic, but Ivy couldn't help the crying. It was like he'd asked her to cut off her own arm; she had a grieving period to go through. He'd given up and apologized and told her she might as well be Violet's friend if she felt so strongly about it.

"Hmm, well, you know. Same as always ..." Violet drummed her fingers on the table, another incessant staccato rhythm. Ivy knew how much Violet hated staccatos—so many times, she'd heard 'play the note in full or not at all!' from her friend during their music lessons long ago. Yet staccatos were a tell, a sign that the music wanted to say something different. What did Violet's staccatos mean?

Stress? Fear? Loneliness? But lonely was more legato, and stress was allegro—it could be staccato, but it didn't have to be. Fear was more staccato, but Violet had nothing to be afraid of, and besides, Ivy associated fear with violins. She wasn't sure why.

Violet's fingers weren't making violin-type noises. Of course, they couldn't, but the staccatos were making more of a waltz pattern, as she tapped with her ring, middle, and pointer finger, and then back again, using her fingernails to accentuate the sound—tap, tap, tap—tap, tap, tap—tap, tap, tap.

Perhaps Ivy was overanalyzing. Violet dropped her hand onto her lap and leaned back, tipping the chair legs up in the way Ivy always told Jordy not to.

She didn't say anything to Violet about it.

"Anyway, I'm glad you're here. It's been ... difficult." She didn't want to go into more detail, but it had been difficult. She was so ready to be done with all the nonsense that seemed to have invaded her soul, making her ungrateful and exhausted. Why, the other day, she'd snapped at Jordy—her beloved Jordy, who'd done so much for her. He hadn't even commented on it, and when she'd apologized, he'd acted confused and assured her that if she *had* snapped at him, it had been in her head.

Entirely possible. Sometimes tone could be everything after all. But if in her head, Ivy had felt like she snapped, her intent had been to hurt, and that wasn't all right by any stretch of the imagination.

"What's been difficult?" Violet leaned forward and narrowed her eyes. "If Jordy's causing you any pain, I will hurt him."

Ivy frowned. "Vi, I wish you and Jordy would stop threatening to hurt each other over me. It makes me worry. I know you don't mean it—"

"Oh, I mean it." Violet's fingers returned to their table-tapping. "If he ever hurts you, I will hurt him, and I'm sure he'd do the same thing to me. Of course, I would never do anything to hurt you on purpose, and I'm sure you'll see that, so—"

"Yes, of course I would." Ivy returned to her washing, dipping her arms back into the now lukewarm water. "I'd know the same of Jordy."

"Hmm, yes, well." The drumming ceased. "You're right, I suppose. But what's the real reason you're sad? For it must be something, Trifle. You were never one to be sad for no reason."

That wasn't entirely true. Lately Ivy's discontent had been without any known reasons. However, she did have one thing. "I wish I had a baby."

"Oh." Then there was a silence. A long silence. "I, uh ... Oh. You probably shouldn't ask me about that. I'd ask Jordy. He has the, um, prerequisites for the ... I can't even make a joke about this. Are you not able to, um–?"

"I don't know." Ivy grabbed a dirty pot and plunged it into the water, causing even more of a mess. "Jordy doesn't want one." Not with her, at least.

"Oh." Ivy heard Violet shifting on the table behind her and felt at once how uncomfortable her friend was.

"I guess I shouldn't have mentioned it." What was the use of embroiling Violet in her disappointment, her shame? Why couldn't she just be happy? "I'm sorry. I won't speak of it again."

"No, but could you, um ... clarify?"

"What do you mean?" She squirmed at the idea of having to admit to Violet that Jordy wasn't interested in having a family with her, and that she wanted to with him, and that that fact was causing her a lot of unnecessary pain.

"I mean, what did he say exactly? Because you like to misinterpret the things people say. So grab a towel, wipe up, sit down, and tell me."

There was something about Violet's tone that brooked no argument. Reluctantly, Ivy stepped away from the washtub and slowly dried her hands and removed her sodden apron before sitting on the chair opposite her friend.

"Did Jordy say why he doesn't want children?" Violet's eyes were dark.

"No. We never ... we never exactly talked about it. He just ... on our wedding night ..." He'd told her he was 'taking care of things' and explained succinctly some biology she hadn't been aware of, and when, some months later, she'd finally gotten up the courage to ask for further details, he'd assured her she'd 'never have to worry about bairns' because of the steps he was taking. As if it were a guarantee that she wouldn't want them.

She had to finish the sentence somehow for Violet without laying any of *that* out. "He said *I* wouldn't want children." That was the best way to describe it, perhaps, without giving further details that she needed to keep private, as much for her sake as Jordy's.

"Then just ask him. He can be reasonable at times." Violet leaned back on her chair and cocked her head. "Have you thought of that, Trifle, in all your wonderings?"

"It's more complicated than that." If she admitted to Jordy that she wanted a child, she'd have to hear him reject her, say that he didn't think she was fit to be a mother. If Jordy didn't think she was worthy ... Jordy knew her better than anyone. Especially now, after this first year, when the scales were sure to have fallen off his eyes. "I'd feel so stupid asking for something that he clearly doesn't want. It's not just the words he said ..." It was the way he said them, the repetitive emphasis, the fear in his eyes. Fear of *her* failure. She knew it.

"Suit yourself." Violet shrugged. "But I think you should try talking. Not that I care about your love life, of course, but that ... Never mind. Other than wanting a baby, what have you been doing?"

"I've been—Oh! What time is it?" Ivy jumped to her feet.

"Close to noon, I suppose."

"I'm going to help the teacher at the village school!" She dashed into the back room. "I have to change and get over there. Will you come?"

"I think I'll just find Heather and catch up on what you're reading." Violet's voice from the other room held, now, a tired note that indicated that Ivy ought to let her be.

Ivy hurriedly undid the buttons on her still-damp morning dress. "All right! She's usually in the woodshed this time of the morning, and there's a chair in the corner with Peter's latest book. Also, a bit of Dickens—it just felt like that time of year."

Violet's moan was audible. "The time of year for depression? No wonder you're melancholy, Trifle."

Ivy shook her head and laughed as she hurried into another dress, leaving the other one draped over the bedpost to dry. With Violet here, how could she be sad?

Yes, everything would be all right.

# CHAPTER FIVE

iolet let herself into the back door of Jordy's office and allowed it to close softly behind her. He was in the front room, talking to a patient, so she sat on a chair in the corner with the book she'd stolen—another one written by Peter Strauss, Ivy's brother-in-law—and read.

Jordy eventually came back in, hid his surprise at her presence, and went to wash his hands in the bowl resting on the opposite counter. "When did ye come intae town?"

"Just this morning." Violet set the book down. "I went up to see Ivy, but apparently she has some sort of ... teaching thing?" She shrugged. Frankly, she hadn't understood what Ivy was talking about.

"Aye." He shrugged as he dried his hands on a cloth. "Aye, she's started goin' tae th' schoolhouse a few days a week tae help oot. I ken she's been restless, so tha' helps."

"She told me she—" Then she stopped, for she didn't want to take away Ivy's right to privacy, not even from her husband. "She mentioned she was sad. That these have been difficult months."

"Ach, she'll tell ye, will she?" His tone was light, but Violet knew him well enough to catch the frustration, the betrayal. *Good.* He'd apparently hurt her Trifle badly enough that he deserved to feel a little jealous. "She willna speak tae me on it. I get th' feelin' she believes I'd be disappointed in her." Jordy scowled. "I wouldna be. O' course I wouldna be. I understand th' winters can be hard here, especially when ye dinna have th' space or th' accommodations she's accustomed tae."

"Right." Plus, Ivy needed someone to serve for happiness. If she wasn't at all times giving everything she had to someone who needed her, she wasn't going to be content. But Violet didn't say that, for Jordy wouldn't understand, same as Ivy couldn't understand Jordy's natural passion for life. Jordy's *joie de vivre* was as real as Ivy's empathy, but they hadn't quite learned how to make the two fit together yet.

Violet personally wondered if they ever would.

"How was this wedding anniversary trip? Aunt Daphne mentioned it to me." She had an idea that some of Ivy's discontent stemmed from that trip, and she wanted to feel out whether Jordy had experienced the same thing.

"It was ... interestin'." Jordy walked back through the doorway into the front room and returned with his bag. Then promptly changed the subject. "I walked back wi' one o' me patients. I went tae his house down th' street, an' he just—"

"What does *interesting* mean, though?"

Jordy paused and narrowed his eyes at her. "Why would I tell ye?"

Violet shrugged. That was fair enough. "Because I'm a person who cares about you both deeply. I've made mistakes in the past, but I would never harm either of you. Ivy and I were talking about this earlier, actually." More or less. "She says I could never hurt her, but of course, if I wanted to, I could. You know I won't, purposefully, and I think I would die of guilt if I did by accident. I wouldn't hurt you, either."

Jordy opened his bag and began removing frightening-looking instruments that Violet was too tired to identify. Usually she would've been able to, of course, as she prized herself on having at least a general frame of knowledge on every field of science. Especially medicine, for she had studied it in depth with and without Jordy, wanting to impress him.

That was a long time ago, though.

It was a while before he spoke, but he finally did. "Why dinna I believe tha'?"

What a silly question. "Because I've hurt you more times than one, and sometimes I've done deliberately harmful things to try to get your or Ivy's attention."

"A'right. So wha' has changed noo?"

"With you or with Ivy?" Those were two very different sources of motivation for this new determination of hers.

"Either o' us. Nae ..." He picked up a handful of the instruments and carried them to the basin. "Vee first, then me. I'd love tae hear your reasonin'."

As if her reasoning would make sense as soon as she tried to speak it to life. There was no reason in a lot of what Violet *said* but plenty in what she *thought*, and it was best when it remained that way. "Almost since I've known Ivy, I've loved her. She does that to people. She did that to you, remember?" She still felt their relationship was greatly motivated by lust given that Jordy had paid Ivy barely any attention before she'd gotten her figure, but that was beside the point. "I realized at the wedding ... I realized a lot of things." Mainly, that the pain in her chest had gotten to the point where, if her own heart didn't take to attacking her, it would probably give up. She'd run. "After I had time to process them all, I began deciding how I would act upon them, and I've decided that action is never seeing her be hurt by me again."

At least, that was the idea. She wasn't sure how well it would work in practice, but she wanted to believe that she had it in her not to hurt Ivy. Not anymore.

Not about weddings that punched her in the gut with every bit of lace, every flower, every vow—or anything else. Not about a faith she didn't understand. Not about a love she couldn't accept.

"A'right, tha' makes a bit o' sense, I suppose. In some ways." He paused for a minute in his thorough scrubbing of his instruments.

"An' me, then?"

"Jordy, I've never wanted to hurt you." Not any more than she had to, of course, for his own good ... or to prove a point ... There were a lot of excellent reasons to hurt Jordy, frankly. However, as soon as she said them aloud, they again would not make much sense.

"But wha' does tha' mean? Wha' are ye goin' tae do?"

"I want to be a better friend." Though *friend* could have a wide variety of definitions. "If nothing else, I'm going to make sure you don't behave like an idiot. I worry that you'll hurt Ivy." Or himself. Or both, if neither of them learned to deal with their obvious issues. They had so many things to address before their relationship could be called even vaguely successful. Violet saw all the disasters, and she only hoped she'd be able to manage all of them before something horrible happened.

"Verra weel, then. As long as it doesna really hurt anyone ..."

"I won't. I won't hurt anyone." Least of all Ivy, and of course not Jordy. She'd sworn to protect and admire him, regardless of his actions, regardless of anything. She'd sworn that on the first day she met him.

*March 1870*
*McCale House*

*That morning had been different.*

*She'd woken up the same as always. Fought her way to consciousness, then fought with Miss Lang, then fought with Mrs. McCale.*

*She'd eaten breakfast. She'd bemoaned her existence. She was just on the verge of her womanhood, so a great deal of bemoaning was in order. At ten, she hadn't known what was happening to her, only things were changing, or would soon, and that it gave her extreme distress.*

Yet she still felt some affection for the McCales, especially for Mrs. McCale, as her feelings for Dr. McCale were more of respect, so she'd waited in the foyer with the rest of the staff and the other students and watched as the carriage rolled up and out stepped their mentor, Dr. McCale, the man whom Violet both loved and hated.

In some ways, he made her life very difficult. In other ways, he was her savior, the man she admired for tearing her away from the wretchedness that had been sure to follow her childhood if she'd been allowed to stay with her parents. The parents who hated her, who didn't want her, who would do anything, anything, to rid themselves of her presence in their life. Including sending her far away to the wilds of Scotland, where she was out of sight and out of mind.

She'd wanted more from her family then. Bitterness hadn't sunk in to the degree it had within the next four years. Yet she was more than willing to give Dr. McCale a chance to redeem her, too. She hadn't believed, fully, in her monstrosity. She was just beginning to realize it. Once Violet began seeing the way people treated her, it was all downhill. She knew they believed she was a monster. She just knew it.

On that bright day, she believed in nothing as she believed in Dr. McCale. In his absence, she had grown fonder, or at least curious as to whether he would once again make the difference in her day-to-day life. She had watched from the stairway, never quite in the group but never quite away from it.

Only he had someone with him.

From the moment Violet laid eyes on Jordy McAllen for the first time, her life changed inexplicably. He was young then, just twelve, and he had his hair somewhat shaggy and ill-maintained. He grinned at everyone, he talked a thousand words a minute in a brogue that was almost too thick to be understood by any Englishman—why, even Dr. McCale would ask him to slow down and repeat himself from time to time, which was definitely unusual, as Dr. McCale traveled to the Highlands often enough to hear everything from a thick brogue to *people who barely spoke any English at all. Some still spoke Gaelic. Jordy knew a little, and she'd later begged him to teach it to her ... but he'd tease her and give her the wrong definitions of words and in general, make himself a pain in her side, as always.*

*Yet she forgave him. That day was the reason why. That luminous day when she'd realized, once and for all, that she had hope, and her hope was in Jordy McAllen.*

*For he made her feel normal. He'd caught her eye out of the crowd and though he hadn't approached her then, he'd done so later.*

*"What are you doing here?" She'd asked the question with as much calm as she could muster. They'd been standing outside, Violet near her favorite bench and Jordy walking up with that cheery grin.*

*The grin had dropped.*

*"I'm here tae help Dr. McCale."*

*"Oh. Who are you?"*

*"Jordy McAllen. Weel, 'tis George, but nae one calls me tha'."*

*"Oh, 'dinna' they, then?" She rolled her eyes, already tired of the brogue even as she was intrigued by it. Honestly, even as she* enjoyed *it. It was thicker, richer, than Dr. McCale's, or anyone else's at McCale House. At times Violet could be made to love different things.*

*"Nae, they dinna." His eyebrows rose, and already at twelve, his posture was that of a self-assured young man. He'd always had that swagger. "Who are ye, an' wha' are ye doin' here?"*

*She let out a soft laugh. "You really are new here, boy. I'm Violet Angel, and you'd best leave me alone."*

*"Frightenin'. But Dr. McCale has told me about ye." He shrugged and lowered himself onto the grass, flopping back with a sigh. "'Tis a lovely garden."*

*Violet had practically growled in frustration. Who was this strange boy who'd come into her life and suddenly thought he could change the subject with no further notice? Violet never allowed people to change the subject. "What will you help with?"*

*"I dinna ken, but I'm tae be a doctor someday." His eyes were*

*closed and his body relaxed—in her presence. Impudent boy. "I'll just do wha' Dr. McCale tells me tae do, an' he says he'll educate me 'til I'm ready for university off in England."*

*"Oh." Almost like a son. Which was the position Violet thought she had with the McCales. No, not son, but child. She supposed they couldn't educate her on the same level, though she was certainly smarter than this long-haired, rough-accented country boy. "Why do you want to be a doctor? Where are you from?"*

*He glanced up at her. "Keefmore. Tae th' north. Me family owns a farm there, an' we raise sheep an' ... Weel, ye wouldna be interested." Again, he dismissed her with a half-hearted gesture and lay down.*

*"I would be." She had to get all the information out of him that she possibly could, after all. "Tell me at once."*

*So he'd told her, about Keefmore and his family and meeting Dr. McCale and his desire to do something big in this world. Though he hadn't said so, she'd at once sensed the difference in him that meant that Violet could, oddly enough, relate to this funny boy.*

*She'd made sarcastic remarks and insulted his intelligence and gone on and on about how much better she was than him, but in her heart, for the first time, she'd identified something new—in Jordy.*

Friend. *He was her friend.*

"Ena!" Ivy let the door of the shop jingle shut behind her. She'd just come from Aunt Daphne's, where she'd taken Peter's latest book back from Violet's grasping claws. She had three more chapters, and Violet's act of thievery had kept her up all night obsessing about it.

"Ena, are you here?"

"In th' back, Ivy!" Ena's voice was chipper. "Lovely tae have ye come this morn! Alistair's been a wee monster today—ach, I dinna mean tha'. He's been a *lad*, as always, an' I love him for it, but if ye could just hold him while I do th' laundry ..."

In moments, Ivy was settled in the kitchen while Ena wrung out tubs of white clothes and sheets and cloths.

"An' how've ye been?" Ena smiled up at Ivy, brushing strands of damp hair from her face. "Obviously no' tae busy, or ye wouldna take time tae sit in this steamy room an' watch me do laundry."

"I'm not very busy this year, actually. I don't really know what to do with myself." Sitting here with Alistair, who was very convinced he oughtn't be held now that he was two and was rambling in half Scots brogue and half gibberish, was all she had to do until Violet emerged next. "Frankly, it's been hard to find joy this year."

Ena nodded. "Th' winter months often do tha' tae me. Let Alistair down, an' we can see if he willna play wi' pots an' pans. He'll take tae bitin' if ye keep him still much longer."

Ivy let him down and arranged kitchen utensils to allow him to make 'music.' Usually she would've protested at this obvious perversion of beauty, but she was at the point in her desire for a child that that didn't matter much to her. Instead, she played with him and listened to Ena talk about how he was growing, how Bridget was doing in school, and so on.

"I admit I'm lonely half th' time." Ena paused for a minute and glanced down at Alistair and Ivy. "I love me bairns, but, Ivy, an adult tae talk tae—more than tha', a husband—is so needed. Ye should understand tha' noo. But havin' ye here at least gives me someone I care about tae talk tae, an' o' course th' teas help."

"I'm glad the teas help." Ivy's sympathy rose at the thought that Ena could ever feel lonely. Why, Ena had so much more to take care of on a daily basis than Ivy did. "Have you ever thought about ... about ..." She wasn't really sure if it was appropriate to ask, but she wanted to.

"Marryin' again?" Ena shrugged. "Nae, I havena. No' really. Although ..." A soft smile appeared, then disappeared. "Ach, never ye mind."

"Tell me! Who?" Ever since having gotten married herself, Ivy saw possible couples everywhere, in the most unlikely places. It had gotten to be a bit of a problem, but with Ena, it was different.

And for the first time ever, something strange happened. Ena blushed. Really blushed, with her face going red from the tip of her chin to the top of her forehead. "I ... he's no' really ... Tha' is, his name is ... Wallace Lennox. He's a farmer, an' a dear friend of me Bob from years past. I havena really seen him in years, but when his wife died, I suppose things got hard in th' village they'd been livin' in, an' he came back tae his family's land." She shrugged. "He's been comin' in here ever since."

"Oh!" That had the potential to be terribly romantic if Ena let it be. "Is he ... What's he like, Ena?"

"He's a good man, or at least he was. An' he's been nothin' but pleasant. He has a son, Willie, an' they live with his da noo, though th' farm is really Wallace's. He had a better time o' it last year an' seems tae be doin' well through th' winter."

"He sounds really nice," Ivy said. Hopefully, he'd come around the store sometime when Ivy was there so she could evaluate him, but she already had a good feeling about this. Could Ena's future be with Wallace Lennox? She hoped so, for she wanted nothing more than her friend to be happy.

"Ach, he is. But ye needna tell anyone I told ye this. After all, he's just a friend, an' we dinna ever talk or anythin'." Ena seemed embarrassed to have admitted that much. "I'm sure he doesna think o' me tha' way. At least, no' much. He's no' a bad man, o' course, but he's hardly ... He's no' Bob."

"But no one will be!" Ena had said so herself many times, so Ivy wasn't shy of reminding her of that fact. "Perhaps he could be someone different than Bob but still someone very dear to you ... right?"

"Right, right." Ena laughed softly. "But let's no' talk about it. It's just somethin' tae think on when there's nothin' else tae keep me mind from runnin' wild. But, in truth, there's plenty o' better things to worry about. I just have tae focus on those an' no' on things I canna control."

That was very wise. Ivy definitely understood the struggle. "Ena, could I ask you a question?"

"When have I ever said nae tae tha', Ivy?"

"How do you ... I think the phrase is 'hold every thought captive.' How do you do that? I want to not think about the empty places I see in my life. Instead, I want to be an open vessel God can fill with whatever purpose He sees fit. But it's so hard, Ena! I have so many things I want. Have I mentioned ...?" She looked down at Alistair, who was currently trying to stack one pot on top of another with mixed results and a lot of crashing noises. "I want a child."

Ena's eyes instantly softened. "Oh, Ivy. I think most women do. But ye ken ... there's nae rushin' such things. They take time, an' some women ... They take time for all women, but for some women, th' time is longer, or it never happens, an' tha' is just another way for God tae grow an' use ye. It's also Him sayin' yer callin' may be elsewhere. So live in th' moment, but ye must be patient, tae. He'll bring ye a bairn when He's a mind tae—an' if no', you will have used all th' time ye have wisely, for His good purposes."

That wasn't exactly the problem, but she still nodded, for it was right in theory even if the actual circumstances weren't what Ena believed they were. Usually, Ivy would have corrected Ena's assumption, but she didn't have the heart to tell Ena the truth of her situation. Ena felt like, in some ways, her only adult friend. She wasn't much older than Ivy, but she wasn't quite her age. Yet she still liked Ivy, still treated her like an adult, still related to her on similar ground.

That was priceless.

Ivy couldn't tell Ena the truth of Jordy's rejection, especially since she might try to talk sense about it, and Ivy wanted it to remain buried rather than sensible.

"Yes," she said at last. "Yes, I ... I believe you're right." Trust God. She needed to trust God to be in control of her life. She couldn't be Alice, in complete control of her own life. She had to just let go and trust that Jordy's decision was the right one.

For she could never even suggest to him that his decision was not the right one.

"I'll pray for ye, Ivy, same as I ken ye have always prayed for me." Briefly, Ena touched Ivy's hand before she returned to her washing. "Besides, this is oot of your control. There's nothing you can do to make this happen, noo is there?"

*Oh.*

# CHAPTER SIX

*March 7, 1884*

For the last two weeks, Ivy had been mulling over her thought process about a baby. She hadn't arrived at anything certain, but she knew that the desire for a child was there.

She felt nothing from God saying, "Do this!" or "Do that!" But she decided eventually that containing all these thoughts in her mind and not discussing them with her husband, regardless of his feelings on the subject, was a poor choice. If nothing else, she ought to clarify her intent—and his—in this decision.

If she never discussed it, what did she expect to happen? There had been times before when her heart had tipped Jordy's in the way she wanted it to go, and vice versa, so what if this was one of those times?

No, Ivy couldn't *not* ask.

Yet neither could she ask. She tried, again and again, but nothing really came of it. Her words were stuck in her throat, because she often got caught in these loops where she'd reword and reword her sentences in her head, trying to plan what she intended to say. After seven or eight tries, she'd be no closer to having vocalized anything. Then she'd give up, without Jordy being any the wiser.

Which was all right in some circumstances. Ivy had long ago

learned the benefit of silence, the way that shutting one's mouth sometimes was the best choice. Honestly, it was the best choice *most* of the time.

However, in this case, she needed to talk. To communicate with Jordy. To ask him why, *why* he didn't want to have a baby with her—even if she thought the answer was an obvious one.

So, on that stormy night with the dinner dishes washed and the food put away, she turned to Jordy with determination and sat across the table from him, placing her arms on the table with palms up. "I have something to say."

"Is it wha' ye've been tryin' tae say tae me for a week, or is it somethin' different?"

If she hadn't been stiff and taut all over from the preparation of speaking about this difficult subject, her jaw would've dropped. Was she really that transparent?

"Look, Vee, I can tell when ye're strugglin' wi' somethin'. But I wanted tae give ye th' time tae talk about it when ye were ready, no' any sooner. Are ye ready noo?"

"No," she admitted. "But I want to tell you now. So make me, Jordy, even if I don't want to."

"Make ye?" He clucked his tongue. "I hate tae make ye do anythin'. I wouldna, Ivy, if there was any way on earth for me tae avoid it. I love ye. So if ye need tae wait—"

"No, no. I ... I've waited long enough with this weighing on me." She took a deep breath. "Jordy ... Jordy, do you want a baby?" That hadn't been quite the question she'd wanted to ask, but at least it would get the subject going in the direction she wanted it to go. Starting was as good as anything.

"Hmm ..." Jordy cocked his head. "Tha' was actually wha' I was expectin', tae."

"What?" How could he have guessed? What had she said or done lately that would've led him to that thought? She couldn't think of anything, and she'd been so careful not to let him know she was discontent. Not that he probably couldn't have guessed some of it, living as closely to her as he did, but she'd at least hoped that he wouldn't guess the specifics behind her melancholy attitude. If nothing else, she didn't want him to think that she didn't love him enough to be entirely happy with just his company.

It was just ... Oh, it was a nice idea, a nice dream. That was the gist of it. Giving up the dream was so hard, especially when she'd always imagined it as a part of that 'perfect life' fantasy that she'd only allowed to flourish, to be a legitimate dream that she thought about during conscious moments, because of Jordy.

His courtship of her had made her believe in that dream for the first time, and it was a dreadful shame that their marriage had completely extinguished it.

"I guessed ye thought o' it for th' first time last Sunday, when we went tae me parents' house."

Ivy scrambled through memories of that day, sitting in the McAllens' happy house with all their children and grandchildren. There wasn't anything particularly different about their behavior or hers, she thought, that could have prompted that line of thinking. "What did you see?"

"It wasna about wha' I saw but wha' ye did. Though o' course, ye could say I saw ye seein' ... Ach, anyway. I caught a glimpse at th' way ye looked around th' room, at tha' big family, at me, an' ye saw me holdin' me wee nephew ... An' from tha' moment, I started thinkin' about how we'd spoken o' children, an' yet I'd never really done much to assure ye ... An' tha's me fault."

"It ... it is?" She couldn't exactly put together what he was trying to say, really. Yes, she'd always admired the McAllens' hearty family. She had quite a few children in her family, too, but there was something about the McAllens that felt big. There was no other way to describe the sensation. And yes, she'd noticed that Jordy was playing with his nephew, Edith's young son, rather too boisterously in her opinion. She'd wondered what Jordy would be like as a father, and perhaps she'd stared overlong as she worked through those thoughts.

All right, she got his point.

"Let me be clear wi' ye, Vee." He reached across the table and took her hands, one in each of his bigger ones. "I dinna need tae have children wi' ye for us tae be a family. I dinna need us tae ever raise bairns together. Me love is no' conditional on tha', an' I assure ye, I would never ask for it. Actually, I'm relieved, in some ways, tha' we've been able tae come tae th' arrangement we have come tae."

"O-oh ..." So he assumed, for some reason, that she didn't want children? He thought she was sad because she wasn't pleasing him, not because she wasn't pleasing herself? Granted, that would make Ivy sad, too, but she was no angel. She was capable of regretting things she wasn't able to have that would make her happy, too.

"Ye see, Vee, I'm ... Ye ken th' kind o' man I am, an' th' kind o' man I've been. Ye ken how many mistakes I made as a lad an' how bitterly I paid for them. An', Vee, much as I love ye, an' much as I think tha', were we both different an' were our circumstances different, we could be able to do it—I think this is a blessin' in some ways. I ... I'm so happy wi' ye!" He squeezed her hands. "Maybe I dinna say it as often as I ought tae, but it's true, an' I love ye. This life I have wi' ye is absolutely perfect."

"I love you, too, Jordy!" She never wanted to miss an opportunity to say that. "If I've been sad, it's not because I don't love you. You make me very happy, and you've done nothing to make me otherwise. But—"

"Ach, nae. No' finished yet." He grinned like a little boy with a frog in his hands, and she didn't have the heart to interrupt him and insist upon telling him her side when he was so cheerful about what he had to say. "Look. I ken I may seem like th' type who would want children, but I really dinna. At least, I dinna want them if they could hurt ye. Ye're more important tae me, truly."

"Hurt me?" Whatever did he mean?

"Aye. I couldna lose ye tae childbirth, Vee. I'd never forgive meself ... Besides, I ken tha' yer anxieties ..." He sighed. "Ivy, I would never do anythin' tha' caused ye sufferin' in any way. I want ye tae ken tha' I really mean tha'. I don't just mean I'll do th' minimum tae keep ye safe. I'll do anythin'."

"Oh ..." Perhaps he was right. Though safety wasn't really a concern when living for God, was it?

"I just ... I care about ye more than anythin' else. I ken I'm repeatin' meself, but, Ivy, ye're me world." He let go of her hands. "Never ask me again about tha'. It's fun tae run this wee cottage together, after all, isna it? I've never had anyone care about me th' way ye have, Vee."

She flushed under the praise, but her heart continued its sinking. He'd made himself clear, after all. Unless some miracle, some accident happened ... or unless God changed Jordy's perspective ... she wasn't going to have a baby. Jordy didn't want one.

At least her thoughts about her own unworthiness were not accurate. She tried to cling to that thought. If only for politeness' sake, he'd never mentioned her mental capacities—except that it might frighten her, which of course it would. Childbirth struck fear into Ivy as it would into any woman ... but oh, she was willing to take the risk. A thousand times, she was willing to take the risk.

He circled the table and gathered her into his arms and whispered those sweet nothings she'd valued so much, and in some ways, still did. However, the 'nothing' element of 'sweet nothings' was beginning to occur to her. There was nothing to their conversation, nothing to his respect for her, nothing to any of these murmurings.

In the end, Ivy must submit to the idea that she would not be having a baby with Jordy McAllen, the love of her life.

That thought filled her with despair. She pretended to be happy the rest of the evening, but she'd learned to lie still, with regulated breaths, until his own breathing became deep and heavy. Once she was sure he was asleep—confirmed by softly whispering his name with no response, for he was a heavy sleeper—dropped her face on her pillow and wept silently.

She wondered how she'd learned to cry like that—*why* she'd learned to cry like that. But she accepted it, for there was no possibility now of her coming to Jordy with this request again. At least, not for a while.

For her bravery had yielded no results, and Ivy believed that when no results were yielded, God must not want her to continue. Besides, He'd called her to submit to her husband—perhaps that was Ivy's hard work in this world. Submitting to a man whose requirements of her, more and more, caused pain—unintentional pain, but still.

Yet how could she bear not to ask?

She cried until she was worn out, then forced herself to sleep.

Ivy was glum.

Violet wouldn't have even bothered noticing this except for the fact that Ivy was glum after what she'd mentioned was going to be a special, private evening with Jordy.

That meant that something had gone wrong with Jordy, unless Ivy had managed to feel great grief over the half of the morning when she hadn't been with Violet. Which seemed unlikely. Ivy was always cheerful about mornings and sunshine and all those other things that, frankly, were sickening in large doses.

So yes, Violet needed to ask Ivy how things had gone. And she was more than prepared to receive an answer she wouldn't like, so that shouldn't be a problem.

They were sitting in the parlor of Aunt Daphne's house, watching Duncan bounce on the sofa and quietly chatting about whether or not they should get him off, and Violet decided now was as good a time as any to ask.

"Ivy, what is it that has you so sad today? You're frowning at Duncan, who I know you think is adorable."

Ivy glanced at Violet, then immediately returned her eyes to the child with a very forced smile. "Duncan dear," she said in a light, empty tone. "Why don't you get off the sofa before Aunt Daphne comes in and decides to be insane?"

"She's always insane," Violet said. "And furthermore, what aren't you telling me?"

"I'm afraid I can't say." Ivy stood and went to scoop up Duncan. "I'll take him to Agnes."

So that was it? After all their years of friendship, Ivy was just going to walk away and not confide in her.

Well. Fine. Violet supposed she should've seen the writing on the wall. She left the parlor behind and ran upstairs.

*October 1881*
*Keefmore, Scotland*

*The church building was everything Violet had expected it to be. Boring and simplistic and ... rustic. She couldn't think of many insults to apply to it, as it was a neat and tidy space full of people who had tidied up surprisingly well, in their own simple way.*

*Ivy was ducking in between the McAllen brothers, fearful of gawking Scots, but Violet stood with her chin raised, unafraid. She never was afraid, really. Or at least she pretended so.*

*"Dinna worry, Vee. They'll tire o' ye soon. Ye're just a bit o' a novelty." Jordy tossed a grin over his shoulder at Ivy as they filed into one of the pews.*

*Violet rolled her eyes. Jordy only encouraged Ivy these days, and he did it in such a sappy way. Jordy and Ivy were getting more and more ridiculous with every hour that passed.*

*Ivy settled between Jordy and one of Jordy's younger brothers, her Bible clutched with white-knuckled fingers on her lap. Violet allowed herself to slouch down next to her aunt in the pew behind them.*

*"Dinna worry."*

*Again with the false encouragement! Violet glared at the back of the younger brother's head. If the whole McAllen family kept* encouraging Ivy at this rate, she'd probably collapse under the pressure. Violet's Trifle was a delicate little plant. How could they smother her so?

"We're no' a bad bunch. Ye just have tae be patient an' let our good side shine through." The younger brother patted Ivy's shoulder, and Ivy's entire body practically collapsed in on itself, proving Violet's point.

Then Ivy turned to Jordy, who spoke to her in far too low a voice with his face far too close to her ear. "I think me wee brother has taken a fancy tae ye."

"Havena!" the brother protested. "I ... I was just tryin' tae be nice! I mean, she's a nice lass an' all, but I dinna even ken her! Really, Jordy!"

Jordy grinned. His eyes even flashed back to Violet for a minute, clearly pleased by the mischief he'd caused. "I was just teasin', Mick, though I suppose I can see how Miss Ivy's looks could go tae yer head." He reached up and tugged at a loose lock of her hair.

Ivy sent him a look that quickly turned into a smile, and Violet tried not to gag.

The two brothers engaged in a round of sparring, and Ivy watched Jordy the whole time with this sickeningly dreamy look on her eyes.

And Violet knew ... for the first time, she knew.

She was losing her two best friends—more than that, the people whose exclusive attention she had previously had complete access to—in the worst way imaginable.

# CHAPTER SEVEN

*March 13, 1884*

Successfully avoiding Ivy McAllen for an entire week was no small accomplishment. However, Violet had managed, if only because Ivy had been distracted.

Her Trifle had a life now, though she didn't know it yet. It was quite a full life—both fortunately and unfortunately. In the last months, she'd taken on more and more to the point where she seemed exhausted half the time. She ran from house to house, volunteer activity to volunteer activity, hurting person to hurting person—and she abandoned her own needs.

Ivy liked it that way. Violet acknowledged that if Ivy had the strength to continue on this path, she would enjoy it deeply. The problem was, Violet's Trifle had somehow managed to do enough that she was wearing herself out, and Violet hated to see that.

Without Ivy to bother her, Violet had had a lot of time to think. Not that her Trifle necessarily blocked her ability to think—though sometimes she did. Lately, Violet's mind had been in the wrong place ... though that was more her fault than Ivy's.

Thinking of Ivy led to Jordy. It always did. That was the problem, though—so did *not* thinking of Ivy.

Still, she didn't see any harm in being in his presence from time to time, and she wanted to see if she couldn't poke her Trifle's relationship with the difficult man in a better direction, which is why she decided to visit Jordy at his office that morning.

He was in the front room with a young boy and his mother. The child's arm was in a sling—from her position in the doorway, Violet guessed that he'd dislocated it and now had to rest it for a while.

She slipped into his back office with the book she'd brought around and half listened to the conversation with the boy and his mother about proper resting procedures, what he should and should not do, et cetera. All basic things, though Violet thought he should've mentioned a bit more about the wear on the socket and the possible issues to be caused by frequent dislocations. That was how she would've done it if she were a doctor.

At last, Jordy sent his patient away and stepped into his office. "I thought tha' was ye." He cocked his head. "Anythin' in particular ye want?"

She set her book down on his small desk. "No, not really." She'd been mulling over what she wanted to say to him. The conversation with Ivy had deeply concerned her, but she also hated to poke into something she didn't want to know about. Jordy and Ivy might have an intimate relationship, but she didn't want to know more about it. There was no need. It was private, and anyway, what Violet didn't know quite literally couldn't hurt her.

She wasn't going to be any more hurt than she needed to be.

Yet she supposed she could ask about some things that might benefit Ivy a little more. In sneaky ways. Ways that wouldn't lead to details.

"So ... Ivy's been keeping busy lately. By which I mean she's working all the time now, which is strange for a woman who usually likes to leave herself afternoons for reading and music."

Jordy walked to the small bookshelf in the corner and began rearranging a couple of books, the stiffness of his actions speaking of an uncomfortable feeling. What about that made him nervous? "No' sure. I dinna understand it. I just ken tha' she canna keep it up for long." She could feel the frustration in his body, and his tight movements, his furrowed brow furthered her suspicions.

"I don't know why she would act that way." It wasn't like her.

"I think she's bored. Which is understandable." His shoulders jerked—half a shrug, half a disgruntled hunch. "Perhaps it's best she does have a few hobbies. I mean, wha' did I expect? There's no' a thing for her tae do here. Aye, a few things, but once th' shine's worn off ..."

Violet narrowed her eyes and regarded Jordy pensively. Did he not know his own wife? Violet could clearly tell it was more than that. Ivy wasn't the type to get bored of something, especially if it involved someone she loved. What Jordy interpreted as simple apathy must be a great deal more—or else Ivy would not have reacted so.

But it wasn't Violet's job to give Jordy romantic advice. He could figure that out for himself.

"And you? What've you been doing? Anything new?" Jordy was always on to some new project. She wondered what he'd started researching lately—usually it was something tied to a psychological issue, which he so delighted in learning more about. It gave him something to observe in the people around him and something to report back to Dr. McCale.

"Ach, nothin'. I'm so busy ..." He left the bookshelf behind. "I need tae clean th' exam room, so come wi' me if ye want tae talk."

Violet did want to talk, so with a heavy sigh, she rose from the chair and followed him into the room, then lowered herself onto the much less comfortable seat by the door.

As he removed a basket of clean cloths from under the table, Violet watched him closely. As Ivy had mentioned, he seemed reserved or at least very focused, which was unlike him. Granted, he had moments of extreme occupation, but they were few and far between, and there was nothing like having a person in his general vicinity to distract him completely.

"How's your family?" That might be a better way to gain insight into what his feelings were at the moment. "I know one of your siblings is married ..."

"Right. Edith." He raised his eyebrows. "Ye were at th' weddin', if ye remember."

"I remember something about it, but frankly, I wasn't paying much attention." It had been a difficult time. "So she's married."

"Aye, these last two years. An' she's a son—David."

"How old is he?"

"A wee bit over a year."

"Hmm."

Again they lapsed into silence. Violet wasn't sure what to say or do to keep the conversation traveling on the path it had been. She did so like knowing the reasons for things. It gave her a kind of delight, like solving a puzzle. Perhaps she was more like Dr. McCale than she gave herself credit for.

"What are your dreams?" she finally blurted out. "All those years ago, you had so many of them. Yet they're not being realized, and therefore, I must believe you've let them drop."

He shrugged. "Me life is different noo."

"Yes, but if it weren't for Ivy—"

"I would be a great deal less happy if it were no' for Ivy." He shrugged. "'Tis a fair trade-off, if ye ask me. An' anyway, I'm no' dreamin' o' th' same things I used to."

She found that difficult to believe. It was more like he had abandoned his past dreams to leave room for a wife who simply didn't fit into them. "Do you remember telling me you wanted to help people?"

"I am helpin' people." He nodded his head toward the front room. "Ye just saw someone I helped."

"Yes, but all those years ago, you meant on a different scale."

"Is tha' less worthy?" He raised his eyebrows. "I dinna see how I canna just be o' use where I am."

"That's Ivy talking through you." She rolled her eyes. "That's not you. You're different—you have always wanted to do more. You said you wanted to change the way all of England deals with the insane."

He laughed as he ran a damp rag over the top of one of the

counters. "I canna imagine tha' I called them insane."

"I don't think you did. I did. It wasn't a direct quote, but all I'm saying is that you seem to see the world through a different lens than Ivy does, but you've seemed to have forgotten that." Was it a strength in their relationship or a weakness? Violet had started believing that it was possible they could find a happy medium, but the more she looked at Jordy's behavior, the more she believed that it was possible that one or the other of them must be uncomfortable for the other to be happy.

"I think we see things verra similarly."

"Nae, ye dinna," she mumbled. "Even if you can lie to yourself, I can't lie to you. I'm not that type of person."

"Aye, yer honesty has always been present, even in me darkest moments." He grunted and tossed the now dust-tinted rag into a basket by the door. Having a system was also not very Jordy. "But, Vi, ye ken I've changed. She's changed me. Perhaps tha's th' beauty o' it. I want tae be wi' her, even if it's no' easy."

"But isn't that going to be disastrous in the long term? You had such dreams, Jordy. Why shouldn't you get to follow them?" Granted, he'd been much younger when those fairy tales had been written, but they had been beautiful. Violet believed there was a great need for the kind of knowledge Dr. McCale possessed, for the kind of program he presented, for his gentle and loving approach to those who were suffering greatly.

Jordy was the natural choice to pass that message on to the nation—and then to the world. He was the one who knew everything Dr. McCale had ever said, written, done. He understood people—and more than that, he could talk to them without becoming brusque, regardless of the type of person he was dealing with. Dr. McCale didn't have that skill.

Besides, more than children had need of that kind of help. Yet few such organizations existed. She'd heard things that were hopeful, of course. There was Dr. Langdon Down, a specialist who had founded his own asylum for the mentally disabled, and a greater understanding was coming to the world of such things through him. Yet that was a different kind of thing than what Dr. McCale treated.

Despite the steps forward, there were as many steps back, and the more Violet explored what was in the world, the more repulsed she was. She knew how someone like her would be treated if admitted to a hospital—but she got out into the world, and she'd yet to hurt anyone. She'd not even hurt herself—not really. She ran her hand over her left arm, which ached from time to time, but that didn't really count. She had to believe it was the only thing keeping her alive some days, so she didn't count it. She couldn't.

Ivy would. Which was why she hadn't told her. And Jordy knew—his eyes trailed to the movement of her hand. She dropped it.

"Still?" At least his voice was gentler.

"No. Just memories." That was only partly a lie. It hadn't been recent, but neither had it stopped as far back as she was implying.

"As long as it's just tha'. Remember, I'll tell Vee if ye dinna keep it under control. An' ye really ought tae let me look at some point—though if it hasna bothered ye again, ye probably havena managed tae get an infection."

She shrugged. She was as clean as she was self-destructive, and she felt she'd be fine. Perhaps she was more confident than she ought to be. That was a common trait in her family, so it wouldn't be unlikely.

"But, as I said, me dreams are fine. They're takin' care o' Vee an' helpin' th' people here. An' tha's enough for me."

"Maybe it shouldn't be. Have you ever thought that you have a great deal to share with others and a great gift in terms of the ability to share it?" She stood and crossed the room, forcing him to stop cleaning and look at her, albeit with more amusement than real respect. "Jordy, you know things the world needs to know. You have a unique perspective—even being Ivy's husband gives you something different to share, but it's more than that. Dr. McCale cannot and will not share as you would be able to do—as you said you would! Granted, someone else could be trained to do the same, but you are qualified and equipped *now*. I know Dr. McCale would support you—

and I know there are places where you could both research and speak. I've been reading about—"

He held up his hand. "Vi, I'm no' goin' tae—"

"But you can help people this way." She placed her hands flat on the top of the operating table and leaned forward, meeting his eyes. "There's so much to be done. I know you haven't changed that much—don't you see how much you could do and how much you could enjoy it, too?"

He shrugged. "I dinna think I'm as interested in this kind o' thing as ye say, Vi. But I dinna want tae talk about it anymore. Why are ye so concerned about me all o' a sudden?"

A thousand reasons. And the culmination of her thoughts wasn't sudden. It was just a crescendo of what had already been there. Though there was still a lot of story to go. At least, Violet thought there was.

"I care about you and Ivy. I've said that, haven't I? I want you to be happy." And they couldn't be happy. They *couldn't*. "I don't think you'll be happy unless you're being your best self, and I don't think you're very close to that—even if you believe you are."

He grinned. "I canna believe ye walked all th' way here in th' snow tae try tae get me tae doubt me entire life." Yet the glimmer in his eye said she'd touched a nerve.

Good.

"Can you tell me why you gave up those dreams? Why was working at Keefmore ever an option? Why haven't you talked about your future?" It had meant so much to him as a young man. Why didn't it now?

"Ye ken all th' things tha' happened, Vi."

Oh. That again? She'd thought he was over the guilt, the depression, the self-pity that diffidence inevitably caused ... a feeling Violet was familiar with. "That doesn't make you incapable. If anything else, it gives you a better grasp on humanity, on the highs and lows of life, on how healing can be had."

"'Tis a different thing entirely."

"No, it isn't! Humans are humans, aren't they?" She glared at him. "That's what I've always been told. That's what your work, your *life* is based on. So accept that fact—and know that you are not unqualified by your past but rather equipped by it."

He stood still then, another damp cloth clutched in his hand. She wondered what he was thinking—usually she could tell, but at that moment, she couldn't sense much from him. He remained still even when she walked around the table and stood before him, head cocked, ready to spring away or draw closer as the situation called for.

He raised his eyes toward her, and a slight smile twitched at his lips. "Perhaps ye're right. I should at least see wha' I can do. Maybe no' noo, but later, as we're more settled."

"Hmm." Close enough, she supposed. It was the confirmation that he was willing to hear her. Jordy was a fool, and he needed her for that reason. She told herself that over and over again on the days when she wasn't at all sure of her own worth or who she might call a 'friend.'

Jordy hadn't been on that list for so long that she didn't know what to think of him. That said, if she could win him back ...

He had promised her that. And so many other things. But that was the primary one that took up the most space in her mind, taunting and teasing her on the dark nights when she doubted every word, every thought, every small choice that had driven him away from her.

That had driven *her* away from *him*.

She placed her hand on his arm. "Jordy, I know you can do this. More than that, we need you. Don't you see that? The world needs more people like you to stand up and speak out in the ways those who are suffering cannot. This is a place you are well-equipped to fill. So fill it. For Ivy, for all the other McCale House students ... for me."

He met her eyes, then cleared his throat and stepped back, and she shook her head. The spell was broken. That was the end of it.

Embarrassed, she, too, drew away. In that moment, she felt as if she'd accessed something different in him. Was that a good thing? Probably not.

She had to get away. Now. Before she thought more. Thinking was ever the enemy, and Violet encountered it often enough to know that running was the only answer to the agony it caused.

She hurriedly collected her book and buttoned up her coat and left after that, but his look stuck with her.

Where could she run to?

*March 19, 1884*

Life just kept rolling along, never stopping, never giving her more than a moment to catch her breath—and as time went on and she worked harder, Ivy was able to truly live. It wasn't easy, of course. However, she was determined, as she always had been, to live a full life, a joyful life, a helpful life.

God had not created her to just sit in the corner and mope. He'd taught her that lesson before her marriage, and she was determined not to lose it in the sometimes methodical patterns her life had taken to in her marriage.

There wouldn't be a child. She'd accepted that. It had been her dream, yes. She had believed it would be her calling, yes. But Jordy didn't feel so—oh, how clearly he didn't feel so! And given the fact that she believed a husband's authority should triumph, she didn't have any choice in the matter.

Not really. She could lie to him, could manipulate him, could even force him. But that wasn't fair. It just wasn't. Ivy wanted to be fair.

Jordy knew her best of anyone, so he must know that she didn't have what it took to be a mother. He'd always been honest with her, always hoped for the best, but the best was being a wife. Being a mother was more than the best. It was an unreachable realm beyond 'best.'

Violet went to McCale House for the spring, for a reason she never did explain despite Ivy's pleadings, and Ivy was alone again, with people who didn't understand her, people she couldn't speak to honestly, and people who didn't believe in her. Oh, but she was trying not to think that way! So she forced herself, that bright spring day, to make the journey to Aunt Daphne's house.

If nothing else, Aunt Daphne always had a suggestion to be active in a world that sometimes asked for inactivity in its more refined ladies. Which, due to her childlessness, Ivy often felt she was. She cleaned the house and cooked and attended church. She'd helped out during the last harvest but not much. Jordy had briefly tried to have her raise a few lambs before removing them because she 'was gettin' tae attached' and 'wasna supposed tae name them.' Ivy still felt she could've handled the inevitable slaughter better than he thought. Yes, she would have mourned their loss, wept for days, even suggested alternatives to butchering—like just keeping them as pets—but in the end, she thought she would've been reasonable. Probably.

But as much for that reason as her lack of children, Ivy felt different. She was a woman of leisure, truly. There was no farm to keep, no 'bairns' to mind, no work to be done. Everything she did, she volunteered to do. There was the music at the church, helping out with the children at school and Sunday school, aiding Ena in whatever she could, the ladies' teas ... but Ivy had far too much energy, as her anxiety was not nearly as severe as it used to be. Not having to deal with spiraling thoughts every day meant her mind was often empty, bored.

She could read more. Go up to practice the piano at the church more. Walk more, now that the days were longer and greener. Sometimes she asked Jordy if she could help at the office, though he never wanted her there.

Yet there must be more for her. God must want more for her. Every night she prayed for a great purpose, because everything she did just didn't seem like enough.

Perhaps it was enough. And that was the agonizing answer she seemed to be coming back with. God had given her enough work, enough to do that would serve Him. And she had to be content in the face of that realization.

But how hard it was!

Aunt Daphne was in the garden at the front of her house, elbow deep not just in dirt but in mud. The entire front of her dress was coated. It had rained last night, but rain the night before never stopped Aunt Daphne from doing anything.

Nearby, Duncan played, similarly covered in mud, but he was just a wee bit more adorable than Aunt Daphne. Not that Ivy judged them, and with a sigh and a glance down at the lavender organdy dress she wore, she realized that in five minutes, she would be just as muddy. She'd put it on for visiting, but she should've known better when it came to Aunt Daphne.

Indeed, in moments, Duncan had thrown his arms about her legs, and she followed him to the flower bed to help make mud pies.

Eventually, Aunt Daphne noticed that Ivy was present. "Thank you for your help, Ivy. Agnes has been absolutely difficult today."

"Did she not want Duncan to get like this?" Ivy said as cheerfully as she could manage.

"Hmph. Agnes doesn't appreciate adventure."

*Agnes will be responsible for cleaning up both Duncan and Aunt Daphne. Of course she isn't terribly enthusiastic.* But Ivy didn't say so, as she knew it wouldn't do much good.

"What are you working on today?"

"I want to plant some trees. I thought trees would be a good addition to this area. Then I can expand to the sides and make a path through them—and think how lovely they'll be in the autumn!"

Ivy glanced about. It occurred to her that perhaps there was a reason why there weren't any trees here currently—mainly, that this was not the place to grow them—but again, there was no convincing Aunt Daphne of anything she didn't want to be convinced of. "All right. Can I help?"

"Always." Aunt Daphne rose. "Hmm. I'm quite muddy."

"Indeed. So is Duncan."

"Very well. I suppose it's healthy for you. The good earth of the land and all that." She turned and gestured toward a few small saplings with their roots tied up in cloth. "Those are the ones we're planting today, but I'll try to have more sent. They have to be special ordered."

"Yes, probably because no one plants trees in Keefmore," Ivy observed.

"More's the pity! What's that bit? Something about trees and poetry and ... Oh, anyway, trees are nice."

Ivy hurried to help Aunt Daphne drag the saplings over to the holes she'd dug. After moving them twice, they finally got them situated where Aunt Daphne wanted them. Duncan loved "helping" to move the trees, and honestly, Ivy enjoyed it, too. There was something fun about getting all dirty and working hard, sleeves rolled up and hair in her face.

"Also, I need you to help with something else," Aunt Daphne continued once the trees were planted. "I'm going to start a gardening club. I thought I could help you put together your first garden as an experiment, and then we could expand to helping the other ladies of Keefmore. Some of them don't use the space they have efficiently, if they grow anything at all. But they should."

"That sounds nice!" Ivy had wanted to organize her garden. "I'd like to grow some vegetables. I tried just flowers last spring, but a lot of them wilted."

"Let's go at once and see if we can't buy some seeds." Aunt Daphne rose and snatched up Duncan, then paused and held him up at arm's length—a considerable feat, for he'd gotten quite chubby. "Hmm. You, too, Duncan? What will we tell Agnes?"

Laughing, Ivy took Duncan, and they all went inside to break the bad news about everyone's state of dress to one exhausted mother.

# CHAPTER EIGHT

Once again, Ivy came to see Ena at the store. She was trying not to spend too much time bothering her friend, but at the same time, she liked to think her presence was somewhat of a welcome interruption to Ena's day-to-day life.

Today, Ena was in the kitchen making tea, which she invited Ivy to partake in. They took it to the store and sipped it behind the counter while they chatted.

Of course, Ivy had her own agenda when it came to this particular visit. She'd been trying to get up the courage to mention Wallace Lennox again. Especially since she'd now met him, or at least seen him, briefly at church with his small, freckle-faced son.

After the basic catching up from a few days ago was done, Ivy cleared her throat. "So ... Wallace Lennox. Has he come around ...?"

"Ivy! I wouldna have thought ye for a matchmaker." Yet the exclamation was good-natured, as was the smile that followed. "Aye, he's come around. In fact ... since last year, he's been in here often, though you hadn't met him until recently. He ken't I had a few things that needed to be done, so ever since he's come back to Keefmore, he's helped me whenever he can wi' things tha' are broke, or just things tha' I canna handle. He'll probably be here today."

"He will? Will you introduce us?" Ivy wanted to meet this man who still brought a slight blush of rose to her friend's cheeks. She supposed no one really was as completely without any silliness regarding romance as they pretended to be. After all, romance was a bit silly. That was the essence of it. All practicality flew out the window in the face of reality.

"Aye, I will, if he comes." Ena shrugged. "But I think ye're reading tae much intae this, Ivy. He's a friend, an' I like him, but ... neither one o' us is far from losin' our spouse. It may be tae soon for him."

"Is it too soon for you?" Ivy knew it was still a bit of a tender subject. But Ena had always said it would be until the day she died ... That didn't mean she wouldn't keep on living in the meanwhile.

"Nae, 'tisn't. But I'm no' th' only one tae be considered here. There's Wallace. He's made nae mention o' any sort o' interest."

"Yet he comes to help you!" Ivy protested. That was a sure indicator of interest, wasn't it?

"Loyalty tae me Bob brings him here. An' I was friends wi' his wife before they moved."

"Oh, then you were good friends?"

"Grew up together. If it hadna been for Bob ... Ach, but Bob was there, an' tha's wha' matters. Anyway, tha' feels like so long ago. It was only eight or so years, but it feels like decades an' decades." Ena's eyes grew wistful. "An' at th' same time, no' tha' long at all. I have a daughter who is nearly eight. Isna tha' a wonder? I remember her bein' a bairn no' so verra long ago, an' since, I've had three others, though only Alistair remains with Bridget and me."

It was a wonder how fast things changed. At times, Ivy's soul would go still and remind her that she was a married woman, and had been so for over a year. That she was an adult in every sense of the word, that she lived on her own, that she hadn't seen her parents, her family face to face in over a year ... and that would press on her.

It was odd how the music kept playing, and at times, Ivy forgot about the simple events that had seemed to spiral out of control, leaving her in a place she was unfamiliar with and yet familiar with, doing things she didn't feel equipped to do but apparently was, for she did them.

Yes, it was strange, and yet it was now normal. Did humanity have the natural-born ability to adjust, or was it just forced to? Ivy would perhaps never know.

They chatted about Wallace Lennox, who was apparently 'brawer than Bob but no' so funny—no' nearly' and his young son who was 'a wee mischief wi' a canny smile.' Eventually, the door of the shop opened, and there was the man himself.

"Good morn, Ena." Wallace shuffled forward with his small boy clinging to the leg of his loose trousers and his cap shoved over his eyes. "I've a few things tae pick up, but I thought maybe I could look at tha' back door? I dinna want ye tae be here alone anymore wi'oot it fastenin' right."

"Aye, today would be a good day for tha'." Ena rose and scurried around the counter. "Let me show ye wha's wrong."

The two then proceeded to the back room, Willie and Ivy trailing behind—although Ena had apparently forgotten to introduce anyone to anyone—and watched as Ena and Wallace were ridiculously aware of each other.

Ivy almost laughed at Ena's blushes and Wallace's mumbling and shuffling, the way they gave each other an overly wide berth and in general acted as if one small movement would make the other one run for cover.

This was the dance, the delicate and, at the same time, entirely *indelicate* dance that a couple performed. Violet would call them 'human mating rituals' and narrate their actions in a funny voice until Ivy laughed. However, Ivy just found them amusing and a little sweet.

Had she ever done this? Somehow she couldn't remember, and yet she was half-convinced she had, for it seemed so universal.

One thing Ivy was absolutely convinced of now, however: Ena was in love with Wallace, or at least falling, and vice versa. It was only a matter of time before they both admitted this and made their two broken families into one whole one.

Jordy would say she was being overly poetic and making assumptions about old friends. As Ena handed Wallace tools and watched him with barely veiled affection, Ivy didn't believe she was reading too much into this relationship, fledgling though it might be.

Yes, there was a definite possibility that Ena and Wallace would soon be a couple. But did they need some help along the way? That was the question.

*April 7, 1884*

Ena wasn't at the ladies' meeting at Aunt Daphne's house that next week, which allowed Ivy a little more freedom in terms of talking about her.

Ivy was determined that it wasn't meddling or, worse yet, gossiping if her motives were pure. And frankly, she had no interest whatsoever in matchmaking in any real way. However, in the little ways? She at least wanted to be informed.

So when Ena had told her that 'Bridie talked me into a trip tae th' coast for th' day, against all logic,' Ivy had realized it was time to ask some pointed questions about the great Wallace Lennox. What did the ladies know about him? Probably a great deal more than Ivy would.

So once the meeting had gone through its necessary Aunt Daphne-isms, including a long rant about the importance of gardening that was half ignored and half borne, Ivy asked.

"What do you all know about Wallace Lennox?"

The pastor's wife, Mrs. Abernathy, smiled. "Ye mean Ena Owen's new lad?"

There was a hum of agreement and a chuckle or two, and Ivy nodded. "That's rather what I wondered, too."

"Aye, he comes around th' store an' fixes things, but if ye come in at th' same time as him, weel, ye can tell how he looks at her."

"An' his lad, Willie, is such a dear! He plays wi' me own sons every day almost, an' such a polite, somber, wee thing he is."

"An' no' badly off." Mrs. Grear nodded sagely. "Aye, he has tha' nice farm, but he fixed me husband's wagon wheel, an' I suppose he does a lot o' work like tha', fixing farm equipment an' odds an' ends. He'd be a wise choice, if Ena's a mind tae take him."

"'Tis no' just tha', though." The pastor's wife leaned forward. "He comes tae see me husband often, an' they talk late into th' night. I suppose he fell away from th' faith for a few years, after his wife passed, but noo he's back an' stronger than ever."

Mrs. Grear cocked her head. "Aye, I remember Wallie Lennox when he was a lad. Honestly, I'm no' surprised tae hear tha' he struggled, though I'm glad he's changed noo."

Mrs. McDermid widened her eyes. "Ooh, aye, I'd almost forgot tha'! He courted Ena Owen, didna he? An' she'd have nothin' tae do wi' him."

"Weel, no' tae speak badly o' Ena, but she was impatient, so ready tae be married tha' she wouldna give anythin' tha' wasna serious as death a second glance. An' her Bob was o' course willin' tae give her th' life she was lookin' for ... Wallie hadna settled down then. He didna until he moved. Did any o' ye ever hear wha' his wife was like?"

"Ach, a sweet thing, sweet enough tae catch an' hold him." Mrs. Grear chuckled. "I love Ena, but she's often a bit more vinegar than honey. An' though she an' Wallace flirted about in their youth, by th' time she turned fifteen, she wasna goin' tae take th' time tae win him over tae her way o' thinkin'. Nae, she was in tae much o' a rush, as always."

The pastor's wife's eyebrows lowered. "As never a good woman should have tae, Mrs. Grear. 'Tis far better tha' Ena followed her convictions than waited for a man who, it sounds like, wouldna have changed for her. But noo tha' they're both grown, an' time has passed, an' Wallace in particular has turned a corner ... Aye, I can see the relationship workin'."

Ivy could, too, and the ladies' information had only confirmed her suppositions. "But you would never say that she didn't marry her husband for love, would you?"

Mrs. Abernathy's eyes twinkled. "I'd never say tha'. No' about Ena an' Bob. But then, I think it came a little slower for Ena, once she was already set on him. Poor Bob never did have a chance after tha', though o' course in th' end, he was th' one who held th' cards. Ye'll get her tae tell ye th' story in full sometime, Ivy, for she'll tell ye things she wouldna even tell us."

That was true, though for now, Ivy didn't want to spend too much time overfocusing on Ena's Bob. She was a bit more interested in Ena's Wallace.

"But," Mrs. Grear said, arching her eyebrows, "I wouldna go as far as tae say tha' Ena Owen's practicality has ever let her hesitate in choosin' th' man tha' would get her closest tae th' life she was lookin' for."

"Mrs. Grear, I wish ye could be more charitable," the pastor's wife said, her tone half scolding. "Aye, she was lookin' tae settle an' start a family, no' tae roam th' country on an adventure, but she loved Bob, an' tha' was always clear tae us all. An' if she chose tae give her heart tae th' man who could give her th' security an' the unity she'd never felt in her own home, weel, if ye canna be practical about th' most important worldly decision o' yer life, wha' can ye be practical about? How could we judge her for somethin' we canna understand?"

Mrs. Grear mumbled and shifted on her seat as she always did, but she didn't say anything further.

The conversation moved on, with Ivy tucking deep into her heart these words about Ena and Wallace. How she wanted to see their love story flourish! She had a feeling it would make Ena terribly happy, and it would likely be good for Bridget, Alistair, and Willie, too.

Eventually, Ivy was able to emerge from her dreams enough to tune back in to the new conversation buzzing around her.

"O' course," Mrs. McDermid was saying, "I doubt I woulda had this bairn"—she patted her round stomach—"if me husband had had his way. He wasna keen tae have another one. Imagine tha', a man carin'!"

"Oh aye, they care. Or some o' them. Me husband." Mrs. Grear rolled her eyes. "Usually ye just hear tell o' men who want more children than their wife or who want a son rather than daughter, but if ye dinna talk about bairns before ye're wed, weel, ye'll pay for it."

Mrs. McDermid glanced around the table. "I suppose we've all been married here, wi' Miss Locke no' bein' present, so I'll say—"

Ivy wavered between jerking to her feet and staying, in utter fascination, but due to the wavering, she stayed as Mrs. McDermid quietly and somewhat gracefully, but with an unbelievable frankness, discussed her husband's opinion on their child-prevention policy. "Which is why I was determined tae only have th' three, but I had th' fourth after tha'. I ken't I coulda stopped it—I didna spend much time with Mrs. Grear before this, so I heard it from th' midwife—but I hadna th' heart."

The pastor's wife looked about as uncomfortable as Ivy was. "I ought tae say tha' me husband hasna ever said ..."

"I'd go as far as tae call this none o' his business," said Mrs. Grear, daring Mrs. Abernathy to contradict her. "Anyway, 'tis a personal conviction, noo isna it? He wouldna be able tae argue tha'."

"I ... dinna ken." The pastor's wife had eight children, Ivy knew, who each had managed families of roughly the same size after they grew up and moved out, so there probably wasn't much discussion about it in her home.

Ivy wished she was the pastor's wife, frankly. If only the discussion, such as it was, had led to eight children, or rather the possibility of eight children—followed by dozens of rambunctious grandchildren.

"An' I'm sure all o' us have had arguments about it, or most o' us." Here there was a slightly guarded glance between Ivy and Mrs. Abernathy. Mrs. Grear was not always subtle. "Th' truth is, at th' end o' th' day, I feel it's me decision. An' men are weak in this concern. If

I want a child ..."

After this, a variety of opinions were brought forth, and Ivy half listened, for she felt that none of them should really be having this conversation at all. She would certainly never feel comfortable sharing about what went on between her and Jordy. Yet there was a curiosity in her soul now that there never had been.

She'd never really thought about having a baby regardless of what Jordy said or did. Practically speaking, a few white lies would be enough to tip the scales on that front if she could have a baby, which she believed she could. If nothing else, her body naturally seemed to maintain itself these days. She was healthy and strong, no matter what Jordy said.

If she were allowed the opportunity, she fully believed she could carry a baby to term.

However, even Mrs. Abernathy's arguments and Aunt Daphne's thoughts were clarifying to her. She'd never considered that there was an alternative to simply submitting to her husband's opinion on the subject, so she needed time and perhaps a great deal of prayer to sort through the idea.

Yet it lingered. What if she was meant to be a mother in spite of Jordy? The idea worked its way into her heart despite her reticence. *What if, what if, what if ...?*

At last, the conversation was turned, with all the might in Mrs. Abernathy's small body, in a different direction. Later, as the ladies were leaving, Mrs. Abernathy lingered behind and apologized to Aunt Daphne and Ivy both for the frankness of it all.

"I suppose it's left tae still be discussed, but I forgot tha' th' midwife has reigned supreme for years. O' course she'd have all sorts o' heathen ideas. But of course we ken it's never right tae stop wha' God would ordain, an' it's no' our choice if we have children or no'." Mrs. Abernathy huffed and left.

"It's clear that touched a bit of a nerve," Aunt Daphne said softly. "I wondered if she was really happy with all those children. I know her daughters have all done the same, too. Yet I like her and her husband very much, so don't take that as judgment, Ivy. The woman is doing her best to uphold her convictions. Yet there's no shame in having one's own."

"Right ..." Though Ivy wasn't at all sure what those convictions would look like herself. She'd never thought she had the right to have convictions of her own on the matter. "What do you think of it all, Aunt Daphne? Stopping babies?"

"Hmm ... I don't know. I never had to think about it." She shrugged. "I suppose Roger and I must have talked about children, but it's been so long, I can't remember. I always knew it wasn't really going to be a part of my life, and that was clearly from the Lord since, back then, I wouldn't have even known how to 'stop babies,' as you put it. That said, as far as I know, there's no real biblical argument against preventing conception if you're not denying your husband or he you. God makes the decision for you in this case, whatever that looks like. But it needs to be one you make with your spouse not without him, so Mrs. Grear definitely has some heart construction needed."

Ivy nodded. If only it were a bit more clean cut. Mrs. Abernathy's suggestion that it was wrong to not have children was one Ivy rather appreciated, but that felt a bit like it was just her own desires talking.

At last, not knowing how to ask for the information she needed to know, she went home, but the thought lingered on in her mind.

# CHAPTER NINE

*May 30, 1884*

Jordy wasn't sure what led him to glance up from the thick medical book that rested on his desk, but his eyes fell on the clock. It was close to eight in the evening.

He sighed, marked his place with a slip of paper, and closed the book. He was already three hours later than he'd wanted to be, so he knew he should hustle home. Yet he'd so wanted to finish at least a few more pages at every break that he'd kept going.

This was how his days tended to run anymore. He did his best to get home on time, but often it was just impossible to do so. He'd have to apologize to Ivy tonight, though she wasn't terribly concerned about him arriving home late, thankfully. He was blessed in her.

Exhausted, he rolled his shoulders before taking up his coat and hat. He'd hurry home through the darkness of the night, though fortunately it was only mildly cold this time of the year. Not unbearable.

He jogged most of the way to the cottage—only to see, from the hill overlooking the little dip where the house sat, that there were no lights on and no smoke curling from the chimney.

That was strange.

He picked up his pace then and burst into the front door. "Ivy, are ye here?"

Only silence greeted him. It was clear no one had been home most of the day. He started a fire in the stove and then poked around the cottage, looking for a clue of where she might be.

He was about to start out in search of her when the door opened, and in stepped his wife.

She smiled when she saw him. "There you are! I stopped by the office because I saw you were there when I went from Ena's house to the church, so I knew you must be home already."

"Already?" It was 8:15!

"Yes, well, I know you've been staying rather late most nights. I suppose it's later than I thought, though." She removed her coat and laid it over the back of one of the kitchen chairs. "Do you want anything to eat?"

Suddenly he wasn't as hungry as he had been before. "I dinna think so."

"I'll just make something little for me, then." She bustled to the cupboards and removed a bowl. "I got sidetracked at the church. I wanted to practice the piano for next week when no one was there, and I've missed every opportunity of late."

"Oh." That made sense. Come to think of it, he hadn't seen much of Ivy lately. How busy was she? "Wha' have ye been up tae this day?"

She shrugged. "Oh, this and that." She hesitated after opening another cupboard. "You know, I think you're right. I'm too tired to eat."

"A'right." Unlike her, but maybe it wasn't. All of a sudden, he was wondering if he remembered much of what had happened in the past several months with Ivy. She'd mentioned quite a few volunteer activities—being busy, being tired, feeling useful. All of which he'd thought spoke of health.

Now he looked at her and saw that she was pushing herself further than he'd thought. He wondered how many days she got home late—

granted, not quite this late, but she often left the cottage with him in the morns. Could she be staying out and working all day every day?

Yet he didn't want to overthink it. As he followed her to the bedroom and watched her prepare for bed with those same drooping shoulders and tired eyes, even as she maintained a somewhat cheerful expression and manner, he acknowledged that he had a lot to do to prove himself to her.

He always would. That was just the way it was. He had to work hard so Ivy wouldn't be disappointed in the person he was.

"You know, Violet is coming back. Aunt Daphne told me when I had tea with her today. She'll be here soon ..."

"Oh. Where has she been?"

Ivy cocked her head. "I think just at McCale House, though I'm not sure if she traveled at any point in between."

"Hmm. Why did she leave in th' first place?" That part he didn't understand. One day Violet had been there, living with her aunt, seeming happy, asking him annoying questions and trying to poke him away from the happy existence he'd developed with Ivy for who knows what reason ... the next she'd been gone, and Ivy had been sad. That much he did know, even if some aspects of her current life were lost to him.

"I'm not sure. She wouldn't say—she said she wasn't sure why." Ivy shrugged. "I don't always understand Violet any more than the next person. I like to think I'm a dear friend, but she doesn't like to communicate."

No, she didn't. Jordy sighed and turned to pick up his nightshirt. If he wasn't going to understand, he wasn't going to understand.

Though it would be disappointing if that meant he didn't understand Ivy. He'd already had a hard time learning her, but perhaps it was worth finding out more about her all over again.

Yet first there were things to do. Tired beyond the ability to think any further, he decided to wait and see.

*June 9, 1884*

Violet ducked her head into Ivy's kitchen through the open back door, then eased in. "Trifle? Are you here?"

"Yes!" a voice called from the bedroom. "I'm just changing into my gardening clothes. Are you the only one there?"

Violet rolled her eyes. "Who would I have with me?"

"Oh, I don't know!" Ivy said as she emerged from the bedroom, minus a dress over her shift, and threw her arms around Violet. "I'm so glad you're here! I was so excited when I heard you were coming back. Help me decide which dress is close enough to being ruined to be further ruined."

Violet moaned as Ivy dragged her into the bedroom. "Trifle, you know I hate helping with fashion choices! That is not the kind of friendship we have. Neither of us are aware of fashion. That's not how we are."

"I know, but surely you'd have a better eye than me for this!" She snatched two frocks off the bed and held them up. "Bleached blue or pie-stained yellow?"

Violet raised her eyebrows. "How did either of those happen?"

"Both are long stories, but the simple answer is that Jordy makes me laugh, and then I spill things on myself, and ... it's a vicious cycle." She sighed and glanced down at the dresses she held out. "I also shouldn't be trusted to clean things."

"That makes sense." Violet stepped up and felt the fabric of both of the dresses—she wasn't sure why exactly, as she had no idea why people felt fabric or what could be gained by it other than sensory satisfaction ... at times sensory overload. "Hmm. Well, wear the blue one to garden. I don't think there's much chance of redeeming it. You might be able to fix the yellow one, though, if you moved the sash up. It's not that big of a stain. And if you ... if you were pregnant sometime, you'd have to move up the sash, now, wouldn't you? That would be perfect."

A cloud passed over Ivy's sunny face. It was clear that was still a sore subject, but Violet had wanted to find a way to touch upon it ... and to have done so within a few minutes of arriving was an immediate gratification of her desires. Yet without saying a word, Ivy placed the yellow dress over the end of the bed and began slipping the blue one over her undergarments.

Violet flopped down on the bed. So the subject wasn't just a bit sore. It was *very* sore. It took a lot for Ivy not to talk to her. The pain of that lack of communication was hard, but it also spoke to the devastation in her friend's heart.

Again, she was angry, at Ivy and Jordy both. They shouldn't have committed to something as insane and as complicated and as near pointless as marriage without the proper preparation. They were so different.

Jordy was the sun, the moon, and the stars. The sun for Violet's earth to hurl around at top speed, always spinning around the inferno without quite committing to a crash. The moon, ominous and of the night, shining light on things that needed to remain in darkness. And the stars, thousands of pricks that looked so pretty—but if she tried to touch the stars, she would die.

Yes, the sun was her best comparison for Jordy. He was bright as the sun with a magnetism that was inescapable. As she basked in his glory, she slowly forgot that she was in orbit at all and went hurtling into the inferno.

Violet hated the hurtling even as she loved it.

Then there was Ivy. Dear Ivy, her sweet Trifle. Ivy would never put herself at the center of anything. But she had a depth that was immeasurable. When one saw her skirting the edge of a ballroom or tucked away at the piano, it was like watching the foam on the shore. So soft, whimsical, light, harmless ... yet confusing.

As Violet watched the tide crash to the sand, she saw how the foam came to be. How it was beaten by the rhythmic tide, a gentle push and pull. The poor foam, shaped by its circumstance. The tears, drawn out by the rough bank.

Violet went to the tide—it flirted with her feet, but she looked beyond. It looked so peaceful. So she stayed for a while. Then one day she looked around and saw nothing but ocean.

No, Ivy was like a current, gentle. One didn't know what one was up against until one was in too deep.

Ivy paused to snatch a hat off a rack by the door then continued out into the garden without a word to Violet, and Violet followed, as she always did.

"Sorry, Trifle." She stood while Ivy knelt amongst the flowers—her little Ivy, entwining but never quite joining. To think of "ivy" as a parasitic plant was laughable now. That's how Violet had always thought before, but the better she knew Ivy, the better she realized that "ivy" was decorative, that she added to the plants, that if there was any relationship other than symbiotic, it must be with complete consent of the host. Who wouldn't want Ivy around them? "I know it's sensitive, so I pressed on purpose. I won't again. It's your relationship."

"I know. And I know you don't always understand how much things hurt." She tilted her head for a brief moment, caught Violet's eye, and smiled before she was back at her weeding. Ivy weeded differently than Aunt Daphne. Aunt Daphne weeded like a woman seeking her own salvation. Ivy gently tugged out each forbidden plant and placed it to the side, as if she regretted even the death of the weeds.

"I don't, and further, I hate to see you hurt. I do. I just don't always show it." Violet sat down behind Ivy on a large, flat rock. "I'm proud of you, though. Your letters don't even mention a child."

"Yet the desire grows greater every day." Again Ivy paused, though this time her face was tilted up toward the sky, her straw hat, tied by a pink ribbon, falling back. "I wonder why that is! Sometimes I think maybe it wouldn't matter so much if I were to go against Jordy's wishes here. I'm not stupid. I know how my body works. Even if I didn't, I could soon find out. But that would be a betrayal. I know he would feel it as such even if he didn't immediately express it. To hurt him in that way? I never could."

Violet sometimes felt more cat than human, and like a cat, there was the absolute sensation of ears perking at times of heavy interest. "So there is some sort of ... prevention ... I suppose?"

Ivy flushed. "I can't talk about it with you, or with anyone, but yes. Of course. Otherwise we'd ... We might have babies. I can't know for sure, but I believe I could have them. And I want at least the possibility of them! But he denies me that, and he has his reasons, so I must trust him." She sighed and returned to her weeding. "God put Jordy in my life, and everything that followed happened under God's will. I must follow God, and He tells me to submit to my husband."

"How ... are you doing it?" Violet had no doubt that Ivy wouldn't respond, yet she might get a hint based on some subconscious clue. Her Trifle was horrible at keeping secrets, any kind of secrets, and Violet had found out all sorts of things just by asking the right kind of questions and watching for the reaction that inevitably came in some form.

"Violet, you know I can't tell you that! Our relationship is sacred. I've already said far, far too much."

"Hmm. You're the kind of woman who gets beaten all her life and no one knows, aren't you?" Violet slid off the rock into a patch of grass and plucked a daisy, twirling it between her thumb and forefinger absently. "I can't tell you how closely I've watched Jordy's behavior toward you for any sign of it. I would trust him with me, but I was worried about you. However, I'm quite sure he would never lay a hand on you, so I've let things be. But, Ivy, do remember there are other ways to suffer if you truly let a man take away all your autonomy."

Ivy let out a small huff that was almost a laugh. "I forget you've not been married. I know you know about a lot of things, Vi—a great many more than I do. And I'm glad to be the innocent. But when it comes to marriage ... I must claim to know a bit more. There's no lack of autonomy in my relationship. Honestly, I have more freedom married to Jordy than I ever did before. It's just that ... that I respect him enough to give him certain things. Well, most things, really." A satisfied jerk of her chin followed this statement.

Violet was glad Ivy felt like that. She could never marry, but Ivy was suited for it. She had stubbornness in her and strength enough for ten women and a kind of trust and honesty and openness that was unmatched by any other woman of Violet's acquaintance. All the things that a woman needed to own a man's loyalty to the point where submission was an option.

Violet's belief in certain teachings of the Bible were shaky enough these days, after seeing all the things she had over the years, that she wasn't quite willing to accept that most women, let alone all women, ought to submit to a man. This wasn't even some silly bluestocking idea. It was self-preservation. Violet thought women ought to want to live, and to live ... well, the Bible could at times make that living hard with high-minded ideals.

For a woman to respect, a man must love. And how few men really loved?

But Jordy must, as all other men who knew Ivy must. So Ivy walked safely through the lion's den again and again, while lesser women were torn to shreds. Violet respected it. It also annoyed her, but she respected it.

Another long silence prevailed before Ivy raised her head. "I hope you're not hurt that I can't say. But it also wouldn't be good for me to tell you such things because, to explain them to you, since you've never ... It would require me to go into ... And I know you shouldn't hear it."

Violet flopped back and twirled the daisy again. "Never mind it, Trifle. I know everything I could know along those lines—you remember how widely I've read, don't you? There's nothing I haven't heard. But I'd rather you be comfortable. And I can probably guess." She knew Jordy, after all, so the only conclusion to draw had been what Ivy would allow. Which was apparently ... anything. A bit disappointing, but what was submission, really, if there wasn't any sacrifice? Even Ivy must bow to that.

Ivy was glaring at her now. "I wish you wouldn't guess."

"I already have, and you can't take it back." She sat up slightly. "Also, a word to the wise. I read somewhere—don't ask me where, for I can never cite sources when asked—that if you use—"

"Violet!" Ivy's voice allowed no further talking, so Violet shut her mouth and began plucking the petals off the daisy.

*He loves her. He loves me not. He loves her. He loves me not.*

The petals always told her the same story. Why did she keep plucking them?

# CHAPTER TEN

I vy was very proud of herself for talking Violet into visiting Ena
with her. Honestly, half of the fun of having Violet there was
getting to expose her to different things. She felt that the homey,
Christian atmosphere of Ena's store, amongst her children, was
perfect for Violet.

Did Violet agree? Not in the slightest. Did Ivy care ...?

No. Not really. She'd stopped caring about some of Violet's
preferences, at least the ones that weren't informed by trauma. Now
she just took Violet places, and Violet was able to adjust and control
herself. In fact, the more often Ivy took her places and forced her to
interact, the more Violet adjusted.

Ivy was proud of that. The pride, very much colored by
happiness, caused her to reach for Violet's hand as they walked down
the street.

Violet of course slapped her away, but it was a nice try anyway.

"I want you to see if you see what I do," Ivy said, pausing outside
the door. "Ena's in love, I think."

Violet raised her eyebrows, looking interested in something for
the first time that day. "Mm-hmm. I shall definitely want to look for
that."

Ivy opened the door and walked through the store, Violet trailing after her, to the kitchen. There was quite a lot of shouting and what sounded like Alistair banging pots and pans, though maybe with some help. Had Bridget finally condescended to play with her little brother?

They went to the back room, only to see Alistair and Willie Lennox playing on the floor with pans while Ena and Wallace sat at the table, leaning toward each other, eyes full of earnestness, apparently involved in a very serious conversation.

But as soon as Ivy and Violet entered, Wallace was on his feet. "Willie an' I had best be gettin' back tae th' farm noo. We're already past time." He collected his boy and scurried out of the door before Ena had even managed to stand.

She glanced over her shoulder at the girls, laughed, shook her head, and knelt to gather the drums her son had now abandoned.

"I ... I didn't mean to interrupt anything," Ivy said, even as sad, slow notes played in her soul. "If I'd known he was here—"

"Ach, never ye mind. We were close tae finished anyway. An' I'm glad ye've come an' brought yer friend. Alistair, please put tha' spoon—aye, tha's me lad. Wallace had said he'd best be goin' home, an' it was me keepin' him tae talk, so ... 'tis just as well."

"If you say so." Ivy turned her head to Violet and mouthed 'See?'

Violet nodded, a smile causing her lips to twitch upwards despite her best attempts at keeping them from doing so.

"But I'm glad tae see ye both. Let me put on a cup o' tea. Violet, how are ye?"

"Well enough." Violet shrugged and slid onto a chair. "I drift about and visit different people, same as always. It's not the best life, but I like it."

At least, that was what Violet said. Ivy longed for her friend to settle, specifically at Keefmore. Aunt Daphne needed the companionship, and Ivy needed Violet near, companionship or no. She just wanted Violet to breathe the same air she did. That was enough to make her happy.

Though technically, since they both lived on earth, they did breathe the same air, in a way. It wasn't terribly romantic, but Ivy did wonder how air worked. Was it all the same air, or did different areas have different air? If not, was there anything to 'taking the sea air'? Certainly the London air felt different, but how big was an area of the same air? So many questions, and Ivy doubted she'd ever have time to answer them all. Violet knew. Maybe that was enough, that Violet doubtless knew how the world worked. Why would Ivy need to?

Contented, she allowed herself to relax as Ena bustled about the kitchen, put on tea, sent Alistair outside, and sat across from Ivy and Violet.

"I dinna want tae talk about Wallace until things are a bit more settled. Then I'll say everythin' one can possibly say tae ye. I promise." She winked. "In th' meantime, mum's th' word. But let's talk about somethin' else. 'Tis far and away better for me tae think about somethin' else these days."

"Very well." It was so hard, especially since Ivy had invested so many emotions in Ena's new love story, but she could be patient if she must. After all, it was Ena's story to tell. Ivy didn't really want to interfere.

"How's Jordy, then? Ye havena talked about him lately, an' I dinna see him around much."

"He's ... busy." Jordy had been terribly busy. He'd helped out with animals at farms, healed the sick and the wounded, and aided those who had no one to help them. Ivy was proud but also a little lonely. Yes, she'd filled her time. She never had a moment to herself, really. But even without those moments, she still felt lonely.

It was so strange to be among a crowd of other people, to be interacting with them constantly, and yet to be terribly lonely. There were places in her heart that were just for Jordy, and there was never enough of him these days. She supposed that was the essence of marriage. It was good she felt that way, and she hoped it wouldn't last forever as the people of Keefmore were able to take care of more things themselves.

Until then, she'd just have to be patient.

There was so much of a need for patience in Ivy's life. Was that a lesson she'd need to learn? She hadn't known until now, but perhaps it was. God must know what He was doing.

"Aye, I've heard he's runnin' around a lot. I suppose tha's put a strain on ye?" Ena poured the tea and slid the first cup across the table to Ivy. "Nae shame in tha', Ivy. Ye miss him. A feelin' I understand weel! Why, ye could spend time with a thousand people at once an' miss th' one ye want most. Tha's a'right. Truly, it is. We were created wi' this cravin', really, an' there's nae shame in it."

With a slight nod of her head, Ivy acknowledged this. "He does his best. Perhaps I ought to talk to him about it, though. He can be terribly single-minded, even on things that he doesn't need to be focused on. Which is so strange because most would say he's scatter-brained. But once he decides on one thing ... Yet it's not his fault. The needs are great, greater than any one man can fulfill."

"Tha's just th' thing, though, isna it?" Ena poured the second cup of tea and slid it across to Violet. "He canna do everythin'. He just canna. Tha's no' possible. Call him back, Ivy, if ye can. An' if ye canna, wait an' pray."

"I'll do that." At least that was something to do, something to work on. Even though she'd have to be careful about how she phrased it, for she knew Jordy never meant for a moment to neglect her. Some nights, he got home at a decent time, and he was terribly thoughtful when he was there. It was just that he often ran off at odd hours of the night, she never saw him in the morning anymore because of it.

But then, though he was present in the moment, the deepest parts of him weren't. She just got the happy, bubbly, silly Jordy, never the Jordy she wanted most.

The Jordy she wanted most was the one who spouted unexpected wisdom, who comforted better than anyone she knew, who always knew what to say, who held her tighter than anyone ever had, not afraid to crush her, all of him invested in her.

"An' ken tha' I'm always there for ye, tae," Ena continued. "But if ye can work it oot wi' just him, do."

Then the conversation progressed, but Ivy felt a little bit better.

Yes, a lot better. Thank God for Ena. She always put things in the sharpest perspective.

*July 10, 1884*

That particular summer was a slow and lazy one, and Violet enjoyed the fact that it wasn't terribly cold. Often summers in Scotland were, but today it was perfectly pleasant. As such, Violet didn't feel like she fit in. She was a lone cloud across the sky, the singular spot of dark in this perfect picture.

Ivy was happy. Of course, Ivy was always happy, but she was extra cheerful today. As they wandered up and down the small hills surrounding her cottage, she chattered on about people in the village, how their lives had changed and developed, as if she actually thought Violet cared.

Violet didn't care about the people Ivy was talking about, but she did care about Ivy, and that led to a lot more listening than she'd ever thought possible before.

It always amused Violet how even her grouchiest days could be diffused by this little spot of sunlight. Well, at least a bit. Ivy had moved on to talking about Peter's latest book, and Violet was able to participate in that one. Ivy's brother-in-law had now dropped all pretense and was writing romances in between slightly more serious works. Yes, he wrote them with a great deal of depth and focus on character, but they were romances.

She wondered what her life would be like if she'd spent a bit more time with Peter Strauss. He was a man she found quite interesting. If there was anyone other than Ivy who could break through her defenses, it was that man.

Yet she was also frightened. Reading his books confirmed her original impression that he was a man of some strength of character, and he was more grounded, more firm in his path than Ivy. Ivy was a vapor at times; Peter Strauss was a rock, and Violet didn't know what she'd do with a rock that could get into the heart of her and start asking questions.

After their conversation on Peter Strauss's book was finished, a long silence began, but it was a comfortable one. They found the peak of a hill and stood, looking out over the valleys and mountains beyond. After a bit, Ivy took a seat and so did Violet.

Sheep formed white spots below, slowly moving their way up the mountain. They were McAllen sheep, Ivy said. Technically her cottage sat in what was just a great deal of grazing area, but it was home.

Did Jordy know that Ivy wanted to have a home of her own someday, separate from his family and in a dwelling that was more house than cottage? He probably knew but couldn't do anything about it yet. Still, Ivy and Jordy lived frugally, so surely it was only a matter of time.

There were things about Ivy's living situation that she didn't seem to mind but which bothered Violet. For instance, Ivy had no piano in her home. How could a girl like Ivy get on with life without a piano?

Violet herself preferred to have a piano. Playing always calmed her, and she enjoyed music theory. But it was more than that for Ivy. Violet's Trifle had always been somewhat of a Mozart when it came to the piano. She'd caught on fast and played easily, effortlessly ... and it had soothed her and grown her throughout the years.

There was nothing that affected Ivy like music, and yet she didn't have music in her home. Was Ivy content with this? She seemed to be. But Violet wasn't living in a music-less house or married to Jordy. She could be skeptical, and she was.

Would Jordy ever see that Ivy needed more from him? More stability, more emotion, more understanding. Ivy needed someone to reach into her soul and read her like a book.

And then again, Jordy needed other things, different things.

Oh, the fools!

"Tell me about the people at McCale House and the ones who have left." Ivy adjusted her skirts and glanced sideways at Violet with a serene smile. "You'd know more than me, if only because you've seen the McCales lately. We'll have to stop in there on our way to England later this year ... but tell me what you know."

Violet took a deep breath. "Well, you know I don't pay much attention, but I suppose they rambled about it. Felix—Felix Merrill, that is—was visiting last time I went through, and he's working for his father's company. He always says they want to get rid of him, but he's a genius with business—numbers, especially, of course. And he seems all right to me, overall. Still a bit psychotic."

"You would say that." Ivy leaned over and began plucking the small, white flowers that dotted the hill. "But he's all right, overall?"

"Yes, I think so. He said he'd come see you sometime."

"I'd love that! I miss him." Other than Violet and of course Jordy, Felix had been the only close friend Ivy had managed to make at McCale House. Yes, she'd been acquaintances with the others, but it wasn't the same. Violet understood. She liked Felix, too, more than anyone else. Perhaps because he was so helpless and without self-control when it came to his compulsions.

"Lenny, I suppose ... Leonard Barton. He's fine now. I saw him at McCale House a year ago. Still talks up a storm, but his family's taken him back, and he's married. Lives somewhere in Yorkshire. I suppose he works outside a lot. His family is rich, so I don't know why." Violet supposed he was just unable to do anything else, but she didn't say that out loud, for Ivy would be sure to scold her if she dared that. Ivy hated the suggestion that anyone from McCale House was incapable of anything.

But the truth was, and Violet had accepted this more and more ... the truth was that there was no such thing as equal ability. Violet couldn't do things some people could do, and they couldn't do some things she could do. And though Violet's condition wasn't such that it absolutely disabled her in any way, there were children at McCale House who faced actual disabilities, and yet ... so did everyone.

Jordy did, for instance. He was unable to focus; he ran about from project to project; he procrastinated everything. These were the things that immediately came to mind when she thought of Jordy's inabilities.

There was no such thing as a perfect person, according to Ivy herself, and of course Violet was able to believe that. Everyone had some hole in their person.

Violet and some others had more holes. That was her personally held belief. It was not, however, Ivy's.

Ivy straightened her skirts, brushing her hands down her front. "I always thought Leonard was so brave! He was fun to play with. That is, others seem to have fun with him." Leonard had been the most extroverted member of the group, other than Jordy, back when Ivy had been at McCale House.

Other students had come and gone. Ivy had seen one and a half years of them. Violet had seen closer to twenty years. Well, seventeen or eighteen anyway. And even now, she was becoming acquainted again and again with new students. McCale House had expanded enough to have twenty at once—twenty mentally challenged, rich children, though new grants were expanding opportunities. Yet Violet was the same. Would she always be stuck in this endless loop?

Squinting slightly to remember who exactly had been present during Ivy's stay at McCale House, she brought up another name. "There's Ella Willis. I'm not entirely sure what became of her. After she left McCale House, around the time she turned sixteen, she just disappeared. I mean, I'm sure the McCales know, but I don't."

Ivy half closed her eyes. "Lord, I pray she's healthy and happy, wherever she's at."

"I never held much hope for her. Such a ill-tempered thing." Violet grunted. "Though I suppose you could say the same for me."

"All the more reason to pray."

Violet caught Ivy's eye and the end of a smile, which indicated that there had been a note of teasing. She almost laughed aloud. Yes, Ivy was grown up, too.

How had everything changed? In Violet's heart, all was the same.

"What about Minnie Kimber? She left before me, so I remember she was going back to her parents."

"She's still with them, as far as I know. Honestly, I never was close to Minnie."

"Probably because she was sweet. You don't like sweet people, remember, Violet?"

"I like you all right," Violet admitted. "But you're an exception. Your saccharine is bearable."

"And Minnie's wasn't?"

"No."

"Very well. I won't question the logic."

"There is none. It's all feeling. Or sensing. Hard to say which."

"You think all your feelings are sense."

Then Violet turned her full body toward Ivy. "My, you've cut right to the root of everything today, haven't you? What's this about, Trifle?"

"Am I snippy?" Ivy winced. "Sorry. I didn't mean to act that way. I just ... Everything is weighing on me a bit. Move on. Tell me about ... Jesse."

So Violet told Ivy about Jesse Andrews and his stutter, and Ivy's body relaxed as the soft rhythm of talking about students continued.

After Violet couldn't think of another single student to talk about, they lapsed into a comfortable silence once again. The clouds continued to make their way across the horizon, each one a different shape. Ivy pointed out a dog, a dragon, and what she thought was either a ship or something very like a ship, and Violet agreed to all her observations even though she didn't see a single one of those shapes.

Ivy and she were very alike but in some ways, entirely different. They often thought the same way, but the differences they did have were huge, and Violet was never quite able to ignore them as well as Ivy did.

Violet had always been good in school. She hadn't spoken until she was quite a bit older, but once she had, she'd done so in full sentences. No baby talk in between, at least none that wasn't practiced in utter privacy. Mrs. McCale always bragged about that, which was good because Violet's parents didn't care.

And once she'd learn to read—which, to the contrary, had been earlier than most—she'd read and read and read. Through Dr. McCale's entire library, to the point where he'd gone to Edinburgh once or twice a week to obtain more books.

She'd read books on medicine, on physics, on math, and on all the sciences. She'd read more history than could be counted. She'd read nonfiction and fiction, poetry and prose.

And Ivy read, too, but never for knowledge. For enjoyment, for emotion, for insight, for wisdom, but Ivy wasn't interested in a collection of facts. In anything academic, in fact. Whereas, Violet wanted to know everything.

So she'd come to know everything and lost her soul. At least, that was what she'd thought. Perhaps she had a soul within her, and perhaps, still, it had the capability of all the things that a soul was supposed to do.

At the same time, Violet rather doubted it. What was the point of a soul, after all? Except to reach up to God in Heaven ...

Staring up at the clouds, with Ivy making soft remarks beside her, she was able to believe that there was such a thing as God in Heaven. In fact, she almost always believed that. But over and over again, the religion that Ivy had clung so closely to throughout her life had hurt Violet, or at the very least, failed to make any real change in her.

Violet found it hard to forgive that. Hard to put her trust again in something that had done nothing for her. Yet there was a God. Years of study had confirmed that there was something, and because Ivy believed it was God, Violet was willing to do so, too.

But what did that mean? How did that affect Violet? Over and over again, she came back to Ivy's thinking, only to bounce again from philosopher to philosopher. Oh, Violet had read all the greats, but none of them had told her anything.

"Violet, can I ask you something?"

She rolled her eyes. "What do you think, Trifle? Is there anything left of me not bared to you?" There were a few things, but it was best that Ivy didn't even know they existed. The guilt of Ivy knowing these things might be enough to do Violet in completely. And Violet's body and soul already bore enough scars from the uncountable times she had given up. What if she wasn't saved this time?

"Oh, I suppose you're right." Ivy sighed. "It's just a hard question to ask. I've been wondering lately if Jordy's reluctance to ... He told me that he didn't want children. Not just because of me, but because ... of him. And I didn't ask too much. I didn't want to embarrass him. I should've asked, but I was frightened. I will someday, perhaps, once I'm able to be reasonable enough that I won't be bitter. But, Vi, do you think it's possible that Jordy's past has something to do with his reluctance to have children?"

Violet's mind sorted through all the information she had on Jordy's college days. The drinking in London, the parties, the women. His guilt was great, but would it take this form? That frankly didn't make much sense to Violet. "I ... don't think so." Her brain tried to draw lines between the two separate things and was unable to find a clear path. "No. I don't think so."

"Are you sure? Because here's what I thought, sort of." She sighed. "And you're the only one I can tell this to, by the way, for Jordy hasn't told anyone. I mean, I told Aunt Daphne, but I didn't want to talk about this with her."

"Yes, she'd probably decide she had to fix him." Violet indulged a small smile. Her unexpected affection for the aunt she hadn't known well until her twenties was always enough to make her lips twitch with suppressed mirth and gladness. "So I wouldn't bring it up unless you absolutely have to."

"And I doubt I shall have to! For I'll tell you." But Ivy was stalling, so Violet scooted a bit closer and placed a hand over her friend's, briefly. That gave Ivy the follow through she needed, and she spoke. "You see, Violet, what I see here is that Jordy doesn't think he's good enough to be a father. And that's not true! But the fact remains. And I wonder if part of it comes from ... from knowing he failed to be as perfect as he wanted to be. Jordy prided himself, when he was young, on being a Christian. He prided himself on his salvation, and I think it was good for that pride to be broken up. I've come to see God's plan in not allowing Jordy to see himself as morally superior. And I think a lot of the time, we posture about sexual sins and say that they're worse, and that's sunk so deep into him. Why, even my reaction might have confirmed that, for I was very upset with him when he first told me." There were tears puddling in her eyes, and Violet looked away, sadly helpless to do anything. Her Trifle was always weeping. There wasn't much to do but sit in silence and let her do so.

Yet she could say a simple truth: "It wasn't your fault if he decided to take it too hard. Besides, you married him, didn't you? And I doubt you've mentioned it since."

"No, except that we had some conversations about it, to clarify his experiences and solidify our desires for our own ... relations. But I thought I gave him grace there. I wanted to." She raised her hand and wiped the tears off her face, sniffling pitiably. "I couldn't bear it if I caused this. It's hard enough as it is, Vi."

"Trifle, why don't you just tell Jordy all of this?"

"Because I've no word from God that I'm supposed to!"

"Well, maybe I'll say something to Jordy." Violet wrapped her arms around herself. "I just find this whole situation so annoying. How dare he hurt you? How dare you not tell him you're hurting? It's absolutely ridiculous in every way, Trifle."

"I know you think it is," Ivy replied. "But I beg you not to tell him! Let me work this through with God."

"All right, fine. But I think you're making a mistake here, especially from a Christian perspective."

"Perhaps. I'll keep praying about it, of course. But it's not easy, Violet. It's not. Nothing about marriage is easy! And I knew that would be true, but I still feel as if I was unprepared."

"Probably because you were quite a bit emotional at the time of said marriage. Reality must eventually seep in." Same as how the reality of all of Violet's life just kept seeping in. Though there was more to it than that, too. Joy was a hard mark to achieve in this world, and Ivy had managed it more than most. Violet? Not at all. Not really. Vague happiness, short-lasting happiness. Never really joy.

Did she even want it?

"But I'll work it out." Ivy's set jaw, the way she tossed her shoulders back indicated to Violet that she very much meant those words. "Or rather, we'll work it out. Thank you for letting me talk, Violet, though I oughtn't to."

"I don't know how to communicate with you that getting advice from family and friends is not wrong, but I'm here to talk any time." Even though it felt like a thousand knives stabbed in her back at times.

If only it could be easier. For, once, she had been Jordy's first confidante. Once, she had kept his secrets, honored him with her silence.

But that had been a long time ago.

# CHAPTER ELEVEN

There was something different about Jordy McAllen. Violet had known it at once, though he'd acted just the same. His actions spoke of an unchanged Jordy, but there was an extra strained edge, an extra dimness in his light.

He was trying too hard, perhaps. That was definitely part of it. But there was something else that she could sense, something that she felt was different from what everyone else could see.

Violet was sixteen, and Jordy was eighteen now, which she felt meant that their special relationship ought to become more special. She'd never mentioned anything like this to Jordy, but she hoped he knew.

Things had changed with Violet. Ivy had changed her, life had changed her ... Jordy had changed her. She was a different person than she'd been when they'd first met—she'd grown and changed.

Jordy had always been a constant. Even throughout his growing years, he'd remained about the same—always ready with a joke, always cheerful, but with eyes that saw through her somehow despite her best attempts to keep him unaware of what was going on in her mind.

She loved his eyes, golden and utterly him, always sparkling.

*There was mischief in his eyes. If she believed a bit in the Scots folklore he'd tell her when he was too tired to think of anything else to keep her from harassing him, she'd say he was a changeling child. She didn't believe for a minute that even the faye could handle Jordy McAllen. They'd probably wanted to get rid of him.*

*But Violet had no interest in getting rid of him. After all, he was her Jordy, and what was Violet to do without him? These last months, with him far away in London attending university while she stayed at McCale House and was utterly bored, had been torture.*

*At least, for a bit, he'd come home.*

*Violet had waited in his room that night while he'd done whatever Jordy did late at night. He'd at last come in, jumped a bit due to the fact that she was perched on a chair opposite the door, then gone to the hearth to poke at the ashes without a word.*

*She stood, crossed the room, and knelt next to him. "So. How was college? As exciting as you'd hoped?"*

*"Tha's one way tae put it."*

*That was when she noticed the catch in his voice, the way his eyes avoided hers. What was wrong? Something bad, for Jordy was never anything but cheerful.*

*"What is it?" She cocked her head, trying to see his face, but he just turned away from her. He'd cut his hair short, and she missed the shagginess, even though before she had always insulted him for it. "Come on. Tell me, Jordy. You know I won't tell anyone."*

*"I've already told Dr. McCale," he mumbled in that same shaky voice.*

*Oh. So that was where he'd come from. He'd been with Dr. McCale for several long hours, so it must've been something serious indeed. "He's goin' tae help me, an' so I dinna need ... We can deal with it." With those words, particularly with that 'we,' his shoulders rose.*

*So Dr. McCale hadn't scolded him for something. He was upset because of what they were 'dealing with' itself. Interesting.*

*"Just tell me. Or you know I'll find out somehow." The words*

were laced with threat, but she had nothing to follow it with. Still, sometimes she had enough venom behind her tone to convince people there was actual danger in her.

Really, Violet wasn't much of a danger to anyone unless she used sneaky tactics, which were not very intimidating in the moment, frankly.

Thankfully, Jordy obliged. "At college, I ... did horrible things."

"I do horrible things every day." Violet shrugged, but she was doing so despite the fact that her stomach hurt. She was doing so because she needed to remain nonchalant or she'd likely scream.

Slowly, he turned to face the fire, and she saw the tears on his cheeks. "At college, I fell in wi' a bad lot. We did a lot o' things, none o' which I am proud o', but I ... th' worst was tha' I've ..." He stopped and sucked in a quick breath.

And Violet knew. "It was about a woman. Or women. Wasn't it?"

"Aye." He spit out the word. "How did ye—?"

She sighed. "I'm not naïve, Jordy. It was an easy enough guess." His guilt, his inability to tell her, how upset he was. She knew that was the unpardonable, unbreakable rule. "And Dr. McCale said ...?"

"Tha' he'd help me. Tha' God will forgive me. It's hard tae believe tha', but he says I just must believe it." He pulled his knees up to his chest and huddled there, looking so helpless despite the fact that he was now technically a grown man. "Vi, this is such a horrible thing. Dinna let anyone tell ye it isna, for 'tis."

"I understand." In truth, she didn't, but she also was going to press for more. She could do her own research, her own thinking.

Jordy spoke softly about the situation, and she listened, but she didn't need to hear it, for she understood. Without any knowledge of why, she understood, and she was so glad of that understanding.

After all, it meant that now she had something about Jordy, something special to just her—well, just Dr. McCale and her—that she could cherish.

And as Jordy calmed down, as his breath and his voice evened, she became calmer, too.

*For at last she had found a way to reach him. And in truth, it reached her, too. She felt she understood him better ... and in some ways, understood herself better, too.*

*July 24, 1884*

Saying good-bye to Violet was never easy, but it was harder than ever now for there was something distant about her friend. Ivy had sensed it the first time Violet had mentioned she was leaving—not to go back to McCale House but to go back to her parents' house in London.

It was almost as if she was punishing herself. Though Ivy couldn't see why. Violet's mind had seemed stronger lately. Usually she only purposefully hurt herself when there was something particularly pressing on her heart and mind. Ivy couldn't see what that would be.

So she gave Violet one last, firm hug. "Write soon!"

"I will, Trifle. Don't look so glum. I'll try to visit sometime ... or you can come see me for a bit if you like."

Ivy would like, but somehow she also got the idea that her visit would not be as welcome as Violet pretended.

Something was definitely wrong. But if Violet was determined not to tell her, Ivy never would find out, so she resigned herself to letting Violet go.

And indeed she did. She watched the coach drive off until it rounded the bend and was gone and then she stood there for a long time, praying softly for her friend.

Ivy had come to accept that sometimes she couldn't make a change in Violet herself. However, it was still hard. When one loved someone as much as Ivy loved Violet, only being able to offer prayers when the needs were desperate, when the danger was great was so difficult. Yet it must be borne for there was no real way around it.

After a time, she recalled herself and walked down the street to Owen's. There, she stepped in to find Ena behind the counter with Alistair sitting next to her. Alistair slid off his bench and ran to be scooped up by Ivy, and Ena greeted her with a smile.

"Violet left this morn, Ivy?"

"Yes, she did." Never had anything been harder to say. How she hated it when Violet left. "I don't know what I'll do with myself now! In this last month, having her here, it's been brilliant." Especially since Ena had been a little bit preoccupied with the courtship of Wallace Lennox. Ivy didn't want to interfere with that, so she tried to stay away as much as possible, and Violet had been a more than welcome distraction.

"Weel, I'll pray for her. Ye mentioned she's no' ...?"

"Not very responsive right now. I haven't the slightest idea what's wrong, and she won't tell me." Ivy carried Alistair around the edge of the counter, doing a slight twirl which sent him into fits of giggles on the way. "So there's nothing I can offer my dearest friend right now except prayer. Which I of course know can move mountains, but in this case, it will never be a mountain I can move. At least, not for a long while." Another tricky fact about Violet's mind was that it never healed overnight. These things took time, and during that time, patience was required. And more and more prayer.

And even then, Violet would never truly be 'fixed.' Yet Ivy didn't believe she needed to be fixed exactly. It would just be a nice bonus if Violet found it easier to live with herself someday.

Ivy didn't even care if Violet was easy to live with. She could bear anything for her friend, but she wanted Violet to experience joy while living in her own skin. At times, that seemed like an unrealistic goal, while at other times, it seemed just within Violet's grasp.

Oh, how hard she prayed for Violet to find joy!

"Thank you for the prayers," Ivy said, setting Alistair down. "I'm sure Violet appreciates them, though she doesn't know it yet."

"Ach, I think she does more than ye ken." Ena took Ivy's hand. "Ye're a good friend tae her, Ivy, an' she kens tha'. Look. I ken she loves ye, an' she'd do anythin' for ye. Aye, we canna ken her heart, but it's clear ye've had some impact."

"Yes, and I'm glad for whatever I have done, although it's only because God sometimes put me in the right place at the right time and gave me the right words to say."

The conversation moved on again, and Ena got to talking about Wallace. Which was fine. It was exactly what Ivy wanted to hear, that they were finally discussing marriage, that it seemed that a serious proposal was imminent. And she rejoiced for her friend.

But hearing Ena's reasons was so hard just then. "An' o' course I want more children, so I'm glad tae be remarryin', or at least hopin' tae remarry. There's nothin' in th' world like me bairns, an' I adore them, an' ye canna imagine how hard it's been for me tae no' be able tae have more! An' noo I'll have th' chance. Wallace feels th' same, tha' though he loves Willie, th' chance tae give him siblings, in addition tae Bridget and Alistair, is important."

Ivy nodded along, and she was surprised by her own acting skills, for she kept it together until she bid Ena good-bye.

But as soon as she left the shop, as soon as the door shut with the tinkling of the bell, she could feel the lines of her face drop like a mask ripped off. Tears pressed at the back of her eyes, and she ran.

She ran between two buildings to the back of Keefmore and dashed up the new steps in the garden and into the house.

The door banged open, and she stood in the foyer, catching her breath. "Aunt Daphne?" she panted out as loudly as she could manage as she shoved the door closed behind her. "It's me. I-Ivy. I need to talk to you."

Aunt Daphne appeared and gestured into the library. "Go in and say whatever it is. I'm listening."

Ivy walked in and took a seat on the sofa. Aunt Daphne sat next to her, and at first, Ivy focused on catching her breath, then realized that she hadn't just lost her breath but also triggered enough panic that she could no longer breathe. She sent a frantic look at Aunt Daphne.

Aunt Daphne put a firm hand on Ivy's back, pressed her forward so her head was tucked somewhere in the area of her knees, and instructed her to breathe. "In ... now out ... in ... now out."

Once Ivy felt she could form proper sentences, she sat up straight and looked into Aunt Daphne's eyes.

And then promptly burst into tears.

She was gathered close, and she dropped her head onto the older woman's shoulder and sobbed.

"That's it. Go ahead and cry. There'll be plenty of time to tell me after that's done. Did you know that crying is actually good for you? I read about it once somewhere. A doctor said, I think, that—"

And on and on Aunt Daphne rambled, with her logical conclusions about this entirely, for Ivy, emotional thing. And once Ivy had again calmed, been presented a handkerchief, and blown her nose, she was able to speak openly to this woman who she didn't know how she'd survived so many years without.

"Tell me."

"I want a baby. Desperately. But I can't have one, and I ... I hate how all I see around me is children. I hate how everyone, *everyone* gets a chance to be a mother but me." Bitterly, she turned her face away. "I don't understand it. Why can't I have a baby? I think I should be allowed to have one. Violet thinks ... Oh, it doesn't matter what Violet thinks. I can tell God is telling me 'no.' But I've never been so angry about anything in my life, Aunt Daphne! I feel as if I want to shout to the Heavens, 'How dare You deny me this?' For I've learned that it is denial. My prayers keep confirming it." She hadn't heard the exact words, but the impression was clear. 'Stop asking until I tell you otherwise.' So she'd stopped.

In a way.

Every part of her was still in absolute rebellion over this, and she was well aware of that.

"Aunt Daphne, how do I stop rebelling over this? How do I be happy when I can't have the thing I want most? More than that, God has given me a command."

Aunt Daphne sat in silence for a long moment as Ivy calmed her breathing for the third time in the last half hour. Around the same time Ivy grasped at a sense of calm, Aunt Daphne spoke. "I know how hard it is, Ivy. Don't think I don't. Yes, I never really felt I was meant for a life of motherhood, but as the years passed and everyone I knew had children, I wished things were different. But they are not. They're not different. Trust me when I say I went through a lot to come to a place of acceptance over not having the thing I hadn't even believed I wanted.

"Besides, I will admit that it helped that there were benefits. This life you are living ... You can have a great deal of impact, reach a great many more people, be used in entirely different ways as a woman without children. I did. I found ways to make my life matter. Never once in the Bible does it say, despite the obviously capability-based, possibly calling-based command to 'be fruitful and multiply,' that all are meant to have children—or to marry. But, Ivy, think of the difference you can make. Even today, you came here and spent time talking to an old woman rather than staying home. Every day is another opportunity to use your specific situation in life to glorify God."

Thank God for Aunt Daphne. Plainly she'd been placed in Ivy's life for a reason. Letting out a deep breath, Ivy enfolded the woman in another embrace. "Thank you. You have no idea how much hearing that, even if I knew it, has helped in this moment. What would I do without you?"

"Oh, there'd be someone else, or you'd survive, but it's hardly a relevant question since I am here, and God has made it so, and nothing can change what is. Now, I'm thinking ..." Aunt Daphne rose and paced over to her desk, where she scooped up a Bible. "We'd best start a Bible study. You clearly need information that I have to give you, so I'll start giving it." She flipped open said Bible, snatched up a pencil and a piece of paper, and began scribbling down notes. "I have a great many ideas, and I hope they'll be helpful to you."

Ivy stared at Aunt Daphne. "Why ... that would be ..." Perfect. Just perfect. "Such a blessing. It would mean so much to me!"

"Oh yes, of course, of course. It must be what God wants, then. Let me see. We'll start our study in Philippians. Just because I want to. Then we'll move on to discussing verses specifically about working for God's Kingdom and discuss practical steps to do so right now." She leaned back, smiling like a cat that got the cream. "Yes, this will do very nicely."

Yes, indeed, it would. Ivy went home that day with a spring in her step.

Thank the Lord for putting good friends in her path who could make a difference in her life in an actionable way.

# CHAPTER TWELVE

*August 1884*

"Miss Ivy! Miss Ivy!" Bridget's voice, tinged with all its usual overexuberant enthusiasm, broke through the door of the cottage before her slim body managed it.

"Good morning, Bridget." Ivy removed her hands from the dishwater and shook them. "Did you bring your friend Mairi?"

"Nae, but Mum's comin'!" Bridget ducked back out of the cottage, her red curls flying every which way.

Confused, as Ena rarely came Ivy's way at any time let alone mid-week, Ivy grabbed a hand towel and followed Bridget into her garden.

Indeed, Ena was walking over the rise, two-year-old Alistair holding her hand and therefore causing her progress to be a great deal slower than Bridget's.

"Ena!" Ivy called, following Bridget up the path that wove through gray rocks and green grass to meet Ena halfway. "What brings you out my way?"

"I hope I'm no' botherin' ye." Ena glanced about, plainly self-conscious, and dropped Alistair's hand to twist her fingers together. "I just thought ye'd like tae be th' first tae ken. Wallace asked me tae marry him today, an' o' course I said I would."

Laughter bubbled through Ivy's lips, and she flew forward and flung her arms around Ena. "Oh, my dear friend! I'm so happy for you!"

Ena returned the embrace, a shaky sigh causing her shoulders to shudder under Ivy's hands. "Thank ye."

Ivy drew back and glanced to Bridget. "And what do you think? Are you excited?"

"O' course!" Bridget grinned and placed her hands on her hips. "He's been fidgetin' around th' store all this year, an' I'm glad he's just goin' tae stay. An' I like Willie just fine."

Ena grinned. "Bridie has it in her head tha' Wallace is a nuisance an' will never be less o' one. An' really, 'tis Wallace an' Willie who will have tae change their lives th' most. They'll be livin' in th' village wi' us, an' a hand will stay at Wallace's farm until Willie is old enough tae take it on. An' th' sons I'll give Wallace, tae, o' course."

Ivy nodded. "Of course." It was that simple for everyone else. If only it were that simple for Ivy.

Yet she shouldn't be bitter, for her friend was happy, and oh, did Ena deserve happiness!

"And Alistair?" She glanced down at the small boy. He'd never met or known his father, and she didn't doubt the transition would be easier for him than even Bridget. "Do you understand what is happening, our wee lad?"

He grinned toothily, glancing between his mother and Ivy. "Mister Lennox?" His voice lilted cheerfully as he struggled to pronounce his words right. "Comin' tae live wi' us?"

"Aye, me lad. He is." Ena ruffled his reddish curls. "An' Willie'll be yer brother, an' then there'll be more bairns."

"Bay-bay?" Alistair suggested, eyes wide.

"Someday, me lad. Someday soon." Ena's eyes were alight at the prospect. She'd lost two children not long before Ivy had met her, and ever since, she'd talked of nothing but having a large family. Bridget and Alistair were a start, yes, but Ena dreamt of having many more.

Ivy sometimes wondered if it weren't as much to replace what she had lost as to build something new, but Ena usually was fairly clear-minded. She must know that some things could never be replaced.

She would never have her husband, Bob, back. She would never have her son and daughter, Bobby and Flora, back. But she had her oldest, Bridget, and of course Alistair, and now she would have Willie and any children she had with Wallace Lennox.

"But where is Wallace? Surely you didn't run off and leave him alone!" Ivy glanced about as if half expecting Wallace Lennox to pop out behind a hillock. After she'd become engaged to Jordy, officially, at her parents' estate in Kent, she'd not let go of him for the rest of the day. Of course, she'd had to, and it had been a good thing, for both of them were suffering from a deadly case of wandering hands at that point in their relationship. It had been good that he went back to Keefmore until a month or so before their wedding.

She still wondered if they would've 'eloped' as they had that October evening if it weren't for the physical side of things. At the time, it had seemed the honorable, the sweet, the romantic thing to do. Now she doubted her own thought process. How clear-minded had she been in those moments? Would she have made the same decision now as she did then?

"Ach, weel, we're no' all free all th' day long." Ena winked. "Wallace came oot tae speak wi' me this morn but had other things tae do in th' village, so we'll have a meal wi' each other this eve, an' until then, I am free. But I couldna sit still at me store after havin' received a proposal. I had tae come tell ye!"

"And I'm glad you did!" Ivy gestured to the cottage. "Do you want to come in? Or perhaps we could sit outside, as it's such a nice day. I could make tea."

"Tha' would be nice. Bridie, do ye want tae run back tae tell Mairi noo?"

Bridget nodded enthusiastically and galloped back over the moors.

Alistair looked after her longingly until Ivy suggested showing him to her cat, Heather, who usually hid behind the cottage, where a pile of wood was stacked up to the eaves. Delighted, Alistair was content to gently hold and pet Heather while Ivy and Ena had their tea.

"You love him, don't you?" Ivy watched Ena's face closely as she asked. "It's not just about the safety he offers nor that he is Bob's old friend. You care for him yourself."

"I wouldna marry him if me heart were entirely closed off." Ena shrugged lightly and stared into her teacup. "An' ye ken I want a fuller household. But nae, th' decision is no' entirely practical. We'll get on well enough."

Ivy guessed that was the most Ena would allow for now. She was an honest woman, always sincere, but as such, she rarely overdramatized anything she said. In fact, she rarely committed to any extreme emotion, and at times, the feeling of being in love was excessive.

Ivy missed those days. She doubted Ena did, as even now she seemed ill at ease with her own heart. For Ivy, the euphoria of first touches, the pleasurable discomfort of not being entirely sure, was an interesting sensation to explore.

It must torture Ena a bit, though. She was the type to be happier past the honeymoon stage.

Ivy had found she wasn't.

As she listened to Ena talk about Wallace and the future of the store and the way they intended to combine their two families, Ivy's mind drifted to the early days of her marriage. Jordy and she had eloped when Alice became so ill that they were forced to cancel their wedding, and the honeymoon had been brief but ... well, perfect. Jordy had met her confusion and fear at every turn with his understanding and gentleness, and he'd wooed her in a mysteriously perfect way.

And surrendering control was easy for Ivy. Grasping her own influence in the relationship was more difficult, but letting Jordy take the lead was effortless. It came naturally to her.

Then they'd returned to Pearlbelle Park. Alice had been slowly recovering, and Jordy and Ivy focused on her when they could.

However, they continued finding time to themselves, and Ivy for the first time had found she couldn't offer much of herself to anyone but Jordy.

About a month and a half later, in early December, they'd renewed their vows at the church with family and friends in attendance. She'd played her part, and so had he, to keep gossip to a minimum. That second honeymoon, with both of them emboldened, had proven a further enlightening experience.

Then they'd come up to Scotland, and ... they'd begun to settle.

And here they were now. Struggling in ways Ivy couldn't comprehend. Oh, she needed to do better!

But it took two to make a marriage work.

At last, Ena needed to go. Ivy embraced her one last time and promised to do whatever she could to put together a beautiful wedding. Ena swore she didn't need anything but a church ceremony to be happy, but Ivy swore she would not allow the wedding to proceed without at least some decorations. Ena laughingly agreed, and then she was off, taking her dear Alistair with her.

Ivy sat on the stoop and stroked Heather and daydreamed of a simpler time.

She'd understood from her wedding night on that life would not be exactly what she had dreamt of. However, she couldn't have guessed it would be so terribly different. She'd assumed she would have a discussion with Jordy sooner rather than later. Before the marriage, he'd not spoken as if they would never have children.

In fact, she frankly wasn't sure how they'd managed not to stumble upon their differences here, as varied and many as their conversations had been.

How had she missed this simple but vital question? 'Do you want to have children with me?' was so basic. She was half-convinced they'd had that conversation. She remembered snippets of it. She certainly had shared bits of her daydreams about being a mother.

So how had they gotten to this point?

Ivy was starting to realize how terrible she was at communicating her own wants and needs.

*September 1884*

The groom kissed the bride just outside the door, pulling her into a brief embrace. Bridget squealed, which set off Alistair and Willie into similar noises of excitement and confusion.

Ena drew back swiftly and smacked Wallace in the chest, but Ivy was close enough to catch the blush on her cheeks, the sparkle in her eyes. Ena clearly adored Wallace, no matter what she said—and, all the more dangerous for her friend's heart, Wallace knew it, knew *Ena.*

Thankfully, the citizens of Keefmore had recovered from the prejudice they'd held toward Ena when Ivy first arrived there all those years ago. Now they embraced her wholeheartedly, celebrating with Ena and her new husband.

Mairi was there, of course, standing next to her best friend Bridget and looking pleased for her. Ivy stood behind her, grinning and squeezing Jordy's hand, perhaps excessively tight.

There was to be a celebration in the town square, and Ivy took Edith's son, David, away so his parents could enjoy a bit of a break. She took him to the pastor's home to lie down in the upstairs bedroom. Mrs. McAllen followed not long after her.

"Me dear, li'l grandchild," she murmured, brushing his brown-red curls back from his forehead. "When do ye think Edith will have th' courage tae cut these? She ought tae, but I took me time wi' th' first curls. They never come back. Ye shoulda seen Jordy about this age! His hair was lighter then, like David's, an' he was quite a wee charmer."

Ivy laughed softly. "I'd have liked to have seen him."

"Ach, someday ye'll have a bairn who looks just like this." She smiled and moved away from the bed. "Though I suppose I oughtn't tae say tha', as we dinna ken wha' th' Lord has planned."

Of course. She'd wondered why her mother-in-law hadn't brought that up before. So now was Ivy going to be questioned about something she couldn't control and could barely understand?

Yet Mrs. McAllen continued on. "I hope Edith and Tris have another child soon. David could do wi' no' bein' th' spoiled only child. Especially since I'm so likely tae spoil him."

Ivy nodded. That was true. She should've been the one to cause him to be removed from 'only grandchild' status, but since she wouldn't be able to, it would of course be Edith who had the next child.

All of Jordy's siblings would probably be married with families of their own before Ivy had a child, if she ever did.

Yet she forced herself to push back the bitterness. That was no way to live a life. *Lord, live through me, for on my own, I am so weak ... and so disappointed.*

This wasn't the life she wanted, but she must make the most of it. She must.

Mrs. McAllen talked on softly about David and his possibilities of having a younger sibling, though Ivy could tell there was an undertone to the conversation. She was tactful and gentle, but she plainly was under the misconception that Ivy was infertile.

In some ways, that might as well be true. But in reality, it wasn't an accurate description of Ivy's situation. God would have to work around human planning if she had any hope of having a child.

Granted, God could do just that if He had a mind to. Ivy believed that, and yet she also believed that that time wasn't now. The restraint on her heart, the barrier she felt whenever she pressed at the topic, confirmed it.

*Yet what about me? What about what I want?* She couldn't help but cry out for her dreams, the dreams that felt so greatly crushed.

Edith came in at last and urged Mrs. McAllen and Ivy to return to the festivities, saying they shouldn't have both holed themselves away for her wee lad, and anyway, now that he was asleep, there was no need to keep so close an eye on him.

So Ivy went back out in the joyous fray, determined to be a light and not a damper.

# CHAPTER THIRTEEN

Not long after Ena's wedding, Ivy received a letter from her mother and one from Alice, which was not unusual in and of itself. However, the contents of both caused Ivy to feel a lovely mix of anxiety and joy.

She read her mother's first, of course.

*Dear Ivy,*

*I was so glad to hear that things are going well with you. I'll respond to your last letter in month depth later, but I have news.*

*Peter and Alice are in England to visit us and other friends, and recently Alice has been asking me if she might be able to come up and see you. My thought was that it might be a possibility, but I wasn't sure.*

*Peter is writing a novel set in Scotland, for the first time, and he wants to turn it into a bit of a research trip. But of course they couldn't go to Scotland without seeing you.*

*I know you've had people stay with Mrs. Daphne Wright in the past, but I wasn't sure if that was still an option. All I know is that Alice and Peter would very* much like to head that way, and I think the ability to do so would be a great blessing to both you and them. I think you'd enjoy seeing Alice. She is much changed, in a good way. You'll get along much better than you have before.

Anyway, I am prefacing all this information that will also be communicated in Alice's letter, though she knows I'm writing some details, so she will likely omit some of this information.

I'll respond more in depth to other things you've been talking about lately as soon as I get a chance.

I hope you're doing well, my dear!

Your mother,

Claire M. Knight


Alice's letter came next.


Dear Ivy,

I'm sure Mother has communicated a lot of this, so I won't offer too much in way of an introduction. Peter and I are in England, and he has things he wanted to look at in Scotland.

Could we come stay near you?

I have other purposes for my visit, but that would be the basics of it. I've missed you, and we never seem to be at Pearlbelle Park at the same time. I have a great many things to say—things I should've said before but never had the opportunity or perhaps, as Peter always says to me, have never quite been courageous enough to abandon my humanity long enough to do so.

There's a lot of bravery in the Christian life, and I've never been very brave. Not since I was a small child. Do you remember when I was brave? For I barely do.

*All that said, I look forward to your response. If now is not a good time, that's all right. We'd be heading that way by October. We'd be there for a month or so. Again, if it's an imposition, tell us. We would hope to stay with Mrs. Wright—the invitation was opened at your wedding, though none of us has yet accepted, so we wondered if it might still be open.*

    *Your sister,*
    *Alice Strauss*

After showing these letters to Jordy and Aunt Daphne, she was able to reply in the affirmative.

But she couldn't help but wonder why they were visiting.

*October 1884*

Alice stepped down from the coach after Peter and immediately moved toward Ivy before he even had a chance to do so. "Ivy, darling!" She wrapped Ivy in a surprisingly tight hug, which Ivy returned with enthusiasm—surprised enthusiasm, but enthusiasm nonetheless.

"Oh, Ivy, it's so good to see you!" Alice drew back with a smile.

Ivy searched her sister's face but saw nothing there but honesty. Could Alice truly be sincere? She seemed so, but sometimes Ivy could be a poor judge of truth. She was sadly prejudiced when it came to Alice, by virtue of her being, well, Alice.

Peter came over then to embrace her and repeat Alice's sentiments. He was truthful, of course, but she'd come to trust Alice a little less with every month that passed.

"I admit I'm more than a little thrilled to be meeting Aunt Daphne again," Alice remarked as they moved away from the coach, where Jordy was seeing to luggage with his brother Mick. "I always found her interesting, and I can't wait to get better acquainted with her. I'm also glad we won't be pressing in on you."

Peter nodded, casually taking Ivy's arm. She liked that about him, too, that he always paced himself with her, that he took time for her. She squeezed his arm and cast a sideways smile at Alice, appreciative of her sister's husband's thoughtfulness. "You know, I wouldn't have come, even though I wanted to badly, if there hadn't been a way to give you some privacy. And I like Aunt Daphne, too."

"Oh, everyone does." At least Ivy thought everyone did. She had yet to meet anyone who precisely disliked Aunt Daphne—or Lady Wright, as some of the people of Keefmore called her—and she felt it'd be an absolute shame to meet such a person. They surely wouldn't be terribly likable themselves. Even the grouchier ladies of Keefmore begrudgingly acknowledged she was a strong woman.

They crossed through the town square and made their way to Aunt Daphne's house. Peter and Alice both stopped and laughed aloud.

"It is funny, isn't it?" Ivy smiled with the admittance. "She's built this grand London townhouse—tall and skinny, almost as skinny as they are in the town—in the middle of a Scottish moor, and she's surrounded it by this Yorkshire cottage picket fence and a funny little garden."

"How delightful!" Peter exclaimed at the same time Alice, apparently not completely changed in whatever way her mother had referenced, murmured, "How odd!"

But Ivy didn't mind either perspective, and neither would Aunt Daphne. Odd and delightful were synonymous to that woman.

Ivy entered through the gate, which was perpetually open and therefore rather pointless, and stepped up the path, with Peter and Alice making random comments about the variety of flora Aunt Daphne had managed to introduce. Ivy, who knew at what cost a lot of that flora had come, made a mental note of everything they said to be relayed to the owner of the garden later. Even in October, there were quite a few things to be noted still blooming or maintaining leaves.

Ivy opened the door and peeked around. "Aunt Daphne? I've brought Peter and Alice, as I promised to." She stepped inside and allowed her sister and brother-in-law entrance before gently closing the door.

Aunt Daphne appeared out of the library. "There you are. I'm excited to have you both stay with me. I haven't had anyone since my niece left me, and sometimes Agnes drives me a bit wild. Duncan doesn't, though. We drive Agnes wild together."

"Duncan?" Alice glanced sideways at Ivy.

"He's Agnes's child. Agnes is my ... everything? She does everything here. I can't cook, and you'll definitely value that fact when you taste her creations." Aunt Daphne whirled toward the stairway, then whirled back around. "Oh, Duncan's her illegitimate son. I suppose I ought to mention that. None of your business, really, but people do seem to get caught up on it."

Peter responded with a somewhat surprised but comforting murmur while Alice said nothing, probably not knowing how to deal with that kind of frankness. Which Ivy couldn't help but find amusing.

Aunt Daphne immediately then proceeded to think of something she'd forgotten and scurry off, so Ivy was the one who escorted Alice and Peter upstairs to one of the bedrooms, which was prepared for them.

"I've always liked this room. It was mine when I stayed here that first time—you know, when Jordy and I were ..." Not courting. She always struggled with the wording for explaining what they'd done, for they'd courted after they'd both considered themselves engaged. Before it had just been stumbling about each other and trying not to fall in love and falling in love anyway, because, after all, that was what God wanted.

Which she clung to on the hard days. *"This is what God wanted,"* she'd whisper over and over again. Nowadays she had those moments quite a bit, when her new Jordy was again not as present as she needed him to be. He was distant, cautious. He worked hard and long at the same things every day. Where was his courage? Where was his devotion, his endless willingness, even eagerness, to take on a challenge? Where was his sense of adventure?

She wanted her husband back.

But she forced herself back to the present, where Peter and Alice were exclaiming over the sweetness of the room and wondering over the intriguing Aunt Daphne who had managed to bring Northern England to Scotland.

"Why would you want to do that, though?" Peter said with his typical Americanness. "Scotland has its own culture, its own way of being. Why make yourself a London townhouse here?"

Alice laughed. "Oh, Peter, you will never understand the comfort of familiarity, will you? Besides, Scotland is just beyond the window. My, this house must've cost her a fortune!"

"I believe it did, but she lives simply now. She doesn't pay Agnes—she just stays on as a friend, and they split the household chores. She has no one else to turn to." Ivy shrugged. Agnes's story was one of redemption to her. She'd always appreciated it—and of course she adored Duncan. Everyone did.

"Is she a Christian?" Peter would, of course, never not be Peter.

"Agnes and Aunt Daphne both are." Both very wise Christians indeed, especially Aunt Daphne. At least, she was when she bothered to slow down.

Just then, Duncan burst through the doorway and into Ivy's skirts. She placed a hand on top of his hand to still him before they both went sliding across the floor.

"And who's this?" Alice knelt and met Duncan's eyes, another thing that surprised Ivy. "Are you Duncan?"

Duncan's eyes widened, but he nodded.

"I'm Alice."

Duncan stuck a finger in his mouth, then removed it and glanced up at Ivy with a confused expression on his face. After all, who was this strange woman in his house? Aunt Daphne often joked that

Duncan was the man of the family and must behave as such, and at three, Ivy was sure he'd started to take it seriously. Yet he still remained quite shy.

"This is my sister Alice Strauss." Which always felt strange to say and probably always would even after Alice had been married twenty or thirty years, which she hadn't. Besides, *Alice Strauss* just had some interesting alliteration toward the end that Ivy could never quite get around. Yet she was sure her sister didn't at all mind being Alice Strauss. She'd come to act rather proud of the fact, actually. "Alice will be staying with you for a bit."

Duncan nodded seriously. "Good morn."

"Say, 'I'm Duncan!'" Ivy encouraged. "'Good morn, Mrs. ...' Or do you want him to call you Alice?"

"I think it's easier."

"Say, 'Good morn, Alice.'"

"Good morn, Alice," Duncan repeated obediently, though he still eyed Alice and Peter warily.

Alice leaned away, seeming to understand this. And when had Alice ever understood anything? Apparently now she did. "Duncan, we'll talk more later. You'll have to show me your room, but for now, I must get settled. Oh, do you think you could show me the house?"

Duncan's face showed something other than apprehension for the first time as a small smile appeared. "Aye."

"Good! Come back and see me in a little bit, won't you?"

Duncan nodded, then scurried out of the room.

"His dear little brogue," Alice murmured absently as she took the carpetbag Peter carried and opened it. "Peter, do you want to tell her?"

"Oh! I forgot. I brought you a copy of my next book, *Matins*. It's coming out this month, and I thought you'd appreciate it. I'll also be writing another book while I'm here—I have a bit of a deadline, I think in December ..." He glanced at Alice.

"Mm-hmm."

"Anyway, I'll try to write fast enough for you, and then you can read the chapters as I get them written in a legible handwriting. Alice will help me with that." He grinned. "She rewrites all my drafts so it's not chicken scratch."

Alice cast him an affectionate smile as she withdrew a stack of papers tied with strings. "But here's this one. Its working title is just 'Katie Grace' on account of the main character's name. *Matins* is in the other trunk if you want it, too."

Thrilled, Ivy hurried forward to take the novel and assure Peter that she would read it in a day and he'd never be able to write fast enough for her. He laughed and gave her a hug and assured her he'd do his best.

Aunt Daphne came in, followed by Jordy and Mick with the luggage, and there was a rush to get everything settled.

After a bit, Peter and Alice were settled enough to be considered useful once again. "Can we see your house today?" Peter's eyes held that eagerness that told her she would love whatever she showed him, whether it was a shack or a mansion.

Ivy nodded. "I want to show you! Let's go now."

"Where's Jordy gone to?"

"He had to get back to the office." 'Had to' being a strong turn of phrase, but that was how Jordy viewed it.

Alice took Ivy's hand. "Take me to see where he's got you living. I shall disapprove greatly of his providing, but never of your home."

Ivy laughed, and the three of them walked together all the way to the little cottage that, though Alice might judge it, was perfectly sufficient. And Ivy assured Alice of this over and over again even as Alice said again and again that Jordy could buy Ivy a castle and she wouldn't be happy.

This led to Peter interfering in the good-hearted argument to declare that though nothing was good enough for their Ivy—that was true—perhaps sometimes a cottage was as good as a castle.

Ivy had always thought so.

"There are some changes we'd like to make sometime, if we've a chance," Ivy murmured, nervous of their opinions now that they had actually come over the rise and stood looking down on her small home.

Peter and Alice glanced at each other and smiled—she wondered, vaguely, if Jordy and she did that and if it were equally infuriating—but they both immediately praised the little cottage.

They walked down and commented favorably on Ivy's garden, though it was growing barer and barer. Apparently Alice's garden back in America wasn't in the best of shape this year due to a lot of gardening, which Peter teased her about—and another of those sweet bickering conversations began, even though Alice couldn't stop laughing.

Ivy couldn't remember a time, even when they were children, that Alice couldn't stop laughing. It made Ivy laugh, too.

Inside the cottage, which Ivy had, when Jordy wasn't about, scoured from top to bottom over the last few weeks, Peter was delighted and even Alice found things to compliment.

Everything was perfect now. Why couldn't they have come earlier?

Though she wondered if, earlier, Alice had been ready to come— and would Ivy have been ready to receive her? Yes, God had brought this trip around at just the right time for everyone involved, and for that, Ivy was endlessly grateful.

"I want you both to eat dinner with me. I've talked to Aunt Daphne about it. Jordy is going to come off work early today, and we can get all caught up. I can't wait to start that book, Peter! What's it about?"

Peter sat down at the kitchen table. "Why don't you just read it?"

"He hates that question." Alice, too, took a seat, gesturing for Ivy to do the same. "He never answers it, even though it's never that complicated."

"If it's so easy," Peter said, "why don't you try it? No, I dare you to. For any of my books, off the top of your head."

Alice shrugged. "Your first, *War of Brothers*, is about two brothers who fight on opposite sides in the American Civil War—and one of them has that sweetheart in Philadelphia. *O Susanna!* is a novel about a girl who travels and experiences a great deal of hardships but is rescued conveniently by a handsome pioneer. *The Death Upon Her Eyes* is dramatic mush that sixteen-year-old girls everywhere love—"

Peter and Ivy both protested, but Alice continued.

"Well, I've got to think of it in that way or I'll think of it as personal, which I hate. It's like being a pastor's child, I suppose—you're ever afraid you're the example. Then *Matins* is a story that I actually enjoyed about a clergyman working through his complicated feelings about God and faith. And that brings us to our next work, *Katie Grace*, which is going to be another romance. It's set in Virginia before the Civil War, and it will be ... complicated to write."

"Hmm. It'll be monstrous to get it published, but I've insisted it will be. I won't stop bothering my publisher until it is, even if I have to give him something else." Peter sighed. "No one wants to hear what I have to say, but they'll hear it nonetheless. And if nothing else, there is a story there."

"Only because of my bullying! You should've heard the ideas he had with no structure, no grounding." Alice clucked her tongue. "Peter loves writing random vignettes with no connection. It's most unsettling."

"I love it because I love my characters! There are a lot worse things I could love. At least it's helpful for my career. But, Ivy, I can't wait until you read *Katie Grace*. I think you'll like her, and some of the side characters, and it'll introduce you to a world I've never had the heart nor the strength to tell you about. But somehow writing is different."

Ivy nodded. As always, there was an understanding between Peter and her. His writing was her music. She only wished music was a bit more easily interpreted into words. Feelings, yes, but at least with his writing he could set out what he meant in simple terms if need be.

Music wasn't like that. Sometimes it could help others understand certain elements of the emotions that tended to overwhelm her, but mostly it was for herself and for God. Unlike Peter's novels that had been read by hundreds and even thousands of people.

And it sounded like this novel was one of the more challenging stories he'd decided to tell. She was curious to read it now.

"What novel will you write next?"

"Oh, I have an outline. Or Alice does. I think it might drift away a bit, though. I've written the first two chapters, and I need to explore the way a few small changes will affect some things toward the end. That's why we're researching—the facts must be in place, after all. Alice doesn't want me to continue until she's approved the first bit and until I've learned a bit more about Scotland."

"I haven't had a chance to read it yet," Alice explained, "so I don't know what needs to change."

"Right." Peter nodded. "It's just a matter of making everything match up right."

"What's the setting exactly?" It was awfully hard to get details from Peter about his book, but Ivy had learned the right questions to ask.

"Oh, around this area. Part of the reason I wanted to come here to visit this time of the year. I'm sure there's something I could draw from the British, as Scotland's culture has morphed into something vaguely English, but I still needed to see this."

Ivy laughed. "Don't tell anyone in Keefmore that there's anything British here, or they'll return to their savage ways."

Of course she didn't really mean it. Though perhaps the people of Keefmore would at times want outsiders to believe what she said.

"I do hope we won't be burnt at the stake or stoned while we're here," Alice observed.

"That would make it a glum vacation." Peter grinned. "But it won't be."

"Tell me about your main character of this Scottish story," Ivy said, and Peter launched into the many details he had accrued about his main characters. His story was apparently something inspired by *Wuthering Heights*, though with some other elements mixed in.

"It's a bit Dickens, a bit Brontë. And a bit me, I hope."

"He's been clever, though, about *Katie Grace.*" Alice smiled at him, but there was just a touch of irritation in her tone. "I've been reluctant to even let him write it. His sentiments bled in *War of Brothers,* but I feel like anything more obvious would lead to ... Oh, all sorts of things."

"We won't be harmed. Not as long as we're careful. As I mentioned, I'll be using that pen name for this publication."

Alice rolled her eyes. "Still such a mean thing to do to me."

"What do you mean?" Ivy glanced between them. "Peter, you're using a pen name for *Katie Grace*?"

He nodded. "I am. Though Alice is right; I was cruel. I told her I would use a pen name to protect our family, but she must let me use the name I wanted. She agreed. And I've chosen P.S. Penn."

Ivy laughed in delight. "Did Riley weigh in on that one?"

"He did, actually! I know it'll be traced back to me—but I want it to be. It won't be obvious to all, but most will trace it back to me. However, I'll make it a little harder to do so. They'll be able to if they've a mind."

Alice held up her hands. "He's brought me around to his way of seeing things. When Peter holds something so deeply in conviction, I trust him. We haven't children, and I'll be careful. He should write this story, if it is what he was meant to write, and though I prefer the slight security of it not being directly his name, and the separation of it not being sold with his other stories, I think there's validity in making it easy for people to figure out. Also, that way we have the freedom to publish with another publisher or more quickly—whatever happens will be easier to navigate without the direct reputation of Peter W. Strauss attached to the book."

Peter nodded. "It's more a business decision than anything. But I am not ashamed of how I feel. I know I have to do something."

"Right." Alice sat down at the kitchen table. "I quite agree."

Jordy arrived then, and Alice shooed Peter and him out of the room so Alice and she could prepare dinner. At first, they worked in silence, but then Alice spoke.

"Ivy, I'm sorry."

Ivy glanced over her shoulder. "What do you mean?"

"I've not treated you well, and you deserve better. You're an intelligent, strong, godly woman, and I've treated you like a child. I don't expect you to forgive me, but I just wanted you to know I see you for who you are." She sighed and shook her head. "I see a lot more things for what they are now, and it's overwhelming but so good for me."

The ladle Ivy held clattered to the ground. Alice knelt, retrieved it, and tossed it in the tub of soapy water before retrieving a rag to wipe up a few droplets of soup.

"I know you're surprised, and I don't need a reaction, but I thought you ought to know. You've been a good, faithful sister to me. I don't know how much Peter ... No, he wouldn't have told you anything. But I am not owed half of what I have received in life. You're a big part of that. I don't deserve you, Ivy."

Ivy hiccupped then, without quite knowing the reason as her emotions had yet to inform her exactly why she was upset, she dropped onto the kitchen table and began to cry.

Alice pulled out another chair and sat down next to her. "Have my handkerchief. Want some water?"

Ivy managed to shake her head, which proved a little difficult while her face was buried in her arms.

"Should I leave or may I sit with you? I would like to, but you can be alone, too, if you need. I don't have to be here."

"Stay."

So she stayed while Ivy, feeling completely irrational, wept.

After the tears had slowed and Ivy had risen and blown her nose and washed her face, Alice asked her why she'd cried. "Was it just because you can't forgive me?"

"No! Oh, Alice, no!" Ivy hiccupped and threw her arms around Alice. "Never that. I'll always forgive you—I have to. You're my sister!"

Alice winced. "I'm—"

"Even if you weren't, it wouldn't matter, because you are my friend."

"Thank you. I'm glad." Alice took a deep breath and let it out slowly. "It fills me with immeasurable relief, for you mean a great deal to me. More and more, I look at my childhood and realize that you were my crutch. I took care of you—and how lost I felt when, for one stupid reason or another, I stopped doing that. Yet I needed to be independent and to grow up, and I felt I could no longer do so with you in tow. I was wrong—I was entirely wrong. But I'm glad that, in spite of me, you've grown up to be the woman you are."

That sent Ivy into another round of tears, though this time the comfort of clinging to Alice made it seem less silly and pointless.

Jordy and Peter came in after a bit, and both demanded explanations—albeit in slightly different tones—but neither Alice nor Ivy could give one.

Alice, of course, managed the closest approximation. "We're sisters, so we had a talk. Ivy, wash your face—and for heaven's sake, let me finish that soup!"

# CHAPTER FOURTEEN

Ivy gasped as Duncan suddenly decided to toss himself onto the rock-laden turf of the hillside and roll down. Beside her, Alice stiffened but said nothing.

He reached the bottom and stood, waving up at them, then began the long trudge up the hill.

"Little boys are frightening," Ivy said.

"They are, aren't they?" Alice took a seat on one of the larger rocks. "But if he's entertained, I suppose it doesn't hurt anything."

"As long as he doesn't fall and hit his head." Nonetheless, Ivy took a seat on a similar mossy rock.

"He's three?"

Ivy nodded. "Four in January."

"Ah. So the same age."

Ivy almost asked 'the same age as who?' but it hit her, and she bit her own lip.

"I can tell what you're thinking, and that's not what I was talking about. I have a nephew who's his age—Barnie. No, my first would've been born May 1882, though I lost him in October of 1881, and obviously Daniel was in August of that year. So they'd both be about two, two and a half. Not nearly as grown as Duncan here."

Duncan arrived then and fell against Alice's skirts. "Are ye goin' tae try it?"

"Rolling down the hill?" She shook her head and laughed, holding his shoulders to keep him from leaving. "Do I look like the type of person who would roll down a hill?"

He shifted from leg to leg, grinning. "Ma-aybe."

"Maybe? That's a surprise to me. Not today—it's a bit damp, and I don't want to change dresses. You go on by yourself, darling."

Duncan nodded and dashed off.

"Isn't he precious?" Alice turned sparkling eyes to Ivy. "He does make me wistful for what might have been, but I'm around enough little ones that the feeling is fading. I'll always wonder, and I'll always grieve—but I'll always hope, and I'll always do my best with what I have now. I think. That's the idea at least. My faithfulness may vary." She leaned back, arms braced behind her, and tossed her head back to look at the sky. "Last year was torture."

"Oh." Ivy didn't know how to respond to that. Alice was ever the strong one, the one who didn't falter. Vulnerability was not something she associated with her sister. "I'd have thought the year before that would be worse."

She shook her head. "No, dear old 1883 just about killed me. Which is kind of ironic, because I'd been doing my best ... Oh, I won't joke about that. But everything sank in, and all of a sudden, my lies and my pretenses were gone. Peter and I had to tear each other apart with every step we took forward. It was incredibly difficult but incredibly good. If Cassie hadn't come to stay with us, we might not have made it. She stepped in for us in a way no one ever has for me before. I learned so much from her about what it is to be a friend, and I will ever be indebted to her."

"I'm so glad." Though Ivy herself had longed to fill the position, she'd been newly married, and the timing just hadn't been right. When Alice's dearest friend, Cassie O'Connell, who had gone to school with her, had offered to accompany Alice and Peter back to America, Ivy's relief had been immeasurable. She couldn't have borne to think of Alice there without someone to support her.

"She just let us both talk to her, which was invaluable. Peter says we abused her greatly, and I'm inclined to agree with him. We shouldn't have used her as our person to rant to—but we needed someone. Talking to a wall isn't quite the same, and prayer is lovely, but God put people on earth for a reason. There was a safety in being able to share with someone who wasn't intimately involved with every situation—and yet knew what we meant. Cassie did volunteer for the spot, and we were cautious about limiting some details and giving her space to herself. Which worked out quite well, as you know. She's quite thrilled with the results of that trip—that's why we came back to England." She winked. "I'm thrilled for her, too."

"But you're better now, aren't you?" Ivy asked. "You really are. No pretenses, no lies."

"I am. Most of the time I feel wonderful. Sometimes it hits me, but in those moments, I just need Peter and God, which is a relief. Having to rely on others was good for me, but I was ready to form a bit more of a family unit. Which, by the way, is just Peter and me and an obnoxious cat and an energetic dog—which I'm sadly only half-joking about." She raised her eyes to the sky. "I married a man who adores animals just for the sake of them being small creatures he can take care of, and it's maddening. I don't personify things, Ivy. I never will. Yet here I am, with a man who talks to his pets. What am I going to do with him?"

"Nothing, I don't think. He's perfect just the way he is," Ivy said firmly. She'd always believe that about Peter, no matter what, so perhaps that wasn't fair. She also didn't have to be married to him, which Ivy realized changed one's perspective just slightly.

"But I'm all right. Don't worry about me. How about you? How are you managing?" She gestured around her. "I won't lie and say I don't think this is lovely and picturesque, but I know life isn't all sunshine for even the happiest of us. Complain to me—I've learned to be quiet, so the skill might as well go to use."

Ivy opened her mouth to say the reassuring, sweet things she said to her mother—that Jordy and she were happy, that he was her world, that she had never loved someone more. That was all true. However, something said that in this case, it would be better to seek some advice.

"It's been good, but Jordy is a bit distant. I wish he spent more time with me and less worrying about work—but I've managed to fill my days. If we had children, that would be different, but of course, we don't." She sighed. "So I either work until I'm exhausted or am bored and discontent. I think working is better—but it leads to some struggles because everything I can think to do involves children, and it only makes things worse."

"There's growth there, certainly. It was the same for me for a long time, but now other people's children keep me from going insane. I used to think I didn't really like children, but the more I grow into thinking of them as real people, the more I appreciate them for their own sake. Not just because I'm related to them or because I want to learn how to be a mother, as I know I may never be one. But perhaps it might be good for us to think of something else you could do. Would the McAllens involve you more with their ... farming?"

"I've been told I don't have the stomach for it." Which was true, if a little exasperating. "Perhaps I ought to just grow up. I shouldn't continually be longing for something I can't have. It says a lot about my heart, I suppose, that I can't get children off my mind." She flushed. When she had so much to be grateful for, how could she allow herself to wallow so often? Though she didn't really wallow, not physically, and she was careful to pick up her spirits and drag them along after a few moments of moping.

"Perhaps. Or perhaps you're not supposed to just drop it." Alice started to stand, as Duncan lay still for far too long on this particular roll, then lowered herself back down when he sprang to his feet and began the climb once again. "There's legitimacy to your dreams, same as there was to mine. Compared to me, you've handled it well, even if you don't quite know it yet."

Ivy couldn't believe that. Her heart was far too rebellious. Alice could only see her actions, read the carefully selected words in her

146

letters. That was nothing to judge by—not really.

"Besides, it's only been ... let me see. In December, two years?"

"In November."

Alice raised her eyebrows but made no comment. "November, then. But still, less than two years. There's no need to despair when the dream may be just around the corner. I tell myself that every day. Still, I see your point. Mother, Aunt Christina, and Grandmother all managed babies sooner—if you look at the Eltons, it was never much more than that, though come to think of it, I don't remember many details. I know Papa was born a little over a year after his parents married, but I don't know if that counts since it's on his side." She shrugged. "I've come to understand that a father's mark may not be as strong in that area."

"Right. Our family is generally like that." Ivy kept the words quiet and regimented, each in their specific place like the marching of soldiers. If only it was as simple as that. "You know you have not ... I mean, I don't need to state the obvious."

Alice hesitated, then shook her head. "It should be different for you. But let's not talk about that now. What I mean to say is that you should not base your experiences on mine, but neither should you cling to what has happened to family members. There are variances. You must remember that you can find great joy in ... oh, in everything. Of course, you know that better than I do, for you have always lived it—and I greatly respect that, Ivy. What you may consider your weakness now has always been your greatest strength. You are ..." She paused and shook her head. "You are what I should have been. I would've laughed at that a few years ago, but now I cannot, for I see the ways I have been caught in my own mind, a prisoner to my own flesh. Peter says it's a common struggle, but when I look at your actions, I see you overcome where I failed. I can't help but respect that."

Ivy swiped at her eyes, and Duncan ran up to pat her cheeks and ask about the tears. She pulled him onto her lap and told him that sometimes she didn't understand why she cried—did that ever happen to him? Duncan didn't think so, and after seeing that Ivy's tears had stopped, he dashed off to explore a particularly interesting rock.

"He's such an only child," Alice commented. "I know a few at my church in Cincinnati. They're a different breed."

"Plus it's an uphill battle for him to make friends," Ivy said. Though the citizens of Keefmore were coming around to Agnes and Duncan, there was still a hesitancy.

"That's a shame, for he's a sweet boy. I imagine there's time for him to grow on people, though, and you'll help, as you always do." Alice glanced sideways at Ivy and smiled. "But you can't distract me. Or at least I won't let you now. I've said my piece about your continued hope, but here's another thing I will say: though you and Jordy could grow stronger with children as without, this time is a blessing. You are forced to grow together in a way you never would have had to otherwise. We as humans are wont to stop our growth during times of peace, but in a marriage, that's not possible unless you are content to fall apart. I don't believe, if either of our sons had lived, that Peter and I would be where we are. I can't say I wouldn't change a thing, I can say that God's ways are best—and I have definitely come to have a greater appreciation of that. It'll be the same for you and Jordy if you let it be."

"Maybe ..." Though Ivy wasn't sure if her relationship with Jordy, rather without conflict or tragedy in general, was comparable to Alice and Peter's relationship. They'd had to fight and struggle; they'd faced great tragedies together. That simply wasn't true of Jordy and Ivy.

"If nothing else, we've had to face the person each other really is, which I think is a hard thing to do before marriage. Some couples do it, I'm sure—and I think Peter got closer to knowing who I really was than I ever did, and I'm still not sure I know him as well as I ought. But in general, there is always something you find out after you're married. There's no way to overcome that—every relationship must develop and change. There's no magical point at which everything is going to make sense and be conflict-free. At some point or another you will come to that point in your relationship; what matters is how you handle it."

Fair enough. "I'm sure there are ways Jordy and I could grow."

"I quite agree! Same as anyone. Peter and I idolized each other before we were married; I think because we are quite well-matched, but also because that's what happens when you're in love. More than that, I think we both felt we knew who we were as a person, and that can be hard because God often has a different opinion than ours. His is the right one, of course, but it can be so hard to see that at the time. And when you idolize someone, any small bump in the road can derail you."

"That's true ..." Certainly, the slight misunderstanding between Jordy and Ivy that had carried into their marriage had made so many things seem impossible. Even though Jordy didn't know it.

"There are so many things about the process, however, that have made me see the good in Peter. But I also don't see his love for me as one of his good traits—he loves me for me, not because he is too good for me, or because he is being too kind, too patient, too forbearing. That's helped. I no longer see his compliments as well-meaning lies. It is an honest outpouring of love. To him, I am the most beautiful woman in the world. He doesn't lie. He means it. And there is so much more worth in being beautiful to one who truly knows you. The world's opinion means so little."

That was honestly a much more pretty way of putting things than Ivy had expected Alice to ever be able to express. "That makes sense. And I'm glad you've come to that realization, for I have always felt you were too harsh on yourself in that area." Ivy didn't understand it, for Alice was one of the loveliest people she knew. Who was she even comparing herself to? There was no one she knew who could match her.

Alice raised her shoulders slightly. "Yes, well, that's what Peter says, and I hope he's right. But about the whole child thing ... has anyone actually talked to you about it? I mean, another woman—an older woman. Because sometimes it can be as simple as ... well, as knowing how things work."

Ivy felt her face grow warm. "Yes. Yes, I'm ... aware."

"Good. As long as you are. We can't know about these things, but there are a few controllable elements."

As Ivy well knew.

"The main thing, of course, is to pray. With Jordy, if you can—I've always found that a great deal of my problems double if they are not shared. Peter needs to know exactly what I'm praying for."

"Right." That made sense. And in truth, Ivy was suffering a great deal more because she was not being honest with Jordy about this particular thing.

But how could she tell him?

# CHAPTER FIFTEEN

*October 1884*

*H*<sup></sup>*e needs to know exactly what I'm praying for.*

That thought rang about Ivy's head in the days that followed. She spent time with Peter and Alice, prayed somewhat hesitantly with both of them on several subjects close to her heart, but still, she withheld this small part of herself from her husband.

What was she afraid of?

Everything. She was afraid he'd laugh at her, mostly, and that he would say she was silly to even wish it. His thoughts on the subject were clear. She shouldn't challenge him. Challenging felt like a word that was wrong, unassociated with her, something perhaps another woman ought to do. But not Ivy. That wasn't Ivy.

Yet, more and more she experienced guilt for hiding things from Jordy. He didn't know, nor seemed to suspect, what was on her mind, yet she knew it must be placing a wall between them. To break down that wall, she would have to open up a part of her soul that he didn't seem to want to hear about. Ivy never forced herself on anyone—if Jordy didn't want to know, she didn't want to tell him.

Yet ... yet this was a marriage. It was unique from other

relationships in its need for transparency. Peter said the greatest risk a married couple could take was keeping something, anything, from each other. There would be little adultery if complete honesty was achieved—and Peter believed adultery extended to any area where a lie created a barrier between a couple.

She wondered were she to tell Peter all, if he would call her an adulteress. Granted, that seemed strict, and she wasn't sure, but that was the thought that propelled her to begin praying.

Jordy and Ivy did pray together every night, but Ivy knew she was not honest. If there was even a chance that she could make a difference simply by letting Jordy have this last piece of her, she was willing to try.

So, softly, she added toward the end of her prayer as she snuggled against his chest, her face conveniently hidden away, "And, Lord, if it is Your will for us to have a child, help us to be open to Your will."

He stiffened but said nothing until she'd finished praying. Then he leaned back, and she was forced to meet his eyes.

Play innocent or admit she knew exactly why he had pulled away? Thankfully, he spoke quickly enough that she didn't have to decide.

"Vee, did ye ... Tha' is, ye dinna want tae ... tae try for a bairn, do ye?"

There was fear in his voice, and Ivy stepped forward cautiously. "I'd rather follow your wisdom more than anything." It was true even if her heart was rebelling. "However, I don't have a problem with the idea of having children if that is God's will for us, no. I never have. And since we are both healthy and have a safe place for potential children, I do feel as if perhaps we are ignoring some rather vital commands from God."

He stared at her for a long moment, then nodded. "I didna ever really discuss this wi' ye, but I have always believed tha' th' church comes down tae hard on newlyweds in tha' area. No' everyone can possibly be meant tae have children—some are no' suited."

"Yes." She would allow him that. And so many people couldn't have children. "Yet I don't feel we are unsuited. I don't even think we would be bad parents. We have a safe place to raise children. Our families would certainly welcome the addition."

"It would keep us here, though." He gestured around. "We could never leave this house, Keefmore—could never travel."

"But where would we go?" Even if they didn't have children, they wouldn't likely have the funds or the time to do so. Besides, she'd been bound here, feeling as if she were stuck in a mire, for months. The extra stability that children would offer would be a purpose not a cage. Didn't Jordy see that?

"I ... I dinna ken." He looked away, his eyes focused on the window in their bedroom. "Perhaps ... I dinna ken. But there are things I'd like tae see an' which I would like tae show ye. We have our independence this way."

"I don't know that independence is that important to me." Actually, it wasn't important to her at all, but she understood that Jordy perhaps valued it slightly more. "I understand what you mean, I think, though."

"But ... but ... but are ye no' afraid?"

"Well yes." Everything frightened her. Yet she did these things anyway. Sometimes even playing the piano or kissing Jordy could be a frightening thing—both had, at one time or another, caused her throat to close up and her vision to wobble, which had proven inconvenient and, in the case of the kissing, difficult to explain. But that didn't make it any less desirable. And childbirth sounded like the type of thing that would overwhelm her. Yet that didn't matter. "Especially after Alice, but I believe my lot might be a bit easier."

The skepticism that slid across his face hurt, but she refused to let herself close her heart again, even though it was tempting. "Vee, I feel it would be tae much for ye tae handle."

Her hands reflexively fisted; both a sharp defense and an outcry rose to her mind, but she wouldn't humor herself. "Yes, I can see why ... why you would think that. All I'm saying is, I'm beginning to feel some conviction about ... about putting matters into God's hands. That's all." It wasn't all, but it was enough that Jordy would respond to her. Wouldn't he?

For a long moment, one that stretched on into a dismal silence that even the beauty of an unsung tune couldn't penetrate, Jordy sat still, then he nodded. "I do see wha' ye mean. But I feel nae such thing. If I did, I would tell ye. But ... perhaps we should give it a bit o' time. Ye say ye're *beginnin'* tae feel some conviction about it. Ye need more time tae think, an' tae pray, an' so do I. Give me six months—tha'll be summer—an' then we can talk."

Six months? That felt like an eternity. Yet after nearly two years, she could wait, couldn't she? If this was what he wanted. "All right. But we must pray, darling. Both of us, apart and together."

Jordy agreed, but she could feel the skepticism in him. He was fidgety the rest of the evening, and he kept her awake with his tossing and turning late into the night.

It was clear she'd touched something in Jordy that she hadn't expected.

Was the problem him and not her?

The sun danced over the icy rocks and crags of the moors as Ivy clutched Peter's arm, her fingers curling and uncurling to increase blood circulation and hopefully keep any extremities from freezing. Before her, Alice walked with Agnes and Duncan. Agnes had decided to join them after a great deal of urging by Alice and Peter, and ever since, Alice had been deep in conversation with her—including a few traces of laughter. Duncan darted about, laughing and playing and capering, self-entertained like any only child who hadn't many, if any, playmates.

Peter placed his hand over Ivy's for a brief moment. "Tomorrow we'll be on our way. I wish we could stay longer, but if we don't leave here before the heavy snow sets in, we won't get back to Yorkshire. We plan on spending winter and perhaps part of the spring with

Uncle Charlie and then move down to Pearlbelle Park. Honestly, as rarely as we get over here, I've no doubt we'll linger, though we must someday go home."

"Right." A sad truth but a truth nonetheless. "I wish I could come with you, but I know I don't want to be snowed *out* of Keefmore. Perhaps in the spring ..." Though Ivy kept saying that and it kept not happening. When would she take a trip down to Pearlbelle Park? It never seemed entirely necessary, and as such, she didn't justify the trip very often.

"I think it's better if you stay home for now."

She glanced up at Peter, for a moment confused, then smiled. He couldn't mean he didn't want her to come with him, could he? "Why?"

"Because, I don't think it's going to be much longer until you have a child, and then you'll want to be here."

She paused and tugged him to a stop with her. "What do you mean?"

"Well, I know you've been praying for a child for some time. But I just think it won't be long now." He shrugged. "I wish I could explain it better than that, Ivy. It's just a feeling. Not anything set in stone. However, every time I think of you in relation to a child, it's impressed on me that you're not praying in vain; it will be soon."

He was being sincere. She could see it in his eyes. "As in, something from God?"

"I don't know. Maybe." Peter smiled, then squirmed, and she realized she was holding rather tightly to his arm. "I shouldn't have told you, truly, for now you'll think about it far more than you need to. Again, I'm not sure. I could be wrong. I just have felt all along that there was no reason on earth for you to not have had a child yet, and it seems like the waiting period is almost over."

So he didn't know or suspect Jordy's part in the whole thing. Though she was grateful, sometimes Peter's insight could be invaluable. Yet she would never explain this to him.

They walked on, and Ivy tried not to think of Peter's prediction.

Yet his words would stay with her, would taunt her for some time. It could be nothing. Though Peter never said anything lightly, occasionally his imagination got the best of him, as with Ivy.

But what if he was right?

Ena was beginning to suspect she was expecting her first child with Wallace, which would mean she was due in June. It had touched a different part of Ivy's heart when she was told; a selfish, desperate cry of 'but why not me?' had leaped into her mind.

Of course she knew why. She did. Yet it had hurt, like a knife shoved into her heart. She didn't wish Ena wasn't with child. She just wished they *both* were.

Perhaps they would be ... perhaps Ivy was next.

*December 1884*

"Merry Christmas, Ivy!" Mrs. McAllen hugged Ivy, stepping back as she did so to draw her deeper into the McAllen's cottage. "Come back tae th' kitchen, daughter. Edith an' I can use ye, an' I havena seen ye exceptin' at church."

Blushing with shame, Ivy followed her mother-in-law into the small back room. She had been avoiding the McAllens' farm. Selfish, but it always reminded her of how long she'd been waiting for a child, another McAllen grandchild.

Ivy was set to work on the remaining steps of the pudding creation. Mrs. McAllen and Edith chatted about what the men had been doing while the cold weather held. Apparently they were repairing a piece of farming equipment, but some difficulty in acquiring a certain part had stalled them. They were trying to replace it on their own.

"An', Ivy, ye must tell me all about how yer family is!" Mrs. McAllen turned to Ivy with a smile. "I hope they're all doin' well."

"They are."

"I ken ye miss them." Mrs. McAllen placed a hand on Ivy's lower back. "Weel, we'll have a good time here, tae. I hope ye can go an' see them sometime next year."

Ivy nodded. "Maybe in the summer. We're talking about it. And it helps when they come visit me."

"O' course."

In no time at all, supper was prepared and all the McAllens sat around the table chatting and laughing. For Ivy, it was a beautiful sight. She enjoyed watching their merriment and even joined in.

She appreciated being a part of this family. They were such a boisterous, funny, welcoming group that Ivy was more than proud to be a part of them. Besides, Jordy held her hand under the table most of the way through the meal, which she found she was still partial to. She'd thought the delight of that simple gesture had faded but apparently not. She smiled at him, and he squeezed her hand tighter.

Everything would be all right. Yes, it would. It must be.

Tristan cleared his throat. "Edith an' I had an announcement we wanted tae share today."

Edith, sitting next to him, set her fork down and nodded to her husband.

"Weel, we're goin' tae have our second child next summer."

"In June or July, we think," Edith added, though her words were drowned out as Mrs. McAllen scooted back her chair and rushed to embrace her daughter, and the brothers laughed and exclaimed. David, Tristan and Edith's son, squealed, and Mr. McAllen congratulated them cheerily.

But Ivy sat still and silent, some part of her having yet to acknowledge what had just happened.

Edith was pregnant. Of course she was. Tristan and she had already had a child, so there was no reason on earth why they shouldn't have another one. Yet Ivy was blindsided, and she sat there, her hands trembling on her lap, for Jordy had dropped her hand to congratulate his best friend and sister on their happy news.

Happy news indeed.

Bitterness welled, but Ivy pushed it down. Deep breath in, deep breath out. She pushed back her own thoughts, her wild feelings, her oh-so-easily-shattered heart, and stood.

In a moment, with tears in her eyes, she had encircled the table to where her mother-in-law stood and embraced Edith. For her part, Edith looked less than thrilled, but Ivy ignored that, taking her hand and sincerely congratulating her.

After all, what else could she do?

The rest of the day passed in a blur. She was happy for Edith and Tristan. Really, she was. However, it was hard to conceal the resentment this announcement had caused, still more as Edith quietly told her mother, in the safety of the kitchen, that she was less than eager to add another child to their family when David was already causing her so much trouble.

Mrs. McAllen offered words of advice that Ivy barely heard. Still, she comforted Edith and told her she'd help, if she liked, and said it would be all right.

But what did Ivy know? She spoke those words out of kindness, but she had no real understanding of what it was to be a mother, to be with child, to manage all these things. After all, Jordy had made it more than clear that he did not feel she was qualified for the office of motherhood.

Who was she to encourage Edith? She had nothing of any real worth or value to add.

At last, the long day was over. They could've stayed the night at the McAllen's, but Ivy begged Jordy to take her home, and at last, he consented to do so.

She was silent on the drive. Jordy asked her what was wrong, and she couldn't reply. She didn't know what was wrong with her. Selfishness, maybe. Or a kind of grief. Yet it wasn't something she could articulate to Jordy.

But she hadn't been inside her own house more than a few minutes when the tears started, and they changed in mere moments to choking sobs that didn't allow her to breathe or think or do anything but force herself to keep living when it felt beyond her grasp.

Jordy held her and begged to know what was wrong, but she couldn't speak. At last, he stopped asking and just kept her still. She needed that—a stabilizing influence in this world so full of shaky things, her body included.

At last, she fell asleep, and in the following days, she determined herself to be more cheerful.

Yet at the back of her mind, the thought remained: *it should've been me.*

# CHAPTER SIXTEEN

*Late January 1885*

The snow now rested in drifts, unusual for Keefmore but rather delightful. Ivy waded through the snow, placing her feet in the footsteps Jordy had made on his way to the office that morning, leaning dramatically to the left to avoid falling over. Her right arm was weighed down by a basket containing Jordy's lunch—she'd taken to bringing it up mid-morning for something to do in the last few months, and even given the snow, she was determined to continue this mission.

She arrived at the office, gave Jordy his lunch, and started the walk to Aunt Daphne's house, where she'd intended to come in with a question about the study they were doing. She wasn't sure if she'd written down the verses incorrectly or if Aunt Daphne had just chosen vaguely irrelevant passages for their study, but either way, she felt a need to clarify.

However, at that moment, something struck her as important, and Ivy paused and glanced up the street to the 'kirk.' After a moment of hesitation, she nodded to herself and scurried toward the building.

It was still cold inside, but she was well bundled. She made her way to the front of the building and sat at the piano, removing her mittens and placing them on the bench beside her.

Yes, there was time for a bit of piano playing. Her soul felt tight this week, as if there were something to be processed and she'd best do so now.

"All right, God, what do You have for me today?"

Before her fingers even had a chance to touch the keys, she heard it. *"October."*

"October?" Whatever could that mean? She'd never heard a date before. She placed her fingers on the keys and began playing an old hymn, with a few added variations, that she'd performed just two days ago during the service.

She supposed she must've heard incorrectly, but still, the month was pressed firmly on her heart. She focused on the notes to give her mind time to clear, paused and took some deep breaths, and then continued playing, but the word remained.

*October, October, October.*

It wasn't going away, and at last, Ivy let her hands drop from the keyboard. "What's happening in October, Lord? Or what's important about it?"

Her arms ached, empty, and she wrapped them around herself. Hesitating, she stood, allowing the bench to slide back. Could it be?

It wasn't anything dramatic, and perhaps it wasn't anything at all. After all, there were other babies, and Ivy was certainly quick enough to think of them. It wasn't necessarily her baby.

Why, Ena was already several months along with Wallace's child.

Of course, Ena's baby would be born long before October. Actually, an October baby would need be conceived—

She hesitated and swallowed. *Hmm.* That was interesting.

Her monthly was due any day now, but a miracle could come. Maybe this month, she just wouldn't bleed—and then she would know.

"Oh, Lord, if that could be true ..." She stopped herself before she could speak the words into being. "Oh, Lord, please. Let Your heart have changed. I beg You. Give us a chance to be parents."

Silence for a minute, then again she heard, like a confirmation,

*"October"*

So this must then be the month. The month that her first baby came into being. Overwhelming peace filled her soul, and she sat back down and sighed.

Then she saw the whole picture. Herself in October with not one but two babies in her arms. Tears welled, and she dropped her face in her hands and let the moisture flow.

She prayed sporadically then, her words at first needing to be forced out and then coming quickly. She thanked Him, and she asked Him to allow Jordy to conform to God's will, too—though if such were the case, it would be beyond his control now.

There was so much to be worried about, yet Ivy restrained herself from thinking about those things. At least for now. Now, all she felt was supreme gratitude. How frightened had she been that permission would never be granted? Yet she had known, somehow, that it would be, and now that waiting had been rewarded.

Jordy wouldn't know, of course. She had an idea that it would just happen, and there wasn't much she was to do about it.

Already dreams were spinning about her head. Everything from the question of whether the baby—no, *babies*—would be boys or girls or one of each—to what they would be like, to what their lives would be like.

Never once did the concept of fear enter Ivy's heart. She found that about this subject at least, she was incapable of feeling it. Yes, Jordy would be frightened, and she prayed God would help him find peace and courage, but personally, she felt no need for either.

She was sure there would come times of difficulties. Of course such times would come. In the meanwhile, there was such a beautiful feeling in her heart, a music lovelier than any she'd heard before.

Surely Jordy wouldn't be too upset with her for rejoicing, would he? For a minute, doubt lingered, but she knew she could count on him at the end of the day, even if at first he would balk. And once he saw God's hand, he'd surely be more than willing to be exactly what he always had been: her rock, her right hand, her dearest friend, the sharer of her joy.

At last, she rose from the bench and put her mittens back on before venturing out into the cold.

She stopped by Jordy's office to collect the basket and lingered, wondering if he'd gotten the same impulse, if he, too, felt this change ... but he said nothing.

He was happy to see her but busy reading some medical textbook for a patient he was seeing in the village. She left him after only a few minutes of waiting about, trying to get his attention.

Yet all the way back to the cottage, she had a skip in her step that led to her almost slipping and falling in the snow more than once.

Yes, she was definitely a bit out of her head, and she hoped Jordy wouldn't notice, for she didn't have the words to explain this change.

When she arrived home, she was faced with an unfortunate discovery: she was bleeding.

How could that be?

Had she dreamt the afternoon, in all its power, only to find that God had lied and her monthly had started?

When Jordy found her sobbing on the bedroom floor a few hours later, he asked her what was wrong, but she couldn't explain. It wouldn't make sense to him, and she didn't want to admit her own frailty.

She was losing her mind.

His arms were tight around her, and she clung to him as she always did in such times, but she couldn't seem to summon words, though she tried again and again.

"'Tis just yer heart," he murmured after a time, when her sobs had softened to whimpers. "Ye're tired, especially as, weel, 'tis tha' time, 'tisn't it?"

Deep breath in, deep breath out. She steeled herself and nodded. "Yes. That's it."

"Does it hurt so bad just noo?" His hand moved to her lower back, rubbing in firm, small circles. "I wish there was somethin' I could do."

"There's not." There was nothing anyone could do—about her foolishness, her pride, her belief that God would work a miracle in her life.

# CHAPTER SEVENTEEN

Spring had come back to Keefmore, and the ladies were plotting their gardens, though how many were doing so willingly and how many were being forced by Aunt Daphne was unclear. Aunt Daphne's parlor had hosted many debates of late on the subject.

Ivy leaned back and listened to the women argue about this and that. She was content being even more silent than normal today; she felt surprisingly exhausted and weak. She had for a few days, actually.

She did just fine until food was brought out, at which point she began to feel a bit nauseous and excused herself to go lie down in her old room. Ena called her back and asked her what was wrong, and Ivy told her she felt sick, which led to Ena asking to come along.

"Anythin' else?" Ena asked as Ivy sat on the edge of the bed and slipped off her shoes. "Other symptoms?"

Ivy sighed. "Just for the last few days, I've been exhausted and can't stand the sight or smell of food. I just don't feel well."

"Hmm ..." Ena sat down next to Ivy. "Where are ye in ... yer courses?"

Ivy sucked in a quick breath. How could she have forgotten? It had felt unimportant to track them lately—hopeless, even. But a quick calculation led to an interesting conclusion. "Oh."

"Aye. Oh."

Ena left, and Ivy lay on the bed in silence, thinking things through and then deciding that, yes, Ena was right. It was likely she was with child. Yes, she hadn't been keeping perfect track of her monthlies, and perhaps she was simply a little under the weather, but that felt unlikely. This was different—not the normal bone-aching heaviness of a cold or the influenza.

What would Jordy say when she told him? Perhaps she should wait until things were more certain. However, it didn't make sense to keep such excellent news from him any longer than she had to.

She excused herself early from the meeting and hurried home, where she paced up and down the length of the kitchen, then attempted to make dinner, which ended with her lying on the floor of her bedroom clutching a chamber pot.

She'd have to try again later. In a month, maybe. She wasn't going to touch a stove until then.

So she breathed in and out and eventually made her way into the garden, where she sat still and took in the fresh air and sunshine and eventually felt much better.

She was aware she'd never feel completely better until she was able to eat, as Ena had mentioned it to her before in the early months of her own pregnancy. However, right now, that just didn't seem feasible. She'd try to nibble on a crust of bread or something a little later in the day.

Jordy came up the path as the sun faded toward the distant horizon, and Ivy stood and greeted him at the gate.

"Why are ye oot here?"

"Oh, I ... I wasn't feeling well." Terror seized her. What if he wasn't happy? What if he didn't want the babies? "I ... Let's get dinner. I wasn't able to ... to cook, but I ..." As if existing just to annoy her, a wave of dizziness washed over her, and she caught Jordy's arm.

"Love! Let's see ye lain down." He escorted her into the cottage and was so gentle and kind and thoughtful, and Ivy so hated not telling him the truth, that she ended up bursting into tears.

"Ach, Vee, wha' is it?" He wrapped his arms tight around her. "Shh, shh, it's a'right. I'm here for ye. Tell me."

"I ... I ..." Yet the words wouldn't come, which led to even more tears which led to her feeling sicker.

Eventually, Jordy got her tucked into the bed. He sat with her for a bit, rubbing her back and whispering soft things. "'Tis yer monthly comin'. It's a'right. I understand."

Just like Jordy to get a sudden rush of understanding about the wrong change. "But, Jordy—"

"Nae, 'tis a'right. Shush noo ..."

She stopped trying to talk and just lay still, miserable.

She was with child, and she didn't know it yet.

Jordy could torture himself with that fact all he wanted to, but it wouldn't change a thing.

What could he do to make things easier on Ivy?

He wasn't so much of an old married man nor yet so far away from college life that he didn't know how to scramble eggs and toast bread, and he could make tea, too. He'd been lectured enough in the last year and a half over how to properly brew the stuff, though it wasn't his drink of choice.

He prepared two plates and left them on the table, then poured the tea and hesitated over dropping a lump of sugar in it. Should he? Jordy normally wouldn't hesitate, as he knew it was a treat his bride appreciated, but something told him to hold off on anything sweet, anything more than leaves boiled in water.

"Jordy!" The voice from the bedroom was half a moan, and he hastened to collect the hot cup of tea, despite the burning in his fingers, and slip through the cottage to their bedroom.

She was still in bed, lying on her side with her knees almost up to her chest and her arms curled around her head. Oh, the dear. "No' any better?"

A slight shake of her head.

"Ach, love, I'm sae sorry." For more reasons than one, though he wouldn't say that to her. He set the cup on the bedside table, rubbed his scorched hands on his trousers legs to eliminate some of the sting, and lowered himself onto the edge of the bed.

After a moment of hesitance, he placed a hand on her lower back and rubbed. He didn't want to risk overstimulating her—he'd fast learned that whenever Ivy was feeling unwell, physical touch only served to add another layer of nausea—but she didn't protest this. And here was a case where there was nothing Jordy could do but offer what comfort he could and be there.

Being there wasn't a lot for a man who liked to fight for those he loved. How Jordy liked to fight, to go to battle for her. But that wasn't what she needed right now. There was no dragon to vanquish, no evil king to dethrone.

Nae, the villain they fought now was far more sinister than that—a thought he winced at but couldn't help. It was a villain he couldn't fight, a villain who would, quietly and steadily and innocently, capture their flag, overtake their castle, and remove them from the fairy-tale dreamland of their hidden world.

He was starting to sound exactly like Ivy, and that fact irritated him just then.

"Love," he whispered after a moment, "this will probably ease if ye're able tae sip somethin'. I brought tea, an' there's toast an' eggs if ye're able afterwards. If ye sat in tha' garden all day as I suppose ye did, weel, I'm worried tha' if this goes on much longer, ye'll be dehydrated. Ye could become really ill."

She shifted slightly. "Aren't I really ill now?"

He tried to smile, but it didn't reach his face exactly. It was more of an instinctive twitch of his lips, but Jordy didn't have to fake cheerfulness externally if she wasn't looking at him. "Aye, an' ye look peely-wally. I ken ye're sick noo, but it'll get worse."

"I can try. Just ... give me a minute." She puffed out a breath, then sucked one in, long and slow and deep. *Good lass.* He'd told her to breathe deep through either waves of illness, as had come during a mild case of the influenza last December, or the panic that tended to follow them. "I'd think ... I'd have thought this would've come on a bit less suddenly. It's only been these last two days. Before that, I felt fine!"

"Aye, I ken. I'm sorry, love; I'm sorry." There was nothing he could do but endlessly apologize. Jordy blamed himself—not that he was the only one involved, but he was the one who had put himself in charge of keeping this situation from arising.

This was too much for her. Didn't God in Heaven look down, see this woman, and realize it was too much for her? She had a weak body, and her anxieties lay just below the surface. They'd talked about preventing this—who was to say that the unfortunate eventuality wouldn't send her into a panic?

At last, Ivy was able to sit up enough to take a few sips of the tea, after which she turned it away, saying the taste was repulsive. Her favorite brew, too! Jordy wanted to fight the unfairness of it all even as he knew he was being unreasonable and childish.

*God, this isn't right for us. This isn't right for our marriage! Why take away our imaginary castle? Why take away this little, private world with just her and me? Why?*

Ivy lay there, so pitiful in the rapidly darkening room. He lit a candle and sat with her and tried not to act too fidgety. He'd suspected for the last several days that her various symptoms were indicators of a pregnancy, and yet he hadn't been willing to admit it.

Now he must.

Again, he'd failed.

Jordy wasn't sure how Ivy's body would handle the adjustment, given that she was so frail and so, well, not Scottish ... but he wanted to believe she would take on that supposed glow and begin to thrive like other women seemed to.

Yet instinct and a rather annoyingly detailed knowledge of her medical history indicated to him that she would have a hard time with the whole process, from start to finish. He felt that, until the autumn, she would be exhausted and out of sorts.

Then the dream would end for real.

Until then, Jordy would care for his invalid wife. And if things didn't go well ...

He had to stop thinking. He just *had* to. It wasn't his habit to get caught in morose wanderings; he almost never did. Jordy just hadn't expected this, and he didn't know exactly what to do with it.

Her fingers slackened in his hand. "I'll try that tea again now."

"Good lass," he murmured. He helped her sit up and let her lean against his chest while she took a few sips of the tea. She was quick to regulate herself—Ivy had mentioned that illness wasn't a stranger to her—and over the course of the next half hour, she finished most of the cup.

She was miserable afterwards, despite the slowness of her drinking, and Jordy didn't like it one bit. But there was nothing he could do—she was right that giving her peace and quiet to rest was the best he could offer to her right now.

Especially since she was again expressing some distaste at being touched as her nausea increased. Jordy was nothing if not a physical comforter.

*Oh, Vee, how can we manage if it is a bairn?*

The baby might kill her, and at the very least, it would be a challenge throughout her pregnancy and then for the many years afterwards as they struggled to raise the child. For it would be a struggle; with two people such as them as parents, how could it not be a struggle?

He winced. That was the key of it, really. Not his fears over Ivy's physical health, though they were great. And not his worries about how she might handle the birth of their child. No, his main fears centered around himself and the simple understanding of his own talents. He was not capable of being a father. He was not capable of offering the support that she needed. And he was not capable of settling down and raising a baby.

During these last two years, while they lived in this honeymoon cottage and made castles in the sky, he hadn't really thought about whether or not he was responsible enough to have a family. All he wanted was Ivy, and she had satisfied him with her very presence.

But now ... now he'd have to be so much better than he was now. He couldn't afford to take time off. He couldn't afford to loiter his way through life. He couldn't afford to be himself!

Of course that would mean his relationship with Ivy would suffer, like it or not. They were losing that mystical, beautiful connection of newlyweds and entering a new phase. A phase neither were prepared for in any way.

Everything was going to be different now.

He walked her out into the kitchen once she was feeling a little better, and had her take the toast, which she was able to keep down. Then he monitored her closely throughout the rest of the evening.

He went outside to draw more water and make sure he'd remember to shut the gate and upon his return, found her sitting at the table with her Bible and a sheet of paper. She slid one piece of paper under another when he entered, and seemed to go back to the Bible reading with a little sigh.

Interesting.

"I could read tae ye for a bit if ye like."

She nodded, and he took up the Bible and read to her, chapter after chapter, as she sat still, occasionally resting her head in her hands, other times staring dreamily at the ceiling.

Finally she went to bed, tired enough that she left Jordy to put away the Bible—and Jordy shifted the papers to see what she'd been writing and then hidden from him. Sneaky ... yes. But it was unlikely Ivy was hiding anything truly secret from him.

It was a list of short words in her curling script. It took him a minute to read what she'd written, but he almost dropped the sheet of paper afterward.

*Nettie*

*Hannah*
*Alice*
*Emma*
*Violet*
*Claire*
*Annis*
*Leanna*
*Edith*
*Daphne*
*Emmeline*
*Georgiana*

*George*
*William*
*Charles*
*Benjamin*
*Michael*
*Albert*
*Fitzwilliam*
*Henry*
*Thomas*

Names.

She knew.

How was it possible that she knew? And how long had she been keeping it from him? Granted, he'd also been keeping it from her, so there was really no guilt on either side by virtue of shared secrecy.

He set the list down under the other paper and walked into the bedroom. "Ivy? I have somethin' tae tell ye."

She shifted on the bed and glanced up at him. "Hmm?"

"Can ye sit up for a minna?"

She pushed herself into a sitting position, blinking at him with drowsy eyes as if she'd been half-asleep. "What is it?"

"Love, I realized tha' ye've missed yer monthly by a few days, an' ye're never late. Combined wi' th' symptoms ... Could ye be with child?"

Her eyes widened. For a moment, she stared at him blankly, then she began crying again, dropping her face in her hands and choking on sobs.

"Oh, love." He pulled her into his arms, lay down on the bed, and let her sob against his chest. "I'm so sorry. If I had any way tae stop this, I would. But it is wha' it is—tha' is, if I'm right. An' I'll take care o' ye. Ye remember tha' ye need never fear for anythin' while ye are mine. It'll be a'right. An' remember, God does everythin' for a reason. He'll take care o' ye, tae."

She sniffled in his arms but said nothing.

"I'm sorry tha' this must hurt ye. See, this is why I didna want ... But, Vee, since it has happened, ye needna feel tha' I will ever no' take care o' ye. Everythin' will be a'right, an' I ken tha' ye shall be th' best mother ..." His voice broke a bit, but he forced himself to shoulder on. "Th' best mother in th' world. I trust ye completely."

"Jordy, I ... I ..." She tried to raise her head but gave up with a small sigh. "I'm sorry. I don't really know why I'm crying. I'm not ... I'm not terribly upset about this. I can't believe it's happened, but I'm not upset. I realized this afternoon, and—"

"Shh, shh, it's a'right. I ken about tha', tae. I saw th' names." He smiled into her hair. "I suppose amongst th' fear an' th' feelin's, there's some excitement?"

She moved her head up and down. "Yes. Did you ... did you like them?"

"Ach, aye. Weel, some o' them. We'll talk about those later." He was in no rush to breathe the truth into reality.

"All right." She sighed and seemed about to speak but stopped herself and shook her head. "Can we sleep soon?"

"Just let me get undressed."

# CHAPTER EIGHTEEN

*May 1885*

Dear Alice and Peter,

D ear Alice and Peter,
I don't know where to begin this letter. I love you both very much, and I felt it was fair to inform you separately from the rest of the family that Jordy and I are expecting. In October or maybe November—Jordy thinks November, and I think October. I suppose we'll see ...

Ivy stopped and stared at the paper for a long moment, trying to think if she should spend more time on the introduction. At last, she crinkled it into a ball and picked up another sheet.

Dear Alice and Peter,
I hope you all are well. I was pleased to hear from Peter about Ophelia ...

No, she'd better not start this announcement with a mention about the cat Alice still complained about in practically every letter she wrote.

It would be far better if Ivy skipped the pleasantries and went straight in with a gentle approach. She whispered a quick prayer and began to write.

> *Dear Alice and Peter,*
>
> *I don't know how to write this. I love you both, and it is a stab in my own heart to watch you struggle through years of loss and infertility. I still pray for you every night.*
>
> *Jordy and I are going to have babies now, in October or November of this year. We're thrilled. It's going to be a dream come true. But how I wish I could share that dream with you, my dearest brother and my dearest sister.*
>
> *But I trust God. I do. Even now. I hope you can share that with me, at least.*
>
> *I thought this letter would be long, full of a thousand reassurances. But what more is there to say? I know you know my heart here. I wanted to warn you. I don't for a minute doubt your own feelings in regards to my happiness, but I would not be strong enough to not suffer if I learned what you are learning now.*
>
> *I love you both so much, and I hope you know that if you would ever be willing to make the trip to Scotland this autumn, we'll need godparents. We would be honored to have you present as such whenever the christening takes place.*
>
> *Again, you have all my love. Jordy, too, sends his love, though he said I'd best write this letter as I know you both better.*
>
> *Your sister,*
> *Ivy McAllen*

There. That would have to do. She folded the piece of paper and picked up another one.

> *Dear Mother,*
>
> *Today I have some excellent news for you! But before I begin, I must say this. I am enclosing a letter to Alice and Peter. Please read it, then pass it on to them if you see fit. If you don't think it should be given to them, please tell them yourself in such a way as you see fit.*
>
> *But the news, which is excellent and explains such vague statements at the beginning of my letter—I am with child. It hardly feels real, but we told Jordy's parents this weekend.*
>
> *I won't come visit for some time, I don't think, but perhaps we can talk about whether it would be possible for you to come here. I want the babies to be born in Keefmore (it's twins, by the way, though Jordy says we can't know and I'm being silly). The babies will come in October or November.*
>
> *I will write more details later, but I just wanted to announce this. Please tell Papa, and anyone else, unless you think it better to wait. I am quite well and healthy. Not always strong and not always perfectly content with the way various parts of me are behaving, but when has that ever not been the case?*
>
> *I'll write again soon!*
>
> *With love,*
>
> *Ivy*

After she set the second letter aside, Ivy turned to Jordy. "There! That's our families."

"Aye." He sat across from her at the table and cocked his head. "How do ye think yer parents will react? I ken ye've talked on an' on, worryin' about Alice an' Peter, but ye ken tha', unlike wi' me parents, this will be their first grandchild."

"Grandchildren," Ivy corrected.

"Born in October, no' November, even though tha' would make them almost a month early." He reached across the table and took her hand. "No' everythin' has tae include some special message from God, Vee. I ken ye believe wha' ye heard, but it's a'right for it tae just be one bairn, born on time, in non-magical ways."

Right. That would be fine. Except that wasn't what was happening. However, she didn't want to contradict Jordy, so she just let it slide.

"I'm going to go see Ena this afternoon. I want to make sure she's settled." Ena's son Hamish Lennox had arrived a few days ago, two weeks early but healthy, and though Ena swore she needed no help, Ivy and the other women of Keefmore stopped by and did random things to make her days easier. Besides, Mairi's mother had practically stolen Bridget and Alistair away that week under the guise of keeping her own children entertained.

"Should I come wi' ye?" Jordy half rose from his seat at the table. "Perhaps I should at least walk ye—"

"No, no, I'll be fine." The last thing she needed was Jordy hovering over her, driving her mad.

"Just be careful, a'right?"

What had she to be careful of? Yet she nodded before she left the cottage behind to hurry out onto the green hills, scurrying toward Keefmore.

Ena was happy to see her, not because she was exhausted or in need of any help, she said, but because she was lonely and bored.

"Ye dinna understand how much I've wanted for conversation. I've everythin' done for me, but ye ken, Ivy, tha' I can manage all I need tae."

Ivy laughed but sat next to Ena with a cup of tea and eventually was given Hamish to hold and coo over. He resembled Wallace in some ways, but she saw a lot of Ena in him, and like Bridget and Alistair, he had a brush of red hair at the top of his head.

"He's so pretty, Ena."

"Aye, isna he? All me bairns have been, so I suppose it isna much o' a surprise." She smiled and took a sip of her tea. "But I'm glad ye think so, for I never would have forgiven ye otherwise."

Ivy laughed. "You know there's not much risk of that. I am forever charmed by babies. And now since I'll be having my own, well, I need all your guidance, and all the time with this wee one, too."

Ena cocked her head. "Ach, ye'll do a'right. Some o' it comes tae ye, an' as long as ye dinna believe ye will be th' perfect mother, an' understand tha' a great deal o' sacrifices will be made, I think ye'll get on well enough."

Ivy hoped she was prepared. She'd been trying to soak in all the knowledge she could from other mothers in addition to asking dozens of questions, and she believed she might be able to do it. She hoped her mother would be about, and of course Mrs. McAllen and Aunt Daphne would help her. Then there was Agnes and Mrs. Abernathy and ... yes, plenty of women who could help her.

The only variable, then, was Ivy herself. But what a great variable she was!

After she finished her tea, Wallace came home, and after seeing that they indeed had something to eat that evening, and the house was in order, she left them behind.

And went home, where Jordy awaited her impatiently, eager to insist she sit down.

Would it never end?

The response from her mother came a few weeks later.

*Dear Ivy,*

*When I read this letter, from almost the first word I knew you had something exciting to tell me. I await more details with impatience, but in the meantime, let me tell you how glad I am for you. A baby is endlessly a blessing, and endless blessings ought to be celebrated accordingly.*

*I had wondered when such an announcement would come. I think I've hoped for it with every letter because I knew you would make an excellent mother, and I think as it is, you must live a rather idle life. I think that for a bit that can be pleasant, but you are my daughter. I know we are quite different, but at the end of the day, I worried for your contentedness. I don't know what I'll do with myself once Rebecca is married. Maybe I'll fuss over grandchildren, but that's altogether a different kind of fussing.*

*I'm not able to leave Pearlbelle Park for a bit longer, but I will definitely be available in October or November. If you give me permission, I'll see if I can't arrange to stay with Mrs. Wright for a few months so I can be near. I know you've told me a thousand times you have ample support where you are, but I'm your mother and, you see, you shall never quite convince me it's enough. I have to see with my own eyes.*

*Though your father would say I've had to see everything with my own eyes before believing it, and it is not just specific to you. Perhaps a small fault of mine, but let me know if you think that would be too invasive. I want to help you, but only if you don't resent the interference.*

*Which, by the way, brings me to Alice and Peter. I delivered your letter to them by hand and let them have privacy to digest it. I'm unsure if you wanted their reaction, but they came to me immediately, very happy for you. Peter was in tears; Alice was not—which is the natural state of things, as you know.*

*They did slip out that morning and go on a long*

*walk, but it's not unusual for them to get away together and just talk. I like how they do that, actually. It shows me that Alice has truly changed. She values time so greatly that it's easy to see any slight slowing of routine is a sacrifice. Yet there they are.*

*That said, I don't know exactly how sensitive the subject is. Perhaps you observed more when you saw them, but to me, they both seem at peace. Alice is godmother to a little boy named Aidan Frederick—her friend Cassie's child. Did she tell you this? I asked, and she talks about him very affectionately, as she does about her nieces and nephews. I think that there comes a point of acceptance, and you needn't have worried as much as you have. I never told you some things that perhaps I will someday, but I think as I've thought about them more, allowed myself to think about them more, I've realized that there is great pain—but in response, great healing. I find that more extremes are covered under Christ than I can even imagine.*

*I'm rambling now. I almost never ramble, so I apologize. This to say, Peter and Alice would like to be with you. They wanted me to broach the subject so you could be honest, but Peter feels that you need them. He asked me to at least put that in word for word; he said you would understand. You know I've always liked Peter a great deal, but I loved him when he said that. I think there are some things about you, my dear, that just have to be understood, not necessarily reasoned with.*

*If you can, write to me—and possibly to Alice and Peter, here at Pearlbelle Park. They would again stay with Mrs. Wright. I wouldn't be so likely to ask her to host so many of our family except that she's offered so*

*many times. I think she cares about you very much,
Ivy. I have to believe it's because of you.*

*At any rate, I'll sign off now and send this letter. I
love you, Ivy, and I'm so excited to meet your child.*

*All my love,*

*Mother*

Ivy set the letter down and turned to Jordy. "Peter and Alice want to come and stay with Aunt Daphne again. Just to be near. Would you mind?"

Jordy turned from the sink where he'd been washing dishes to allow Ivy a few minutes off her feet—in his opinion, she pushed herself entirely too hard. Ivy barely moved, so she wasn't sure what he meant, but he'd been so unbearably anxious lately that she couldn't bear to contradict him. So she sat and was bored. At least she had glorious things to dream about now.

"Why would they come?"

"Peter thinks it's best."

"Ah." He scrubbed a plate in silence for a few minutes, then nodded. "Aye. They ought tae come, then. No' tha' I understand why, but ... I mean, I willna tell ye tha' yer Peter canna come. Though I will regret it for every day tha' Alice is here, probably."

"Alice has softened." She said that to Jordy every time her twin sister was brought up, and he always scoffed, but it was true. When Jordy had first met her, she'd done everything possible to discredit him and having not succeeded, was bitter for the rest of the wedding period.

That was, until she'd tried to take her own life. And Ivy hadn't known. She'd been too preoccupied with her wedding, too selfish, too lost in her own life to see that her sister was suffering ...

She'd never forgive herself for that. Not quite.

Besides, just then, Ivy needed Peter's help. She needed him to stand by her and be her dear big brother who loved her and understood her in a way no one else could. There was something precious about his entirely platonic, entirely sweet love that always brought her just the encouragement she needed at any stage in her life.

Peter cared about her in a way no one else had ever been known to do, and that in itself was vital. Jordy's love was at times without understanding. Her mother was right that sometimes Ivy couldn't be reasoned with. There wasn't much need in finding reason when it came to love, to friendship, to family, because to Ivy, these things were more important than reason. Reason didn't need to be consulted.

Peter understood that. Understood *her*. Even Jordy hadn't reached that point—at least yet. The only person other than Peter that had come close was, of course, Violet.

How Ivy wished Violet could be there. It would be nice to have Peter, and Alice of course ... if Alice was in a helpful mood, which at times she could be convinced to be these days. However, Violet would've been helpful in an entirely different way. Violet would've brought both reason and understanding—her caustic remarks tinged with gentle love, her snippets of reason laced with hesitant affection. Violet was her sister at heart, whereas Alice held the superior claim of having seen her grown up.

But in some ways, Violet had seen Ivy grow up, too. She wondered if Violet wasn't the truer sister.

However, Ivy would never state these things aloud, not even to Peter. Oh, he would understand. He would always understand, even if it was at the detriment of his own wife's place in Ivy's life. However, that didn't mean it was right. Ivy didn't feel it was entirely right for her to prioritize Violet over Alice, her own blood.

Not that ... It wasn't proven, but Ivy had a sneaking suspicion that Alice wasn't her blood, but she was in every way that mattered. She wasn't going to ask for clarification. Honestly, she didn't need to hear it. It mattered not one bit.

There was the matter of Jordy's behavior of late. She loved her husband entirely and unconditionally, and she felt confident in his love, too. But love wasn't everything.

For the past month, he had smothered her with affection, made everything easier, seen to her needs before she'd known they were even vague inclinations. In short, he'd been the sweetest and most loving man in the world. Almost unlike himself in his complete lack of any priority but her. He didn't even want to leave the house. At times, when she suggested he should try taking a walk or going to see Tris and he assured her he wanted to do nothing of the sort, she wondered if he hadn't somehow lost himself. Where was her Jordy?

She liked his adventurous nature. She felt it balanced her out well, kept her from falling asleep in a haze of books and music that led to no personal growth. She wanted him to push her, challenge her, make her better, not simply do everything in his power to make her happy.

Sometimes making one's spouse happy could be remarkably similar to placating. Of course, there was nothing sustainable about this system, in which one's definition of *happy* was being in a safe bubble where nothing could interfere with you being yourself, even if 'yourself' possessed a sinful nature.

It wouldn't last; it didn't lead anywhere but through wandering woods of empty promises and lost folks searching for fulfillment where none could be found ... yet Jordy continued. It wasn't like him. He was the most self-improving and fellow-human-improving person she knew.

He was scared. She could feel his fear everywhere. He was scared about her being ill and hurt. He was scared of losing her. He was scared of ... well, either them being parents or her being a mother or himself being a father. She wasn't sure what. A mix, perhaps.

Honestly, he was supporting her in all the wrong ways, and it was starting to get on her nerves a bit. If only he'd just be Jordy for her. That was what she needed. Did he think she'd married him with the assumption that he wasn't the best thing in the world for her?

Perhaps he did. Perhaps he thought she'd married him in spite of his faults not because of them. How could he believe that when she so adored him?

Yet there it was. Jordy didn't really trust her with himself when he was struggling. What she'd rejoiced in, he'd taken like a death sentence, and 'for her sake,' he wasn't being honest about it. She'd asked more than once, but he'd never been willing to talk about it, and pushing for information never helped with Jordy, so she'd let it go.

Yet as she found paper to write back to Peter and Alice that of course they were welcome—and she'd just make sure Aunt Daphne was all right with it, but she was sure she would be—she was sad. For, after all, why did she need Peter and even Alice so desperately?

The point of a family was to be a unit of self-sufficiency. There was that 'it takes a village' mentality, but it simply wasn't accurate. That wasn't what God had said. He'd said 'it is not good that the man should be alone,' and so He had created woman—not an entire village. The family unit should exist in such a way that it should sustain itself but didn't necessarily need to.

She sighed as she stood from the table. "I suppose I can wait to go up to Aunt Daphne's until tomorrow, and I can't really finish this letter until then. What would you like to do this evening?"

He blinked at her, then glanced outdoors. "'Tis entirely tae chilly for a walk if tha's wha' ye're thinking."

It wasn't chilly at all. But he insisted it was, for he was so frightened. So entirely frightened that something would happen, that she'd be hurt.

*Oh, Jordy, how can you be so afraid when we have God taking care of us?*

# CHAPTER NINETEEN

*June 1885*

The familiar coach rolled to a stop in front of the inn, and Ivy stepped forward, Jordy directly behind her. Peter's face lit up when he saw Ivy. He paused to help Alice down, and she ran forward and took Ivy's hands.

"Oh, Ivy, we're so excited for you!" As before, her smile was all sincerity and no bitterness. "I hope you don't mind us coming back, but we couldn't very well be away from you just now."

"Of course!" Ivy needed them in her life, truthfully. Though she appreciated the people she had in Keefmore, sometimes she needed Peter and Alice—like now, when Jordy was again not as present as she needed him to be. When he refused to talk baby names, when he avoided setting up the nursery, when he talked about everything but the upcoming babies. Being in denial wasn't really an option, though. It was becoming increasingly clear to even the casual observer that Ivy was with child. Yet Jordy had, for some reason, decided to pretend this was not happening.

If that wasn't just like this new Jordy, this frightened Jordy. Where was his courage? Where was his devotion, his endless willingness, even eagerness, to take on a challenge?

She forced herself back to the present, where Peter and Alice were walking toward Aunt Daphne's house, Alice telling her something Rebecca, their youngest sibling, had done during their visit. *All right. I need to stay in the moment and enjoy the time I have with them.* Appreciating the blessings was vital, even if it was difficult.

They made their way to Aunt Daphne's house, and Peter and Alice continued chattering happily. Yet Ivy's mind still wandered elsewhere.

Aunt Daphne came out and greeted everyone before leading the way inside her home, followed by Jordy and Mick with the luggage, and there was a rush to get everything settled. Jordy told Ivy she ought to sit down, and Ivy insisted she must help Alice unpack, but Alice sent her away, assuring her she could handle hanging a few dresses in a wardrobe.

So Ivy was sent away to sit in the parlor, properly immobile. She was going to kill Jordy at some point. It was a simple fact. She wanted to be upstairs with her brother and sister. Instead, she must rest. Instead, everything was 'too exciting' for her. But she felt fine. Actually, after the first two months, her body had rallied, and now she felt stronger than she ever had in her life. Granted, also bigger but certainly healthy.

How much of that was natural and how much of that was due to Jordy's being overprotective? She wasn't sure, but she did know she felt better on the days she was left to her own devices and was able to do more walking, spend more time outdoors.

Jordy went back to his office, as he had an appointment, but Ivy didn't feel like she could move. Not when she'd promised she wouldn't. And so she waited.

For the last two years, she'd wanted more of Jordy's time and attention, but as it turned out, these days having Jordy's time and attention was a bit more of a heavy weight than a blessing. Though she shouldn't think that. She shouldn't. He wanted what was best for her. How could she be ungrateful?

She could do one of two things. She could keep blaming Jordy and grow increasingly bitter, or she could find a way to move on. It was an obvious choice but not an easy one, like so many things in marriage. In any relationship, truly.

After a bit, Peter and Alice came down. "Are you feeling all right? Maybe we should walk you home." Peter's eyes were worried, and she supposed some of Jordy's anxiety had gotten to him.

"I'm fine, but let's go home."

Alice glanced around the library. "Where's Jordy?"

"He had to get back to the office, but he wanted me to rest here before I walked back. I'm not tired; I feel healthier than I ever have, actually. But he doesn't seem to see that."

Peter laughed. "Speaking as a fellow husband, I understand the impulse. But of course I married Alice and smother-loving was never really an option."

Alice shrugged. "I know my own boundaries."

"No you don't." He accompanied this statement with a half-incredulous laugh.

"All right, perhaps I don't. But Ivy does, don't you? You've been taking care of your health since you were quite young, and I've never known you not to regulate yourself. So tell Jordy that! Come on, Ivy. I know you can have courage. I've seen you have courage."

If only that were true.

Back at the cottage, they talked about nursery plans and baby names until Jordy came and then Ivy was recalled to herself and, with Alice, started dinner. Peter and Jordy slipped outside at Alice's command, leaving them alone once more.

"So how are you feeling, really? I know you would talk about just about anything with Peter, but I had an idea that you wouldn't speak of this." With surprising efficiency, Alice chopped carrots while she spoke.

"Oh, I'm all right. I was horribly ill for the first couple months, but for about these last two weeks, I've felt fine."

Alice nodded sympathetically. "Well, if you ever feel sick again, I have a wide variety of random tips and tricks. Most of them are not things I've experienced, but some of them, I have. It's a shame

Mother isn't here. She's likely experienced much of what you did."

"Mother will be here as soon as she can manage. But in the meantime, it's good to have you here." She'd forgotten that Alice had been with child, had carried to full term ... though she wasn't sure about asking questions about it.

When Ivy had been engaged to Jordy, Alice had come back from America with Peter. She'd lost the baby just a few months before, and she had acted fine ... but had not *been* fine.

Ivy had hated herself as much as she'd feared for Alice. For she hadn't known. Her twin had been suffering more than anyone had a right to suffer, and Ivy hadn't known. To her, Alice seemed surprisingly peppy, but it was really just an act.

Only Peter had known how bad she was, but he had been too broken up himself to speak of it.

If only things had been simpler, but they weren't.

At least Violet was honest with Ivy about her struggles.

Or Ivy thought so. She'd worried about Violet a great deal about that, wondering what secrets weren't visible to the naked eye. Wondering in what ways, daily, she must fail her best friend.

For a variety of reasons, Ivy had never asked Alice about the pregnancy or the lost little boy. Peter had told her some things but not all, and she wondered still if it would ever be all right to ask.

Perhaps not. Alice did deserve privacy, after all.

Yet apparently that wasn't the case, for as Alice slid a handful of carrot slices into the stew, she spoke again. "I don't know if this has ever occurred to you, but I was with child. I had many of the normal experiences; I wasn't sicker than most, and until the actual labor, everything went normally for me. I don't mind talking about it. It's painful, but it's a different kind of pain as the years go on."

"Oh." She wondered what exactly Alice meant by that. When Ivy thought about the pain of losing a child, especially losing a child without ever having the chance to properly meet him or her, it must be excruciating. Ivy would almost rather die than have that happen to her.

Alice had plainly felt much the same, that death was preferable to life in such a case. Ivy had contradicted her when Alice had ever brought up the idea that she might be better off dead, but in her heart of hearts, she had understood the sentiment as she looked at her own longing for a child and just how broken, how empty she would likely feel if that desire was denied in such a cruel and unnatural way.

Violet would say, of course, *"What is more natural than death?"* But death was not natural. The story of the Bible readily communicated that truth. The reason Ivy rejected it as too cruel was because God Himself did not wish death on anyone. Not, at least, without a life to follow death.

"Do you ... do you ever think that you'll meet your babies in Heaven?" Ivy forced the words out before courage faded.

Alice paused for a minute, then continued in her chopping. "All the time. I pray for them, I dream about them ... When I was coming out of being in a coma after I ... *after* ... I thought I saw them. In Heaven. For a few brief minutes. Peter doesn't believe me, which is funny because I would've thought he'd be the first to say it was possible. He humors me, but he doesn't believe it."

Ivy would've thought he'd be the first person to validate Alice's dream or vision or whatever it was, too. But Peter had been deep in grief at the time, and even now he seemed to hold the whole situation with more seriousness than Alice did. She'd felt a restraint in him when it came to Duncan that she never had before.

The tragedy had changed Alice one way and Peter in another. He was more cautious with his affection to strangers now. He'd usually have approached Duncan first, spoke to him, and been best friends with him by teatime.

Maybe Ivy was reading too much into an already brief interaction. Alice had changed for the better. She'd let that be enough and not worry about Peter.

"But I think it could be grief that holds him back." Alice turned from the stove briefly and sighed. "It hurts too much. Both to think about them in Heaven and to think about not seeing them for years and years—and to think that I have seen them while he can't. I wouldn't blame him for that. I'd feel the same if I were denied a chance he got."

"What did you see?"

"Oh, vague images. I mostly remember holding my younger boy—Daniel, for that's what we called him—and wondering at how real he was ... and yet not real in the way we think of as real. More real in a ... a spiritual way." She shook her head. "I can't explain it."

How interesting. Alice was always able to explain and reason away everything. Maybe that was why she was so changed. She'd been confronted, over and over again, with situations out of her control, with things that were unexplainable and random, and she'd come to accept that what mattered were spiritual explanations, many of which humans couldn't comprehend.

"I can't wait to really meet them. To ... to introduce you, I suppose. Two little boys. It'll be good to see them again." Alice turned back to the chopping board and selected another carrot. "To see what they're really like, for one thing. I feel as if I got a glimpse, and now I'm starving for more. That's what it's like—starving. Not that I've ever really starved ... I've been hungry but never starving. Kirk—Mr. Manning, I suppose—has been, and he told me about it. What he described is what I feel."

"Oh." Ivy had no words for that. An experience distant from her, and yet, only having carried a child within her for a brief four months—under three that she had known about—she already felt that she would willingly die for the sake of her child. She wished she could share that feeling with Jordy. Make him realize, somehow, that the pregnancy was real.

"But don't you worry for me." Alice turned away from the counter and smiled. "I was sincere when I said you can ask me anything. I care deeply for you, and I want you to benefit in any way you can from me. That's why I wanted to come here."

"Mother said Peter felt he ought to come."

Alice laughed. "Yes, he did. You know how he is. So determined.

He wanted to see you, and that was that. He doesn't ... You've often said you hear things directly from God. An almost audible voice. Peter doesn't—I don't think very many people do. But he seems to have a better idea of what God wants from him than anyone I've ever known, and now, when he says to me, 'God told me this,' I listen."

Ivy nodded. That seemed wise, for Peter surely knew better than anyone what he was about. He was so close to God. She often envied his wisdom and knowledge of the Bible and of Biblical history, for it was clear that it far exceeded her own.

Yet there was another level to it. His grace, his faith, the way he truly lived out his beliefs in his day-to-day life. She was proud to call him her brother-in-law and prouder still to be his sister-in-law.

These were the days when she wished that—well, no, she didn't. She didn't wish that in the slightest. She just wanted Jordy. She wanted him to be as he always was, not as he now behaved.

If only he hadn't changed toward her since she became with child. If only things were the same as they had been. But he seemed so wracked with fear, and even with guilt, and there was no breaking past it. At least, not that she could see. Perhaps if she kept trying, but she wasn't at all sure what to try.

"Jordy ... Jordy doesn't want the babies."

"Hmm." Alice turned back to the stew and began to stir. Funny to see her so domestic, though Ivy supposed Alice could likely say the same about her. They'd definitely both ended up in places they wouldn't have imagined. "You say babies, but you don't know that, now, do you?"

Ivy cocked her head. "Didn't I tell you? I do know. I heard from God that it would be twins. I only don't know if it'll be boys or girls or a mix. They're coming in October, not in November, no matter what Jordy says."

"Ah." That quiet sound was full of doubt, but Ivy felt no need to prove anything to anyone. "Has Jordy said why he doesn't want children?"

"Oh yes. Any number of reasons." This time, she couldn't keep the bitterness from her voice. Like a boil lanced, the words came tumbling out. "He thinks having the babies will hurt me, or even kill me, and he's worried that it'll cause me anxiety, that I'll slip into depression. His fears have overwhelmed him, and he's not the man I married. He used to be brave and bold and to push me to be more than I am. Now he smothers me. It's not just that—I think he's afraid to become a father as much as he is of me becoming a mother. I'm not sure what else there is, for he won't talk about it with me. He says it'll worry me."

"Ah yes. 'Don't you worry your pretty little head.' The words of a coward without an explanation." Alice withdrew the wooden spoon. "Come tell me what you think of this brew, darling. I have absolutely no idea what I'm doing."

Ivy came forward, accepted the spoon, and stirred the stew. "Ready, I think."

"If you say so. I'll set the table. Now, here's what I think. Talk to Jordy. Just tell him everything you're feeling here. You have a voice in this marriage, too. You can speak to him, you can reason with him. Sometimes you speak to God for him. Did you ever think of that? If you're a 'help meet' created for him, and the Holy Spirit is our Helper, that means a lot about what it is to be a wife. Peter likes to point out that particular connection to his friends. He's a great champion for women, Peter is. Personally, I don't care too much, but I do think it's interesting."

Ivy took a deep breath and let it out slowly. Of course, Alice was right, but it wasn't easy to admit, nor was it easy these days for her to talk to Jordy. "He's so reassuring that I can't get in a word edgewise, and then he makes me nervous with his fear, for it is great."

"But do try." Alice placed four bowls on the table with a clink and turned to face Ivy. "Again, you're my brave sister. I fully expect you to do what you must—as you always have."

The table was set, and Ivy walked outside to call in Jordy and Peter, feeling peppier than she had in weeks. Her sister Alice cared about her, loved her, and was willing to go to lengths to develop their relationship.

What more could she ask for?

She supposed that, once she followed Alice's advice in regards to Jordy, she'd have nothing to wish for at all. And she prayed that Jordy would listen to her. He had in the past. She had only to hope that her pleas now would be sufficient.

And that he still believed in the stronghold they'd built in their early marriage and even before that.

"I wonder if you comprehend fully how much light you bring." Alice adjusted the basket on her arm that she'd wrestled away from Ivy. "Ena had her child in May, correct?"

Ivy nodded. "Correct."

"I'm sure no one else is still tending to her needs, yet here you are." A small smile flashed across Alice's face and then was gone. "You do realize she has a husband and a half-grown daughter."

"I know. It's about friendship." Besides, with Alice there, her load was even lighter, and she had time to experiment with baking, which often left her with more breads, biscuits, and cakes than Jordy or she could ever use.

"Fair enough. Besides, if I eat any more of these biscuits, I'll have to order a new corset."

Ivy laughed. "I'm not far off from that, either—for different reasons, though, obviously. But I am bored enough these days that I actually eat, which I don't think I ever have before."

"I know! Isn't it strange? I fill my time as much as I can, and Riley and Peter take the rest of it, but if I do have time to myself, I find myself often turning to the pantry in boredom. Which is a mistake, because I have a whole train of followers: Peter, then our dog, Juno, and our cats, Ophelia and Cassius."

Ivy found herself giggling at the mental image. It would indeed be amusing ... but inconvenient. "Perhaps I ought to get some more pets. I think Jordy wouldn't mind having a dog around." Plus, her brother-in-law Ben had offered her a puppy sired by the McAllen's dog, Bean, lately. She should've paid closer attention instead of turning him down immediately.

"Oh, you wouldn't like to have a dog, Ivy!" Alice gestured to the left. "That's the butcher's, correct?"

"Yes, for us village folks, few as we are. He also does butchering for some of the people in the area who are unable to do it themselves." She shuddered at the thought of those little lambs.

They arrived at Ena's house and were greeted by Ivy's cheerful friend, baby in tow. Ivy swiftly relieved Ena of Hamish, even though she knew it was no true relief. For a new mother, Ena had told her, relief came in terms of washed dishes and clean laundry. Having her child removed from her arms was the last thing a woman needed.

However, Ivy had been greatly blessed in a generous mother-friend, and Ena didn't protest having Hamish taken. Ivy cooed to him and exclaimed over his growth and laughed at his gurgles. After she'd had a few minutes of this, she offered him to Alice, not wanting to be rude despite the fact that she lacked any desire to give him away, and Alice took him and was similarly delighted by his sweetness.

"How are ye feelin'?" Ena looked Ivy up and down. "I ken ye're delighted, but ye can tell me anythin' wi'oot me thinkin' less o' ye. 'Tis no' easy, noo, isna it?"

Ivy laughed. "Not easy, but it's delightful. They squirm about inside me now. It's stranger than anything, but I like it. It reminds me that these are babies."

Ena grinned. "Or a babe, singular. Ye willna be tae disappointed if 'tis no' twins, will ye, Ivy?"

"Oh, no, not disappointed but surprised." After all, it would mean that whatever she'd experienced hadn't come from God, which would seem quite strange given all the ways it had proven accurate. Though she wasn't technically due in October, either. Based on her last monthly, Jordy had estimated November.

However, so many things lately had proven that Jordy wasn't always right.

"I'm beginning to lend more credence to her, Ena." Alice looked up from Hamish at last. "She's never lied before nor exaggerated. I'm inclined to believe she must be right."

"Hmm. I dinna disbelieve her exactly ..." Ena paused as Hamish began fussing, but when Alice rose and rocked him, he swiftly quieted. "He's a bit o' a needy one."

"That's all right. I prefer them needy." Alice winked. "But I suppose I ought to surrender him to his mother all the same. And we'd best be on our way now that we've dropped off our basket. We're due at Aunt Daphne's for a lecture."

"Bible study," Ivy corrected. Aunt Daphne was trying to give Ivy a Biblical introduction to motherhood, which given that she'd never had a child herself, had proven ... interesting. "It's not a lecture; it's a Bible study."

Alice smirked. "Whatever." She passed Hamish back, one hand lingering on his fluffy hair overlong. "I'll come visit you again soon, dear one. Ivy, lead the way."

# CHAPTER TWENTY

*July 1885*

Violet once again stepped through the gate—*oh, lovely, now there is a useless gate*—at her aunt Daphne's house. She'd been compelled to come back by dozens of letters, which begged her, pleaded with her to come support her best friend.

How could Violet support her, though? She knew plenty about pregnancy, childbirth, and babies from a scientific perspective, but beyond that, it wasn't a subject she exactly specialized in.

Yet she'd come, unable to resist the siren call of her dear Trifle, even though every instinct screamed at her to stay away. She'd come, and here she was, ready to cause chaos, more like than anything.

But Ivy would never admit that. Ivy would never believe that Violet was capable of causing pain to her. Yet it happened. Again and again and again.

How could she comfort Ivy when her heart was tugging in another direction? She circled around Jordy's orbit, keeping her composure, still holding herself back from crashing into his fiery inferno.

The magnetism of Jordy was inescapable, but the tide that was Ivy continued to tug her toward the shore—and then back out again.

Yet she knew which was steadier. The tide came in and out, day and night. The sun was 'sure as day' until the dusk came—then it vanished.

But Ivy always tugged her toward the light. Or just a different world entirely. Violet's fairy tales were dark and musty, a dungeon of her own making, yet Ivy's tangled vines wove their way around them, until the castle collapsed and yellow rays of light made their way through the rubble.

It was a walk through the Forest of Arden, and all the fairies, good and bad, melted at Ivy's words. It was a trip through Wonderland, and yet Ivy lived in a dream she understood.

And Violet was the Hatter.

Taking a deep breath, she stepped through the door and into her aunt Daphne's house. For better or for worse, she was here, and momentarily, everyone would know she was there. Now she had just to remain strong for a bit longer. If strength was even the required element in this game.

"Miss Angel?"

Violet turned to face Peter Strauss, Ivy's brother-in-law. She cocked her head. "I don't think anyone on earth has ever called me that but you. What's the point? That's my sister—or her daughter, I suppose." She shrugged. "I forget Dory's married now. But I assure you, she was never Miss Dorothea—she was Miss Angel. My parents hardly remember I was born, let alone that I'm the eldest."

"Well, at the very least, I remember." Peter glanced around the foyer. "Did you bring anything?"

"Yes, but I've paid a boy to bring it up."

"Good, good. Your aunt Daphne isn't here, and Alice is upstairs, changing from clothes that got wet while we were helping Ivy with some laundry. But Agnes set out tea for us, and you're welcome to join us."

"I think I will."

She followed him into the front room where Aunt Daphne always took her tea on a small table. In short order, Violet was sipping tea while Peter talked quietly about this and that, as he always did, asking questions which she only bothered to answer with nods and murmurs.

"I admit I wondered why you left—and now why you've come back. I know enough about you from Ivy to understand that this is your true home, and yet you've fled again and again." Peter Strauss's eyes didn't cut through her like other insightful people's did, but he definitely saw through her. However, that seeing held so much compassion that she couldn't even hate him. Which she rather disliked. If she was able to properly hate the man, she'd feel so much better.

"I haven't any home."

"Yet this would be your home if you had one, wouldn't it?"

She glanced about her and shrugged. "I suppose so."

Peter Strauss leaned back on his chair with a sigh. "That's what Ivy said."

"Yes, well, she's often right, isn't she?"

Peter nodded. "That, we can both agree on with ease. I'm glad you've come, and she will be, too. She said you ought to be here."

Violet sighed. "I don't think I ought to be here, frankly, but I can understand why Ivy thinks I ought to be, so I am."

"Do you remember that subject we conversed upon at length, before Ivy and Jordy were married?"

His face was so solemn that Violet almost wanted to make a joke. But she couldn't, for she did remember, and her soul shuddered with the memory. Slowly, reluctantly, she allowed her head to nod.

"I worried ... When you left, I read restraint in it, restraint that Ivy could neither see nor understand. When I heard you were returning, I wondered." Peter Strauss grimaced. "I pray I am wrong. However, if I were so much as to mention the name Jordy McAllen—"

Before she could help it, Violet winced.

"See? That's what I mean."

Violet rolled her eyes. "Here, hand me the teapot. I can be the lady of the house, if your wife is late."

The teapot was passed, and for a few minutes, the calming ritual distracted even an American like Peter Strauss. However, it could not last. He had no respect for teatime and never would.

"Miss Angel, I fear you're playing with a bigger fire here than you know. But I suppose it won't do for me to just jump into this. I suppose I ought to ask you questions to lead up to that." He smiled then. "Am I losing my touch?"

"Oh, it only makes sense that with age, some things would slip away." Yet he hadn't changed in any real way, Violet didn't think. He was calmer, perhaps, maybe a bit less nervous. But he still saw through her.

"How do you feel ... about the babies, I mean? Or baby, if Jordy is to be believed, but I think, as Ivy's waistline continues to expand, he's beginning to give her beliefs some credence." Peter grinned. "Wait 'til you see her, Violet. Even you must be delighted, for she is blooming."

Violet rolled her eyes. "I doubt I shall be delighted. And like Jordy, I'm skeptical of her claim that she knows she's carrying twins—how could she know?" And yet she'd gotten in trouble for doubting Ivy before, so perhaps that wasn't the best idea. "And if she and Jordy want to have a family, Heaven knows I can't stop them."

"Yes, but that doesn't mean you're happy for them, Miss Angel."

"What does it matter?" Very little. No one every consulted Violet's happiness, and in this case ... even she wasn't as unreasonable as to believe she ought to have any say. It was entirely within Ivy's and Jordy's right to start a family together. In fact, it was a miracle they hadn't done so sometime before. Most people liked children, and Ivy certainly wanted them, so there was no argument against babies on that part. And if Ivy was thriving ...

Yes, it was all right. Or Violet ought to think it was all right, at any rate.

"It doesn't, except as it might affect your spiritual state and the way you relate to others around you."

Violet shifted on her seat. "I should go see Ivy now." She had come for that purpose, after all, not to chat with Peter Strauss or anyone else, for the matter.

"Perhaps you ought to. But if you ever want to talk—"

"I assure you, I shall not."

"But if you do—"

"I don't." She frowned. "Please leave me be, Mr. Peter Strauss, and allow me to deal with my own feelings toward your sister-in-law and her husband. I am quite in control of them."

"Are you?" He raised his eyebrows. "That doesn't seem to be the case, Miss Angel. Pardon me, but I think you have a lot of sorting to do about how you feel for Ivy as well as how you feel for Jordy. For to neither of them have you given the regard you ought, as close friends, and yet they both hold a place in your heart that they ought not. Am I wrong?"

"I haven't anything to offer on whether you are wrong or not, for I don't know quite yet how I feel." Violet shrugged. "There is much to be sorted. But I must do that work on my own. Have you ever been able to arrive at a conclusion more swiftly once you were bothered about it again and again? Don't poke at me, Mr. Peter Strauss, for I know nothing more than what you do."

"I'm sure you know a little bit more."

She rose and turned to the door. "I'm quite sure that I do not."

As she ran out of the house, she whispered the first prayer she had in a long time, only it was not perhaps the most holy thing uttered. She whispered, "Let me have both." Was that even a prayer?

Perhaps not. Yet the choice lingered before her, the choice Peter had laid out before her. She could not be a friend to Ivy if she were a friend to Jordy, and the love she held for both of them wasn't exactly the holiest of types.

How did one choose?

And yet there was so much more at risk these days.

"'There's two of them,'" Violet muttered to herself, quoting Ivy's letter. "'There's two of them, and just like us, they'll be the best of friends. I know it. So come and help me realize this dream, Vi, for I need your presence for safety ...'"

Lies, all of them. Violet was the last person Ivy needed.

Particularly for 'safety.'

"You tell me that like you could possibly know. You clearly don't know anything," she mumbled as she walked toward the hills, determined to get away for just a short period of time. "If only you knew the kind of friend I've been. If you knew, you'd curse the day you heard my name."

*Violet Angel. Violet Angel. Violet Angel.* It echoed in her heart, increasingly ironic as time went on. 'Angel.' Violet wasn't an Angel. She oughtn't to be. But Lucifer was an angel, too.

"'There's two of them.' You rejoice." Violet scoffed. As if it wasn't twice the knives shoved into her spine, the pangs squeezing her heart. She topped the hill and whirled to face down on Keefmore, and her eyes strayed farther, to the north, where Ivy's cottage was tucked into another small valley, amongst the sheep pastures of the McAllens.

Tucked away safely. Yes, Ivy was safe these days.

Or was she?

Violet turned and began to walk again, quick strides, hectic strides. "As much as I fear for myself, I fear for you. For you? Oh yes. Yes, I fear. If you knew, you'd think me heartless. But I'm not heartless ... or perhaps I am."

She scrambled down a rocky hillside, her feet sliding on the sharp rocks. She gasped and panted, but she made herself keep going. She must. She couldn't stop. Not now. Not while her heart threatened to beat its way right out of her breast.

"Perhaps I'm not heartless ... or perhaps I am." She turned her eyes to the blue sky overhead, turning to golden colors as the day dipped toward evening. "I've given away my heart and not received one in return. Does that make me heartless?"

There was no answer from the clear sky above. It didn't match her mood, and she turned from it with anger and continued scrambling over the rocks.

"What does it feel like to have three hearts inside you, Ivy?" she whispered. "For I have none."

She slipped to her knees, and her hands followed, and she cried manically, dry sobs with no tears. Trembling, she took a rock in each hand and held them, a stabilizing force in this inner maelstrom. "Just let me leave. Don't call on years of friendship, on my own salvation. You were the beginning of me, so be the end of me, too. There can't be 'two of us' anymore. There's a divide. Don't you see? How can I tell you?"

She calmed her breathing at last and gained sufficient vocal control to let the next words grate out strong, like so many stones falling to the earth. "I want him."

Didn't Ivy see? How couldn't she see? Her naïvety, her innocence, her belief in her good friends, had deceived her.

But there couldn't be 'two of them' anymore.

"I love you, too," Violet murmured, "but if I stay, I'll never forgive myself."

In Violet's heart, there were 'two of them.'

There was Ivy, with tears on her cheeks, calling her back. God, love, salvation, grace, hope ... sins. She claimed her, named her— *"Violet, my sister, my friend."*

Then there was he.

Golden eyes, a head full of reddish curls, flushed cheeks.

And he claimed her, named her— *"Vi, ye wee demon, where've ye been?"*

Violet squeezed her eyes shut. "You'd scold him for the 'demon,' but it's true, isn't it?"

Yes, there were two of them. Both in her heart, both her saviors, one way or another. One drew her to Heaven, and the other—

"God, help, help, help me," she cried. "I'm tempted, and I know how far I'd fall."

Was there coming back from that?

"But who do I choose?"

She didn't want to choose. She wanted to run.

"Ivy, let me run."

Yet she rose and dropped the rocks and walked slowly back up the hill, shoulders slumped. She would go to Ivy, and the cuts on her hands and the rip in her dress would be mended, and she would be undeservedly fussed over.

What else could she do, after all?

Ivy would not let her run. Her letter had made that clear. Violet was to come and 'be supportive.' Violet was to come and love Ivy, in some ways 'for a change' and in some ways 'as she always had done.'

But Ivy didn't know the choice she was forcing Violet to make.

When Violet arrived at Ivy's cottage, she thought she behaved herself well. Her hands were bandaged and her skirt mended, and Ivy fussed over her quite a bit. And Violet hated herself quite a bit, too.

Then she went home, too late to eat dinner, though she'd insisted she would get something at her aunt Daphne's house when Ivy had begged her to stay to eat with Jordy and her.

And she went to bed without supper, punishing herself for her own idiocy.

She couldn't choose, and yet, as much as she could, she must side with Ivy.

Yet she had no control over her dreams, not the nighttime ones, at least. They did what they would.

Were they dreams or nightmares?

*She felt, as if in reality, his lips brushing over hers, as they had a few scattered times before. The taste of his mouth was always a relief of sorts, like coming home, like finally finding something that could satiate the constant uproar inside her.*

*Violet knew the feel of his hair under her fingers, the strength of his arms around her, the scent of antiseptic ... She'd tell him to change his clothes before he embraced her, but he never would.*

*All these things that could've been hers.*

*All these things that, perhaps, in some way she couldn't even put into words, should have been hers.*

*Or perhaps she just thought that because she was losing her mind, for the taste of him was driving her insane.*

*There could be all the domestic things, then. There could be a cottage that Violet would keep very badly. There could be white washing hung on lines and an overgrown garden and curtains in the windows.*

*There could be children, too. Violet wouldn't mind that. Maybe. At least in dreamland, could she take care of a baby? Love it, give of herself to it?*

*No. She couldn't. Even her dream refused to allow the little things in. No, it was just the idea, separate from a family unit, of being loved, touched, cherished, of having someone say, 'You are my one and only,' and meaning it ...*

*But as always, the dream distorted. Jordy was leaving her, walking away, toward Ivy. At first in the dream, it was a torrid affair, a passionate case of adultery. And Violet the betrayed.*

*She liked to be the betrayed. It helped her overcome the fact that, more often than not, she was the betrayer.*

*Which was the direction the dream soon took. The direction of reality.*

*And she had to watch Ivy's pain. Had to watch her emptiness. Had to feel everything Ivy felt, and bear the blame and the guilt of having caused that pain.*

*And that sin. For Ivy would not be able to turn a blind eye to a discrepancy of that type. No, she would know Violet for what she truly was.*

*For such an act, there could be no grace. No repentance. No ... no nothing. No future, no life after the death of that sin.*

*If Violet were to commit it, it would tear apart the seams of her entire existence, and that of Jordy and Ivy.*

*Jordy was always blameless in these scenarios. He could not help it, nor would Ivy or Violet blame him if he could.*

The dream continued to become more and more nightmarish until the shouts and jeers of an assembled crowd, stoning her to death, caused her to jerk awake with a gasping sob.

Where was hope if the nightmare became a reality?

# CHAPTER TWENTY-ONE

*August 1885*

Ivy ran her hands over her abdomen and sighed. "And yet you want to say it's not twins?"

"I'm no' sure, Ivy, but tha's exactly th' point I am tryin' tae make. Ye canna ken, as I canna." Jordy looked up from where he sat on the edge of his bed, having just pulled on his boots.

"Yet look!" She turned to the side and again examined her figure in the mirror. "Does this feel like it could be just one baby?"

"Maybe ye're right an' ye're due in October, though th' dates dinna make as much sense." He shrugged. "There could be all manner o' explanations. Some women just—"

"But on the first pregnancy?" she persisted.

"Perhaps." There was a trace of skepticism on his face.

Ivy had given up trying to convince her husband with any kind of spiritual reason and had since begun using every physical sign she could think of to convince him that she bore twins.

Jordy used to believe her when she said she'd felt something from God. Where had that belief gone?

The midwife's daughter had told Ivy, though, that she believed she felt twins—that Ivy was right. And Ena believed that the midwife's daughter knew what she spoke of, despite being younger than her mother. More and more, Ivy trusted Marsali Dunmore over her mother, who could be, at times, unpredictable. Marsali was steady as the sun and wise beyond her years.

Ivy wondered if, perhaps, Marsali had been the hand that had really kept her mother in line. And now, as she grew and began setting off on her own, Mrs. Dunmore was losing her touch.

"But you heard what Marsali Dunmore said, didn't you? And, Jordy, if you could feel the way they—"

"Him or her, you mean."

"If you could feel the way they, meaning both of them, move within me, you would not doubt." She came to his side and placed a hand on his shoulder.

He looked up, met her eyes, and smiled. His smile faded as he looked into her face, and he closed his eyes. "Honestly, love, thinkin' o' th' possibility o' twins ... I shall have tae face th' reality o' one child soon, or at th' least, I am tryin'. But two? Give me a wee bit more time."

Her hand slid off his shoulder, and she stepped back. "So. You do know what you're doing." Somehow she had wanted to believe that he didn't know. That he had stumbled upon his manner of behavior in these last months.

She turned from him and started to walk out of the room.

"Wha' do ye mean, Vee?" His voice was innocent, but he must know. He must know how he wounded her.

Emotions boiled to the surface, sharp and quick, faster than any she'd ever felt before. "How dare you neglect me for five months and refuse to participate in the preparations for the children you created with me?" She turned to face him, the heat that had rushed behind her eyes making her see red. "Jordy, how could you do this to me?"

He stepped back, eyes wide. "I didna ken—"

"Of course you didn't know! Because you're an absolute idiot. Do you have any idea how I felt? Alone in my excitement, unable to share my feelings with my husband. Jordy, I love you, but what am I to do with your disdain for the one thing in my life that I have desired more than you?"

He was white as a sheet. "Ye never said a word."

"What was I to say? I love you, Jordy, and I want you to be happy. But God has promised me this. Can't you just believe me when I say that? We changed nothing about our intimacy, and still, we have conceived. The change was that God made the decision—"

"An' 'tis no' entirely without room for error, which I've said before is—"

"No! Don't you talk." She stamped her foot. "You've hurt me so badly, Jordy. These months have worn on me. Without you, I have relied on Alice and Peter. Even Violet has offered me more comfort than you have! Have you any idea how difficult this has been without you?"

She stopped talking, panting, the anger rushing out of her as soon as it had come and being replaced by shame. Surely she could've found a gentler, softer way of communicating the same sentiment.

She sat down on the edge of their bed, dropped her face in her hands, and began to sob.

The mattress bowed under her as he lowered himself down next to her, but he had given her space, and she only vaguely knew that he sat there except for that shift in weight. She eventually grew short of breath and a handkerchief was presented to her, but he said nothing.

"I just ... I can't ... I can't do this without you," she choked through her sobs. "You're ... you're the only one who can really help me, Jordy. N-no one else can."

Slowly, his arms came around her, and she collapsed against his chest, allowed herself to be drawn close. He shifted her a few times to make room for her somewhat different shape, but they managed, and at last, held close and safe, she settled down.

"If I had ken't tha' ye felt this way, Vee, I woulda told ye long ago tha' ye can tell me anythin'. Doesna matter wha'. Ye must tell me wha' is on yer mind." He sighed. "I'm so sorry I have ever led ye tae believe tha' I wouldna support ye, regardless o'—"

"It's not just that. You ... you have supported me in some ways, Jordy." She had to admit that he'd tried. "You just didn't give me what I needed. You've smothered me in trying to keep me safe, but you've never ..." Rejoiced with her. Helped her with the delightful tasks of setting up the nursery, of choosing names, of planning futures. They still hadn't talked about anything practical. "It's as you said. You haven't admitted yet that it's real."

His chest shuddered against her cheek. "I ken. I ken I havena. But I didna think ... I didna think me simple inability tae process somethin' would hurt ye so. If I'd ken't it ... I woulda done somethin'. I dinna ken exactly wha' tha' would be, but I'd have done it. Vee, I love ye, more than anythin', an' I ... I wish I were a different man."

"Yet you are the man I chose." She tilted her head back and rubbed at her eyes. "I ... I don't suppose you can deny that."

"Nae, I canna. Wha' I can deny is tha' I am or ever have been any good for ye. Ye are me better in every way."

"That is just not true. You're my ... my knight in shining armor."

"Yet I've failed ye. Our castle in th' sky has long since crumbled tae th' ground. Ye ken wha' I mean, dinna ye? Wha' we talked about on our honeymoon?"

Vaguely, she remembered lying in his arms, half-awake, flirting about the castle he would buy her someday, a cloud castle in the sky that would house all her wildest dreams.

Yes, she supposed she could recall that, but she had to squint to see the details. There was something about it just being the two of them, away from all civilization, with nothing to do but love and serve each other.

What she hadn't realized was that Jordy had apparently taken that a bit too literally.

"Jordy, you've never been thinking that was my dream, did you?"

She saw a flush creep up his cheeks. "No' exactly. More like, 'twas mine."

She blinked. Jordy was never one to be a daydreamer. Usually he prized reality. "Really?"

"Aye." He lowered his eyes and sighed. "Truth is, Vee, when we created tha' castle, I was thinkin' o' this cottage tha' I prepared for ye. An' I thought about how ... how there wasna really a place for a nursery. I wondered if I ought tae see tae it right off. But then I thought, 'We shall never have a child.' An' we didna for so long tha' I believed ... I believed I was God, I suppose. Tha's th' truth o' it."

Believed he was God? Whatever did he mean? She waited patiently for him to continue.

"I thought ..." He sighed. "This will sound silly."

"Go on."

"I thought I could stop nature. We were no' bein' as careful as we could be. But I believe tha' I ken't enough tae stop it. An' I rested safe in tha' belief. Because I couldna bear tae think o' anything otherwise."

She knew that, for he'd said it again and again. "But why don't you want us to have a baby, Jordy? For there is nothing on this earth I desire as much. At first, I didn't. At first, it didn't matter. But that night, our wedding night, when I asked you what you were doing ... 'It'll keep us from havin' a child.' I felt my heart shatter. Yet I locked myself away, and I didn't let myself think of it, for as long as I could manage. But a few months in, I thought of it again, and then again a year ago ..." She shook her head. "Jordy, in the year leading up to these babies, I have thought of little else. I begged God to change your heart. When He did not ... Jordy, I have never wanted something as much as I wanted you to want to have a child with me."

"I understand tha'." He hugged her close. "An' in truth,'tisn't ye. I was sincere about tha'. Never was a woman a more natural-born mother. An' yet I feared losin' ye. Th' most vital part o' me life. Ye have given me happiness. Ye keep me grounded; ye make me content with a life tha' I didna believe I could be content wi'. I have been verra happy, an' ye are th' cause. I feared tha' ... ach, any number o' things."

"Such as?"

"Such as ... such as God needin' tae take ye from me. Tae ... tae keep me from ..." He shook his head. "Tae keep me from lovin' ye tae well. Above even Him."

"Would you say that you do, Jordy?" For, flattering as it might be, it was the last thing she wanted. If she didn't possess the second place in Jordy's heart, she would be terribly disappointed in him.

"I dinna think so. But I fear it. An' I fear losin' ye. I'm fair petrified at th' thought, Vee." He shuddered. "An' anyway, I feared ... I wouldna make much o' a father. I can manage bein' a husband. At least, I believe I can. I ken we've no' been married long, but for me, at least, lovin' ye is no' a chore—it's a blessin'. But bairns? I was scared, Vee. An' I've been a fool tae no' see tha', o' course, God can ... He can cover this, tae."

She sniffled and nodded. It hurt to hear him admit, again, that he didn't want children with her, but at least he thought she could be a mother. That, perhaps, could be enough.

"I don't know if it makes a difference, but I think you could be a good father. You're good with Edith's boys, and with my younger siblings, when we're with them, and ... I think you could do it."

He squeezed her close for a moment and chuckled. "Doesna matter, I suppose. I will be a father whether I like it or no'. I suppose I have feared more than I ought. I should trust tha' God kens wha' He's doin'. If He's given us bairns tae raise, we must be meant tae raise them. I canna question tha'."

"No, we can't. And, Jordy ... can't you see my perspective?" She cupped his face in her hands and forced him to meet her eyes. "Can't you see the blessing in this, just a little?"

He smiled. "Perhaps if ye tell me, I'll see."

She took a deep breath, let it out slowly, and began to share her dreams. And he listened—calm, quiet, his heartbeat slow under the hand she kept resting on his chest. And she wasn't sure how much he agreed with, but at least he was there and listening.

Eventually, she felt him relaxing more, and she believed he was beginning to understand. He asked quiet questions then, easy ones but questions nonetheless—would she rather have boys or girls, when had she first decided she was having twins, what was the significance of

October in her mind?

And she answered them, and again, he listened.

She wasn't sure if that was enough, but it might have to be.

"Wha' is it, do ye think, tha' has hurt ye most about ... about th' way I've behaved?" His voice shook a little, and Ivy stilled in his arms, then raised her eyes again to his face. There was a definite darkness there.

"I don't know." Yet she did, and she was lying when she said she didn't. "Perhaps the fact that you ... you have treated our babies like an illness and tended to me like an invalid rather than an expectant mother."

"I see." The words were forced out rather than spoken. "I wish I had ... but ye see, I canna ..." His voice trailed off, and he shook his head.

"What is it?" she asked softly. *Please tell me, Jordy. Please. I must know. Let me glimpse the inside of your heart again.*

"Nothin'. 'Tis nothin'." Again, he jerked his head back and forth, and she felt him move away from her, as if he could no longer bear to touch her.

"And that hurts," she whispered. "How you won't touch me. I'm at a time, at present, Jordy, when people keep touching me more than I even want. Peter and Alice and Ena and everyone, except maybe Vi, want to feel baby kicks, and the midwife and her daughter poked and prodded—and even professionally, I have seen you do the same. Yet you don't even touch me for that. I asked to meet with Marsali Dunmore, but I expected some concern. It's like you don't even really believe we're going to have children."

He grunted, his back turned to her now. "How ... how could I—?"

"I don't know! I just know what I sense in regards to you. You don't talk to me about the children, and you barely respond when I bring them up." She swiped at the remainder of her tears with the still-damp handkerchief, then crumpled it and dropped it on the pillow. "I suppose I can see a bit why you are so disconnected. You haven't even ... When even my brother-in-law is more connected to my child than my husband, in some ways, I can see why you would ... why you wouldn't feel it's real. It's my body that has borne the changes, and you have not ... You have done nothing to be involved."

"I ..." He did not continue anything after that one syllable.

Ivy placed a hand on the small of his back. "Tell me, Jordy. Tell me why."

"I canna ... canna be a father." The first two words were slow, and they broke and shattered and forced him to rush the final four.

She scooted closer, mindful of the fact that any forward momentum was harder to control these days, and pressed her face to his back now, her hands on his shoulders. "I love you no matter what, but I'm not going to comment on that until you explain it in full so my absolute disgust of that statement is backed by fact—not just emotion."

A small laugh shuddered its way out of Jordy's chest, and she realized it was that damp kind of weeping laugh. Still, she waited.

"I ... I canna provide a good example for a growin' lad or be a man who a young lass would turn tae as an example o' manhood. I canna be tha' ... tha' man." Again, his voice broke, and again, she caressed his back, pressed a kiss between his shoulder blades even though he would not be able to feel it through his shirt and jacket.

"Keep going, Jordy."

"I havena wanted tae think about any o' this." His words were half hysterical now, and the rest were rambled, panted. She'd never seen him cry before, not really. "Wha' will happen? Wha' will happen when they're born, an' I canna ... I canna be enough. I am enough for ye, but I can never be enough for ... for bairns. Tae be a father is a commitment o' years. Tae be a father is ... it's impossible. Vee, I canna do it."

"Yet you have, haven't you?"

He let out a small, choked laugh. "Right, right. An' tha's all there is tae it, I suppose, is whatever bit o' fun I had. An' noo I'll run off an' leave ye, I suppose, an' ye shall rely on Alice an' Peter an' Ena an' Vi an' yer aunt Daphne tae sustain ye. Aye, tha'll be fine an' dandy. I havena even fixed th' room for ye. It's just a storage closet, but we're tae have bairns there in October—or November—but I think part o' th' reason I willna believe ye, other than th' obvious scientific reasons, is because I canna have it be October. Even a few extra weeks is th' difference between th' day me failures become obvious—an' this time I canna squeak by an' love ye an' nae one be th' wiser—an' tha' tae love these bairns, well, I—I would have tae ... an' yet I canna ..." This time he was unable to speak again when he stopped, and his shoulders shuddered under her hands.

She sat in silence for a long time, rubbing and crooning and letting him work the worst of it out. She wasn't quite sure what he most needed when he wept, for he never had before, but she prayed over him and eventually felt she needed to give him her words.

"I have a few things to say," she whispered. She opened her mouth for the first serious issue and felt an ominous chord, so she approached it from another angle. "First, that I heavily resent the implication that making love to me is just 'a bit o' fun.' That is holy and good, first and foremost, but it's also much, much more than 'a bit o' fun.' I know you don't really think that, but you're hurting, so I forgive you—this once. Don't you ever let me hear you disrespecting me in such a way. Especially when you're so sweet during and after. It makes me think I can't believe a word you say, Jordy McAllen." She purposefully kept her tone light and was met with a slight, broken chuckle.

Good. The ominous chord ended, and she felt ready to proceed.

"Second, my love ... you are the father of my children, and you will not leave me to do this by myself. Is that what you fear? That you'll leave? Because you won't. I know you. I know you better than you know yourself. Can I acquaint you with the Jordy McAllen I know? It seems you two haven't met."

He stiffened, then nodded. "A'right, go ahead an' introduce us."

She leaned on him again and closed her eyes. How to put this into words? For her Jordy was a complicated man, like any, and there was so much to say that knowing where to begin felt near impossible. Yet she'd try, for she knew it would mean a great deal to him, if she could find the right words for the task.

"I have the pleasure of introducing you to my husband, Dr. George McAllen, only he goes by Jordy, so please refer to him as such." She smiled. "Isn't he 'braw'? But I can't get too hung up on that, for he's a great deal more than that. He's a doctor, and he works hard to give to people, even when they can't afford to pay him, even when he has very little left to give. I can't count the nights when he's run from a warm bed into the cold to help someone, out of the goodness of his heart. He gives to the people of Keefmore long hours, exhausting work, with often minimal pay. He goes above and beyond the call of duty, and for these last two years, I have watched him be steadier than the sun. Certainly, he works a longer day than that lazy star, for he is up before it rises and he falls asleep long after it."

Little by little, his posture loosened and his shoulders straightened. Had she reached him with that?

Oh, but there was so much more.

"Despite the said minimal pay, he provides for his family amply. I never have wanted anything since he became my husband. I have never even had to ask for anything I wanted, because it was provided for me quickly and without hesitation. I am well fed, well clothed, well comforted. I love my home. With the exception of a few months this year when he has held a horrible darkness in his chest and not allowed light to penetrate as it ought, he has always tended to my emotional and spiritual needs, too. He leads me, he supports me, he understands me ... better than I understand myself. And he believes in me. When he is not sunk in his own fears, as that darkness has made him sink, he pushes me to be the best version of myself." Tearful now, she pressed her face against his back and sniffled. "How could I ever not love such a man?"

"Vee, I—"

"No." She pushed herself back then, took a deep breath, and forced herself to be calm. "No, I have more to say. Give me half a minute, and I shall say it, but don't you speak until you must."

After she had managed to, with strength not her own, compose herself, she began to speak again.

"Jordy McAllen is also a family man. Why do I say that? Oh, because he is. He takes care of his other family members, too. If his brothers need advice—whether the advice be on subjects spiritual, educational, romantic, or otherwise—they come to him first, before their own parents. Especially Mick and William. When he plays with or holds his little nephews, I see how dearly he loves them, how tender he is, how he would gladly risk all for them. He respects his parents and has them both for excellent examples of how to raise his own children—he is the eldest, so he can clearly see the work that went into it. Though he claims that most of his siblings' raising happened while he was gone, due to his absence through much of his young manhood, I do not miss the way his mother tells stories of leaving his brothers with him—and those are not the stories where the mishaps happened. No, my Jordy is good at keeping children safe. He is my stronghold, and I know that when our children are born—"

At that, he turned and pulled her into his arms. With a frightened squeak, she nonetheless went and cuddled close to him.

"I love ye," he said somewhat fiercely into her hair. "Wha' on earth would I do wi'oot ye? Me greatest blessin'."

"I didn't even get to talk about your relationship with God!" she protested.

"Oh, dinna go tellin' me there are observations about tha' side o' Jordy McAllen, tae, for he's neglected it shamefully o' late."

"Well, I know that can be rectified. God loves you so much, Jordy, that He keeps pulling you back in no matter what happens. So I know He's waiting for you with open arms."

For a few minutes, they sat in silence, then Jordy spoke again. "I'm no' goin' tae th' office this morn. They can find me here if they need me, but I've work tae do."

"What's that?" she whispered, a bit dazed still, for it felt like all the energy had suddenly drained out of her body.

"I have tae get tha' nursery set up for ye. I'm already behind, so I'd best start noo."

With that, some of the energy was renewed, and she enthusiastically hugged him, then rose. "I have so many things to show you, Jordy," she called over her shoulder as she walked toward the doorway. "Alice and I have all sorts of little things collected, and everyone in the village has made me something. It's going to be so lovely. We have these darling clothes—"

In the nursery, where boxes and boxes sat, only the beginnings of the many supplies she would need but that were thankfully arriving more as blessings than expenses as of yet, she took the box from the top where she'd stored her very various things and pulled out a christening dress, all white and lacy, and turned to face Jordy, now standing in the doorway.

"See?" She held it up. "And there will be another just like it, once Alice sews it. I thought we'd ask Alice and Peter to be the godparents to one of the twins, and Violet and one of your brothers—Ben, perhaps?—to the other. What do you think?"

"I think tha's an excellent idea. Though I admit I hesitate over thinkin' tha' Vi will guide me child toward ... Wha' is it tha' godparents do again? But I can understand wha' it means for ye."

"Vi came to be with me when she clearly didn't want to." Ivy sighed. "I don't know why, but I know that she didn't want to come, and so I appreciate that sacrifice."

"Likely 'twas just selfishness, Vee, though I ken ye'd like me tae give her th' benefit o' th' doubt."

Ivy opened her mouth to protest further but stopped as she felt the babies move, as they did more and more often these days. "Come here right now."

He raised his eyebrows but came to her nonetheless, and she took both his hands and placed them on her stomach.

For a moment, they stood thus, then he jerked his hands away as he, too, felt the soft kick. She took his hands again and placed them where she'd put them before.

"You're not allowed to move."

"I ... was surprised ... is all." Again, his voice was thick with emotion, but she hoped, prayed it wasn't pain this time. She prayed it was an entirely more positive feeling.

He kept one hand where she'd placed it and circled the other around her back.

"Oh, Vee ..."

"Do you see?" she murmured. "These are our babies, Jordy. I can hardly wait to meet them. Please, try to feel the same."

He leaned over and placed his forehead against hers, eyes closed. "Love, I'm goin' tae do better noo. I promise ye tha'. This time, dinna be afraid tae push, a'right? Aye, it hurts like anythin', but it's worth it. I'll try tae listen. Keep me near tae ye—make me love ye properly. I've been an idiot."

She wasn't about to protest that he'd been an idiot, so she didn't say anything. She just let it be a perfect moment.

There was time enough to suffer without interrupting the beautiful minutes that came and went in every life.

Perhaps, after all, they would be all right.

# CHAPTER TWENTY-TWO

Jordy sat on the edge of the bed and took Ivy's hand. His eyes were soft and gentle, and yet she could feel the pulse threading through his body and even into the air ... hectic, fast, strong. He was afraid. "I'll be back in a quarter o' th' hour. Will ye be a'right?"

"With all these people around me? Of course." She pushed herself up, determined to show her own strength. As of yet, the pains weren't bad, and as of yet, she hadn't so much as made a peep about it. She wanted to instill confidence in Jordy now—but eventually, she would be weak. And when that time came, she wanted to remember the times when she was able to be strong.

So Jordy went off to collect a few items from the office, and Alice immediately took his place.

"How are we doing?"

"Well enough." Ivy smiled, though she could feel her lips tremble a bit. Oh well. "I wonder how long it will be."

"I wouldn't have you compare my only experience to what you will likely have. Ask Mother when she comes back in. She'll have a similar experience to what you will probably work through."

"Though," Mother said softly as she entered the room, "you are in far better health than I was when you were born. When you were born, I was weak—tired—and more than that, downhearted, dispirited. Everything is different here. But all the same, I survived, and so will you."

Ivy released a nervous laugh. "You're not being terribly encouraging."

"Aren't I?" Mother perched on the edge of the bed. "I mean to be. I know you shall be all right, and I'm not worried in the slightest. You shall have excellent care, and you are built for this."

The hours stretched on. Jordy came and went, as did his mother, but as the pains increased in length and intensity, he didn't leave her side.

In the seventh hour, Ivy begged for Violet to come to her side, and she came, and Ivy took her hand, too. Alice and Mother both seemed more efficient in terms of fetching and carrying things, in encouraging verbally, but she needed to touch both Violet and Jordy just now.

And the day continued on, and the pains kept getting worse, until Ivy was not at all sure she could bear much more.

Everyone seemed to think she could, but then, they were not present in her body, experiencing the overwhelming suffering.

Would it never end?

Violet hated this.

Hated every small moan and pant, the way her Trifle had been forced to writhe on the bed, weeping.

Everyone else seemed terribly calm, and Violet wanted to believe it was because every one of them had seen more babies delivered than she had.

But that was not entirely fair, for Violet knew quite a bit about childbirth. Probably more than anyone present, in theory at least.

However, when it was her dear Trifle ... that was an entirely different matter than a hypothetical woman with a hypothetical baby.

Violet, for her part, did the best she could to stay out of the way, and everyone churned around her, doing everything they could to help.

But it was plain from Ivy's expressions, from the words she managed in between contractions, from her strangled cries that not much was helping. It was just to be gotten through.

So Violet shuddered through her best friend's pain as much as Ivy did, never releasing her hand for so much as a moment. She would not leave her side. Not while she looked like *that*, not while it was clear that Violet had been a fool not to worry more than she had.

As one contraction ebbed to make room for another, Ivy turned her face to Violet. "What time is it?" she panted.

"I'm not sure, Trifle," Violet whispered, laying her head on the pillow next to Ivy's. "But nearing dusk."

"I'll light a lamp," Ivy's sister, who had been doing most of the fetching and carrying, said. "You're doing so well, Ivy. You're almost there. You just have to be strong for a little longer."

Violet wanted to shout out a protest. That wasn't fair! It had already been far, far too long. Yet Ivy jerked her head in a sort of a nod, made no protest, and then gripped Violet's hand with an astounding strength. A bone-shuddering groan was ripped from her lips in the next moment, and Jordy was whispering something near to her ear, about her breathing or something of the sort.

Ivy gasped in a breath but was otherwise unable to reply or obey whatever he'd told her to do. Violet understood that Jordy knew about these things, but she still wanted him to leave Ivy be. After all, he couldn't understand what she was going through.

And neither could Violet. She couldn't begin to understand it. Never would her body bear anything more intense than the mild cramps that accompanied her monthly—and she didn't have that with any sort of regularity, either. She would never have this particular experience in womanhood. Yet her Trifle, her innocent Trifle who had never done a thing wrong, must suffer so for no reason.

*Oh, Lord, bring her through this. Please. I ... I'll do anything. If You just don't let her suffer much longer, I'll do anything.*

With the next contraction, Ivy briefly arched her entire body off the bed, then she writhed and groaned again. "Jordy—"

"I ken, love. I ken. Shh. Mrs. Knight, should we—?"

Ivy's mother nodded succinctly. "We're almost there, dearest. I promise. Alice, can you—"

Their voices faded off. Violet focused in on Ivy, on watching her expressions, on hearing only the noises she was making.

"What can I do?" she murmured, low and soft.

"Nothing," Ivy panted. "Just be here."

But Violet wasn't talking to Ivy. No, she knew there was nothing she could do, nothing of this world. She could only offer prayers. Violet didn't know how to pray properly. So what was she doing?

Just whatever she could to make things easier.

*Lord, please, save my Trifle. Let the babe—or babies, I suppose— come quickly now. Not another hour. A few more minutes ...*

Yet the minutes ticked on, and Ivy still suffered.

Until at last, nearly an hour later, with blood and sweat now practically causing the humidity in the air, there was na infant's cry.

Alice was the one who carried the first baby away to be cleaned while everyone else remained with Ivy, and a few minutes later, what at least felt like a slightly less intense experience led to a second child.

Then Violet leaned back, for Ivy was begging Jordy to hold her, and he pulled her into his arms and held her steady, whispering to her again. She heard the tears in his voice.

Violet eased out of the bed, left the room, and stood in the kitchen, staring straight ahead of her. She became aware that Alice knelt by the stove, a large pan of some sort in front of her. Coals were raked out onto the ground, glowing a soft orange beneath the pan.

And an affluence of lace and wool rested in the pan.

Violet raised her eyebrows. "Pardon me, Mrs. Strauss, and nothing hostile meant by it, but out of curiosity, do you intend to cook and eat your sister's child?"

Alice looked up with a smile. "This is what Jordy told me to do. Mother should bring me the other in a minute, but he said we needed to immediately keep them warm until Ivy is ready to hold them—and then perhaps only by shifts so they can stay here."

Violet walked over and knelt next to Alice to view a tiny, wrinkled, red, old-man face peeking above the wool. "So small," she murmured, reaching down to touch the cap of a downy head.

"I know! I can hardly believe it. But its lungs are healthy, as the other's seem to be, from what I heard a moment ago, and I want to believe that Jordy is right—that at six weeks early, we should not have to worry as long as they are cared for well. All the same, taking precautions seems well worth it."

"Have we a boy or a girl, then?"

Alice raised her eyebrows. "You didn't hear?"

"I was not listening to anyone but Ivy at any point throughout the birth. Seemed rather pointless." She removed her hand from the child's head.

"Both girls." Alice smiled. "Beautiful, isn't she? Ivy will be so pleased. And of course she was right."

"She is always right."

"For once, I am inclined to agree with you."

Ivy's mother came in then with another bundle, and the two were laid to rest one beside the other.

"We'll have to figure out a better way of managing those coals," Mrs. Knight observed. "I'm going to help Ivy get cleaned up. See if Peter can't help you arrange something more permanent."

Peter Strauss entered the room then, glanced about, and came to kneel behind Alice, placing a hand on her lower back. "So these are them?"

"Two girls," Alice confirmed. "Both alive, both breathing."

"Has Jordy—?"

"Not yet. But I imagine he wants to make sure Ivy is well first."

Peter nodded and shifted. "I imagine so."

Mrs. Knight went back into the bedroom, and Peter helped Alice rig a system to make it easier to transfer coals into some foot warmers that could be placed around the babies to provide the necessary heat.

Violet eventually found water to wash herself, but she felt oddly disconnected from everything. Linens were carried out past her, babies were fussed over, Jordy came out and sat by them for a bit, and again, he wept.

"She's told me she won't sleep until she gets to hold them both, so I suppose we'd better arrange it."

"Aye." Jordy stood but kept a hand on one of his daughters, whose temporary bed had now been moved to the table. "She ought tae hold them noo, before they begin tae fail for lack o' love. Tha's wha' me mother told me tae do, an' I ken tha' years o' doctorin' canna hold up tae some good woman sense."

"I think we ought to give Ivy some privacy," Peter said. "Jordy, you take one, and Miss Angel, you take the other and bring them in to Ivy. We'll see to dinner, and you can call if you need anything."

"But I can't—"

Before she could protest, Peter had moved around the table, the sneaky devil, lifted one bundle, and placed it in her arms. And Violet stood, her arms awkwardly wrapped around the tiny thing with its downy head and not at all sure what to do.

Jordy picked up the other baby as easily as one would pick up a bundle of sticks and started into the bedroom.

Was she just to follow him, then? How could she even walk for fear of dropping the most precious thing she'd ever held?

It wasn't Violet's opinion, of course, that made the thing precious. It was the fact that it was Ivy's precious thing, Ivy's blessing, Ivy's baby. Ivy loved this child with an intensity that at times frightened Violet.

When Ivy spoke of her children, it was always with a hint of, *"And I would gladly take a knife to your throat if you ever so much as insulted them,"* which was a new element to her Trifle. An element she liked—and disliked—and rolled her eyes at a bit, for taking a knife to someone's throat involved blood, and blood was one of the things

Ivy did not care for very much.

At last, Violet managed to prevail herself forward into the bedroom after Jordy. He was already kneeling next to the bed, transferring the first bundle into Ivy's arms.

Ivy was pale—far, far too pale, and she was often pale; right now she was gray. Her eyes had those dark circles under them, and in the lamplight, she looked more dead than alive.

But her eyes were alight, and she made a soft sound, like a gasp or a croon or both, as her child was settled into her arms.

"This is th' elder," Jordy whispered. "Look at her! She's just slightly bigger, but it's hardly noticeable. They're both fine and strong. Here. Me mum said—"

Again, Violet began the process of tuning him out. Whatever he said led to his having Ivy unbutton the front of her nightgown—Violet glanced away briefly to give her the privacy to randomly disrobe, if such was her choice—and settling the firstborn against her chest before tucking the blankets back up around her.

"Vi, bring the other so I can look at her at least," Ivy whispered. Her voice had a hoarse edge, and Violet checked to make sure someone had thought to bring her water and tea—the glass and the mug on the bedside indicated that they indeed had. "Jordy, come back quickly, but can you see how that dinner's coming along? I'm dreadfully hungry."

He pressed a kiss to her forehead, then slipped out of the room, and Violet took his place at the bedside.

"Here." Ivy shifted ever so slightly to the side. "Sit so you don't have to bend. This is the firstborn, so we've decided on Margaret. I just think it's a strong name, and Jordy says we shall call her Little Molly."

"That's pretty enough." Not the nicest name Violet could think of, and she was surprised that Ivy hadn't chosen something a bit more literary rather than just choosing a random name—unless she was thinking of Margaret Dashwood or Margaret Hale. Which she doubted. Still, she could accept it.

"More specifically, Margaret Alice. We made a promise to each other eons ago, Alice and I, that our firstborn daughters would be named for each other." Ivy reached her free hand out and tugged at Violet's arm. "Let me see."

Violet managed to maneuver the bundle into a position to where the face was visible from Ivy's angle. "There."

And she found herself, in a way, blessed that she was able to see Ivy's face at the moment she first looked at her younger daughter. For it was breathtaking, truly.

"You're quite beautiful," Violet mumbled before she could quite help it.

Ivy blinked, her eyes briefly leaving her child's face before returning. "The baby?" she breathed.

"No. You looking at the baby."

Ivy laughed dismissively, but she couldn't change the fact that it was true. She did look lovely, with one child tucked just under a cover in her arms and her eyes glued to the face of her other.

"They look like Jordy," Ivy observed, although it wasn't even vaguely true. They looked like little raisins. "Look at her ears! Shaped just like Jordy's. And her nose. And even her mouth, a bit."

Violet couldn't be bothered to see it, but she still shrugged, which was good enough for Ivy.

Ivy adjusted the blanket to look down at her other child then. "Molly," she whispered. "My Molly. I'm your mother, and I love you." Then, without any warning, her voice broke, and, without moving her body very much at all, she managed a sob. "You're so b-beautiful."

Violet blinked, unsure what to do, but she managed to balance the baby in one arm and find a handkerchief in the nightstand drawer with the hand. "Here."

Ivy accepted the handkerchief. "Th-thank you. I'm s-sorry." She dabbed at her face with her free hand and hiccupped. "I just have never felt like this. I don't know what to do with it. Oh, Vi, this is what Heaven is like! I'm sure of it."

This was what Heaven was like? Then Violet wanted nothing of it, for the scents of blood and sweat still lingered, Ivy looked like she was about to die at any moment, and the babies weren't even human-looking yet. However, looking at Ivy's face, she could tell her friend truly believed what she said, and Violet didn't have the heart to contradict her.

Wanting to give Ivy something to think about other than her emotions, Violet asked a question. "What will you call the other one? Have you decided that?"

"Oh! Yes! I thought I'd said." Ivy shifted upwards slightly, adjusting the child sleeping against her skin, and put her free hand on Violet's arm. "We're going to name her Violet."

All of the blood in Violet's body rushed to her ears and thudded and made her feel faint. She tightened her hold on the bundle, then loosened it, dreadfully afraid of crushing it. "A-after ... me?"

"Yes, of course! Oh, Vi, who else could I name her after?"

"She could have her own name," Violet suggested. "Like Elsinore or something."

Ivy looked quite amused by the suggestion. "From *Hamlet?*"

"Well, it's ... classical." Plus she thought it was one of the more elegant names, but she wouldn't say that now that Ivy had made fun of it.

"It's a castle."

"Some women are built like castles. They have a little of your mother's blood in them, don't they?"

Ivy shook her head, grinning. "Well, I've no connection to *Hamlet* or to castles, but I do to you. And I can't imagine a better namesake or godmother for my second daughter."

Violet now felt nauseous enough that she feared for whatever remained in her stomach—namely, that it might make a sudden appearance—but Ivy continued.

"Jordy likes Violet Leannan. He said he'd give me anything if I just accepted that it was 'sort of Gaelic,' whatever that means. He says it's Irish, but no one will ever use her second name, and he thinks it's pretty. I suppose it can be spelled with one *n* or two, but I would do two, so it would be—"

With that announcement, Violet's heart had lightened a bit, and she spelled the name out in Ivy's stead: "L-E-A-N-N-A-N. Like Leanna but with an extra *n*. Yes, I'm familiar with Leannan." Though as a part of leannan sìth, or leannán sídhe, a member of the Aos Sí, the name for the mythological creatures of Irish folklore.

Many years ago, she'd learned Irish folklore just because Jordy told so many wild tales and she'd wanted to outdo him but with something that would frustrate him.

She'd fallen in love with the fairy-lover myth as both a muse and a bit of a vampire, depending on the variation, and Jordy had humored her, hearing her tales, teasing her about being a bit of a fairy lover herself.

Oh, and she'd loved that teasing, relished it ...

"I think it's pretty, at least, and he's right that we won't use the second name much. So it'll be Violet Leannan, who we will call Letty to simplify things, and Margaret Alice McAllen. My two girls." Ivy flopped back again with a small smile. "Do tell me you're happy with that, Auntie Vi."

Violet swallowed. "I ... I am. Happier than words can say." She understood now that it was not just an empty gesture. It was a gift from both Ivy and Jordy, thought through on both of their parts.

And she knew then that if there was a choice to be made, well, she could not make it. She must choose the both of them. For they were equally her dearest friends, Jordy and Ivy. They both knew her best, loved her best of anyone in this world.

Eventually, Violet helped her switch one baby for the other—Little Molly for Little Letty. And then food was brought, and everyone fussed again.

Violet went home happy that night and excited to return and spend more time with her namesake—oh, and Molly, though she was already of the firm belief that Letty was the superior of the two.

But she thought that, perhaps, she could do that. Be 'Auntie Vi,' as Ivy had referred to her as already. Play the supportive best friend and pseudosister. Love Ivy and Jordy and their children. Exist in their lives and yet not be the ruination of their lives.

She could do that, couldn't she? She could love them enough for that, couldn't she? Surely it was attainable.

And she must, after all, or God would be sure to strike her down, for she'd promised, in exchange for Ivy's life, to run if the temptation became too strong.

And how could she bear to part from Ivy?

# CHAPTER TWENTY-THREE

I vy loved the quiet days that followed, though she'd been told they'd be the hardest of her life. Yes, she was exhausted, but with as many people as were hovering around her, and beloved people at that, she didn't have much to do.

Of course, feeding Molly and Letty was a full-time job. She found that she went from nursing one to nursing the other to napping, and such comprised her days and nights. She ate while she nursed, thanks to Jordy and Alice and Peter and Mother being on hand to make sure that happened, and everyone was extra careful about protecting her energy.

But she was so grateful that first, she was able to nurse them, and second, they were able to latch on, both variables Jordy had been quite fussy about but that she didn't much care.

Especially since nursing gave her an opportunity to hold and admire her babies, who everyone in Keefmore seemed to want to hold, much to Ivy's dismay. Yes, she was flattered by the admiration they received, but they were so fragile, and fear and longing threatened to tear her apart whenever they were out of her arms, let alone her sight.

After all, they were her babies. Her babies. What a delightful thing to be able to say, at long last!

As for Jordy, she found herself checking in with him more than once a day, and there was honesty in his eyes when he told her he was happy.

It was beyond wonderful to have Jordy be happy, sincerely happy. It made him that much better.

His happiness made her happy, and in time, she felt her happiness had the same effect on him. And, of course, seeing him smitten with the daughters he hadn't even wanted was delightful.

For he, like Ivy, couldn't keep his eyes off them. He fussed more than she did, too—he was wary of everyone who touched them, protective to the extreme of both their twins and her.

Ivy knew these days wouldn't last forever. Jordy needed to work and her mother to return to her own children, and Alice and Peter must return home to America, and Violet would go home, too, perhaps. Ena and Aunt Daphne would remain in Keefmore, but they both had lives of their own. Yes, the reprieve from having to do much of anything was brief, but it was a reprieve nonetheless, and Ivy enjoyed it thoroughly.

Today, Alice and Peter had taken the day to themselves, at Ivy's encouragement, and her mother was actually packing at Aunt Daphne's house, as she would be returning to England and Pearlbelle Park the following day. Meanwhile, Jordy had decided to take the afternoon to check in on some patients. Already Ivy's support system was wavering ... but Violet was here, holding Letty in the crook of her arm and a book in her other hand, and that was enough.

Molly at last finished nursing and fell asleep, and Ivy rose from her chair to transfer her smoothly into the bassinet.

"There," she murmured as she smoothed a soft blanket, knitted by Nettie and brought by her mother, over her child. "That's my wee Molly."

"The only other person in the world she could be is Letty," Violet whispered, smirking. "Though I confess they are hard to tell apart."

Ivy scowled over her shoulder at Violet, who sat on the kitchen table chair they'd brought into the nursery. "That's not true. They're as different as night and day."

Violet raised her eyebrows. "Oh, do tell. For now, at least, they've the same blue eyes, and the same light hair, such as they have, and they're about the same size. What more is there?"

"Well ..." There were things, but Ivy couldn't quite put them into words. It was rather one of the disadvantages of being so close to them. And yet also one of the advantages, for she knew she could never mistake one for the other. "It's clear they're not identical. Despite that small size difference, their faces are structured differently. Letty is leaner, her nose a slightly different shape, and I don't know. You can already tell they will have wildly different personalities." Like Alice and Ivy. Perhaps even like Ivy and Violet.

"Can't you tell the difference?" Ivy asked, tiptoeing over to Violet and lightly touching the top of Letty's head. "She's very like Jordy, I think."

Violet squinted and seemed to consider this. "Hmm. Maybe ..."

"About her mouth, I mean, and her nose, too. I can see it." Of course, beauty might be in the eye of the beholder, and Ivy was very determined to see elements of Jordy in her babies, especially since everyone, especially her own mother, talked about how much they looked like Ivy.

She was flattered, yes, but she could look in the mirror if she wanted to see herself. Which was perhaps the wrong analogy since she could also just look at Jordy if she wanted to see Jordy, but she wanted to see Jordy *everywhere*. Seeing herself everywhere wasn't nearly as much of a draw.

But if every day of her life she could look at these babies and instantly be reminded of the simple but beautiful fact—*"these are the babies made with the man I love"*—well, that was the perfect life, wasn't it?

But they were also their own little people. It was strange to think about that. They were small, but more and more, when they opened their eyes and looked up at her, she thought she saw recognition.

Jordy thought they probably weren't recognizing anything but the fact that they were loved, safe, fed, and changed right now, but Ivy disagreed. After all, these two had rested beneath her heart for eight long months. Surely there was recognition there—that she was the one who had carried them, nourished them for all that time?

But it was fanciful, and Violet would laugh if she spoke any of these words aloud. So she didn't.

"You know I love you, don't you, Trifle?"

The words were entirely unexpected, though not unwelcome, and Ivy looked up with a smile. "Of course. I love you, too, Vi."

"Do you know ... I would do anything for you. Risk anything for you. But ... but I'm afraid of hurting you. Especially since you've taken so many risks, done so much for me."

"I haven't taken any risks that haven't paid off. Your friendship means the world to me and always has." Violet was closer to her sister sometimes than Alice. Well, maybe less so in these last few months, when Alice had become vital to her, but in general, it was true.

"You have, though. More risks than you know." Violet stood. "Here. I'll put her down and we can talk in the next room ..."

Ivy helped Violet get Letty settled and then they walked into the kitchen together and sat at the table.

"You see, Trifle, I ... I need to change the way I have been about something." Her shoulders slumped and her eyes cast down to her hands, clasped before her. "I intend to be a better friend to you from now on. A better aunt. When I saw ... You're a very strong woman. And I feel like I've hurt you in so many ways—"

Ivy held up her hand. "Vi, I've told you before—I'd forgive you for anything. Sometimes you're not yourself! So what type of person would I be if I blamed you—?"

"Nevertheless, there are areas where I have very much failed you, and I want to do better. I am going to do better. I've always ... Trifle, I've always imagined my life a certain way but had no way to realize it." She gestured toward the nursery door. "In these last two weeks, I have imagined my future in an entirely different light. One involving you and Jordy and ... and the girls. Mostly the girls, really. I think, with a little practice, I could be an excellent aunt, even if I am not quite there yet."

"Oh." Yet Ivy didn't understand, not completely. All she understood was that this meant a lot to Violet, so she reached across the table to touch Violet's fisted hands. "Violet, any involvement in my life, and in Molly's and Letty's lives, from you is entirely welcome and appreciated. I hope you will be an aunt to them—their dearest aunt, who they can go to with assurance that you are as safe to them as their own parents and that you love them as much. I trust you completely."

Violet let out a shaky-sounding breath and nodded, somewhat manically. "Yes. Yes, I want that. Trifle, I think ... I think I can do it. I didn't think at first I was strong enough, but I want ... I want your friendship more than anything else."

Hmm? What was that? Ivy leaned back slightly. "What do you mean by that?"

"I mean ... you're good and holy and clean, and I think that's what I mean. I want more that's clean. I never feel clean, and I ..." She stopped herself then, clenched her teeth, and looked away. "I want you to be my salvation."

*No.* Not even from Violet would she take such talk. "Violet, Jesus is your salvation, not me. He's the only One Who can save you."

"I know that, but I need time to come around to it. For now, be my light until I can find something greater to cling to. Please."

Perhaps ... Ivy would have to have some serious talks with Violet about this way of thinking, but she understood vaguely what her friend meant.

"I want to have ambitions and passions of my own, though, too. I think I ought to get back into music some. I've had some ideas ..." Violet was rambling now, her eyes bright in a way that came near to scaring Ivy. "I want to make a difference in the world, the way you do, but in my own manner."

That much made sense. Ivy could understand it. "Yes, that sounds perfect, Vi! I'd love to help you with it."

"And you will! See, I just need you to stand between Hell and me for a bit, Ivy, until I am strong enough to stand myself."

"You mean until Jesus Christ is strong enough in you—"

"Yes, yes. Of course that's what I mean." Violet tossed her hand in disdain for Ivy's specifics, even though they were absolutely vital to the meaning and the function of what Violet was suggesting. "Thank you, Ivy. I ... I need some time to think this out. Will you be fine by yourself for a bit?"

Ivy nodded. "And Alice and Peter will be back in an hour, so even if both my girls wake up and overwhelm me for a time, I shall manage well." Not to mention she needed to figure things out by herself at some point.

"Good, good." And with that, Violet rose and left the cottage behind.

Ivy watched her go in absolute puzzlement.

What had gotten into her Violet now?

*They were curled up on the floor of Ivy's living room, sheet music spread about. Molly had some in her mouth, and Violet pried her sticky fingers open and tore it away.*

*"Soaked," she pronounced. "Heavens, Molly. There's a reason your sister is named after me and you after your aunt Alice."*

*Ivy laughed. "Let me take her. I'm afraid a year is a bit young to start with music, dearest."*

*"Nonsense. I was hardly older." Nevertheless, Violet passed Molly over and collected up a few scraps. "So what do you think? Am I getting somewhere?"*

*"I hardly know. I can hear parts of it but not all of it together. Yet. But it's coming, Violet—I can feel it. It'll give us something to do, at least." She held up a sheet. "We have to redo this one."*

*Violet squinted. "What? That's part of the allegro, isn't it?" She launched herself forward and snatched the sheet away. "That part is perfect. You're an idiot."*

*"Can't you feel how garbled it's going to sound? Especially if you have all the violins playing this section, which requires some interpretation—" She tried to take the paper back, but Violet stood.*

*"Shush, Trifle. I know my own symphony. It's late, you know; should we get supper for these wee heathens of yours?"*

*Ivy blinked and glanced at her watch. "Oh, heavens, it's five thirty! I'm sorry—without Jordy coming home, I never think about dinnertime. Thank goodness you're here."*

*Violet coughed. "Right. With him at McCale House, it just seemed ... best."*

*She scooped Molly up and passed through into the kitchen. "How so?"*

*"Oh, you know. He's there. You're ... here. Alone. And you must need me, Trifle. I'm so necessary." Violet's flippant voice behind her, rambling about Ivy's utter incapability, faded into the background as she began preparing for dinner.*

*"Well, I'm glad you came here, though I'd rather hoped you would stay in Edinburgh and take care of Jordy. I can't imagine what he's eating; he can be so irresponsible."*

*"Mm-hmm ..."*

*Music was scattered over her piano now, and Violet was scribbling frantically while Ivy kept her fingers flying, catching every note almost before it was played.*

*"What's this one, then?" Violet asked as the last chord trailed off.*

*"Oh, I don't know." Unlike Violet, Ivy didn't compose symphonies. She wrote pieces for the piano—complex pieces, granted, but solos or on the very rare occasion, duets, though they struggled to get those put down. And they didn't have cohesion to them, necessarily, either.*

*Violet threw up her hands in a halfhearted gesture of frustration. It wasn't true frustration, not after all these years, though perhaps that made it truer. It was expected frustration, frustration one knew one would have, which was the best and the worst kind. "What feeling were you experiencing as you played, Trifle?"*

*"I was happy but a bit sad." She cocked her head. "Motherhood, perhaps. I thought of Molly, and the rest of it just flowed out. And I thought of how hard it is on Letty."*

*Violet chuckled, a small sound of bitter amusement, but she smiled. "She'll be fine, Trifle. She has her own life, all right? She won't be alone forever. Independent, is what Letty is, even despite Molly. She'll find something. So is this 'For My Violet'?"*

*Ivy shook her head. "No. Other pieces have been 'For My Violet,' and those were for you, and this wasn't for Letty, either. This is 'Inevitable Changes.'" Ivy laughed at that, too, and shook her head. "I'll think about it later. Let's work on your latest piece now; I feel I can just taste the finishing touches."*

*Ivy dropped to her knees, covered her face with her hands, and let a sob escape. She'd been so good—so very good—and she hadn't let go until now, until the casket was lowered and the mourners moved down the hill, away from the graveyard.*

*A few members of her family lingered, almost unsure what to do with her. It was Violet who stepped forward, placed a hand on her shoulder, squeezed.*

*"Shh, Trifle. It's all right. I know." Her own voice was thick. "I'm here, all right? I'm here. 'Dinna fash yerself,' wouldn't he say? Come away now."*

*Ivy rose and walked down the hill, because she had someone to lean on.*

Perhaps it was just about reframing her life around one goal—a friendship with the only person who had ever believed in her.

What good would an illicit affair do? She'd never cared for romance anyway.

# CHAPTER TWENTY-FOUR

T here were dreams and there were nightmares. Sometimes they were both. Violet went to bed that night without expecting either. That was, perhaps, why her sleep was fitfully possessed by those types of dreams that faded in and out of pleasantness.

Eventually, though, the nightmares consumed her.

I'm not human.

*That was the context of the dream.*

*The words somehow softened her actions. If she whispered them to herself over and over again, she didn't feel the guilt over not holding herself to a level of 'humanity.' Of course, humanity was so flawed that using 'humanity' to refer to guilt and kindness and all that was nonsense. It always had been.*

*Yet she went a step beyond humanity into 'not human.' And that made it easier to feel all right about what she was planning to do.*

*The veil rested perfectly over Ivy's face, but somehow Violet could read the sparkle in her eyes through it. Somehow ... Violet hated her for it. That happiness. The way she smiled right now. The way she* always *smiled.*

*Violet wanted to ruin that happiness. And she had a few words that would change that forever:* I'm in love with him.

*She wasn't kind; she didn't have to hold them in. And to see that face, that brilliant face, crumple into agony, she'd be cruel. She had never pretended to be any better than that.*

I never was.

*Never had been normal. Never had been kind or loving. Yet Ivy had loved her anyway. Had been kind anyway. Had kept her from the darkest places, had entered the darkness herself to drag Violet back out.*

*Ivy looked beautiful. Ivy was a saint. Ivy always loved Violet.*

*And Violet was no angel.*

So why are you expecting me to act like one?

*"Violet? You seem sad." Ivy's face was twisted then, though the grief wasn't full. It was more like passing concern.*

*There it was. Her opportunity. She could say exactly what was on her mind. She could ruin today. She could make Ivy hurt as much as she herself was hurting.*

*"No, actually, Trifle." Violet smiled. "I'm just thinking about how hideously long today shall be, with so many of your relatives—and of course I just hate weddings. You'll keep me close to you?"*

*"Of course!" Ivy squeezed Violet's hand, her face brilliant again. "Of course I will! I will forgive you if you have to act up, too, so don't worry. Today wouldn't be quite so special without you near."*

*Of course it wouldn't.*

*Violet wasn't human. She never was. But Ivy expected her to act like one. And today was Ivy's day.*

Violet jerked awake, but this time, she didn't weep as she always did when she woke up from the dream.

Instead, she lay in the silent darkness and thought.

Ivy looked sublime as she once again sat before Violet, her younger twin cradled in her arms. "Violet McAllen," she said softly. "Our Little Letty. Aren't you beautiful? Vi, I always knew I would name a child for you. I wondered about Violet Alice or Alice Violet, but I'm glad we had two so we could manage it easier."

"Well, I'm touched you thought of me." Yet today Violet felt like saying anything but those words. Today she felt ... today she felt like she was still dreaming.

It was still a nightmare.

Violet felt if, today, she held one, cradled it close, looked into its face, touched its small hands, she would somehow realize the reality in a different way.

For after last night, her mind had begun to process the little ones in a different way. A less shining light. Now they sat in shadows, threats to her happiness, and Violet was trying to fight them ...

But she couldn't stop thinking.

That *he* had touched *her*. That they had been intimate, closer to each other than any other. That, based on the little glances and the happy smiles and the joy in their faces, they both enjoyed all that touching.

She was starting to feel insane, or at least a bit touched. And if she didn't do something soon, she was likely to explode.

She didn't stay long that day, despite the fact that Ivy clearly wanted her to be there. She ran out onto the moors behind the cottage, and she kept walking, though the wind whipped away her, threatening snow and at least cold.

"Let me die out here in the elements! I deserve to die. Why. Can't. I. Just. Die?"

Yet she didn't spontaneously combust, so instead, she was forced to keep walking. Walking, pacing, running, whatever this was, she kept her legs moving until her chest was tight with lack of breath.

And still she moved.

"How dare she name one after me? It's like a knife in my back. How dare she? I want to die. He's lain with her, of course, again and again until they slipped up and conceived. He doesn't even want babies! What were they thinking, being intimate? They should've ... kept it ... platonic."

If there was anything unreasonable about that, she wasn't at all in the mood to unpack it right at this moment.

The wheeling thoughts brought her to a halt, and she collapsed on top of the hill then, allowing her body to sink onto the packed dirt amongst the larger rocks. And there she lay, body shaking—not with sobs but with rage.

*How dare they? How dare they? How dare they?*

Violet loved Jordy, and she had loved him longer. She ought to have him. And really, there was no reason she shouldn't.

Except Ivy. She owed a lot to Ivy. How could she reconcile the two?

Betray Ivy and yet save Ivy? Love Ivy and yet love Jordy? How, how, how?

The visions reeled. Jordy's arms around her as he taught her to ice skate, even though, as it turned out, he hardly knew how himself. Reading books with Ivy, being told stories she already knew, that were far too young for her, and seeing them in a new light. Searching the Scriptures with Ivy, wandering through the grounds of McCale House with Jordy.

Oh, there was the choice again, and she could. not. choose.

There was no choice to be made. She wanted them both. She wanted Ivy, her salvation, her friend, her encouragement, her dear sister. And she wanted Jordy, to prove her worth through his lust, to make him hers, to erase her very existence by making her give up everything.

It felt as if once she had Jordy, his attention and his longing, she would not need anything else. And surely, since she wanted nothing else, this must be true.

But how? How? How?

Ivy was surprised when Violet, who had left several hours earlier, returned to the house. The day was quickly darkening, but it would be another hour or so before Jordy returned home.

"Violet!" she exclaimed, turning from the stew pot she was stirring. Slowly, responsibilities had begun to pick back up, and now she was cooking again. Alice and Peter would leave soon, and then it would just be her and the occasional help of citizens of Keefmore.

But, she felt, she was ready.

"Hello, Ivy. I have something to tell you." Violet's hair and clothes were in disarray, and she was pale save for a bright dot on either cheek that told Ivy more than even her sharp breaths that she had run all the way here.

"Are you all right? Sit down." She put down the spoon, covered the pot, and turned to the table. "Can I get you anything? Water, perhaps?"

"No, nothing. Please sit. I have much to tell you."

Ivy cocked her head and sat down. Though she didn't know what Violet could be referring to, she did know that it was something serious.

Or perhaps, at least, serious in Violet's mind. It might be something silly, or perhaps it was something a bit insane. But it was important to Violet, and that was enough for Ivy.

Violet's entire body straightened, her chin raising and her eyes becoming focused on a distant point over Ivy's head. "I am in love with Jordy."

Ivy had thought that, seated and without anything in her hands, it was impossible for her to cause any shocked-related harm, but her entire body jerked, causing the silverware on the table to rattle. "What?"

"I'm in love with Jordy. Dreadfully so. Have been since I was twelve years old, in fact, or at least that's the earliest date of which I have recollection. It might've been longer. And frankly, I got a bit tired of not telling anyone, so I'm telling you."

Spiraling thoughts filled Ivy's mind. She couldn't seem to catch onto one, though she did try. Violet in love with Jordy? Since before she'd even known her? What did that mean? Why would Violet tell her? More than that, why wouldn't she have told her years and years ago, when they were still children, before anything mattered?

For now everything mattered. It mattered, and it mattered in excess. Every action, every word, every thought must be held captive when you were an adult; there could be no passing inclinations. There was no safety within the freedom they offered, and all growth must be done in such a way that did not break vows.

And Ivy took her vows quite seriously.

She didn't know what to say or do now.

"I just thought you deserved to know. Since he's, well, presently yours." Violet cleared her throat. "I ... I don't know what else I had intended to say. I could speak for hours about my emotions on the subject, but it would do little good. The basics are laid out in the simple three words: I love him."

Trembling, Ivy gripped the edge of the table, still unsure if she entirely understood Violet's full meaning. "Why are you telling me this?"

"Because I think it's fair that you know. I care about you, Ivy, but I thought it fair to inform you that I want him, that I'm longing for him, and that if I had the chance to take him, I would. I know you won't believe it of me, but, Trifle, I need you to know that it's only a matter of time."

"Only ... a matter of time?" Utterly confused, Ivy leaned back on her chair and regarded her friend with what she hoped was a tinge of grace, though she mostly felt a sort of empty deadness that allowed for no true reaction. "Whatever do you mean, Vi? I ... I don't understand you."

"Only this." Violet leaned forward. She seemed to have regained some confidence now. "If I had the chance to take Jordy to bed, I would. There can be no hiding it now."

Then Ivy's mind seemed to snap to the present, and she jerked to her feet. "Do not—and I repeat, do *not*—talk about him that way. I know you're just in a dark time and trying to hurt me, but I will not believe it of you. That said, you are not allowed to talk about my husband that way. Not now, not ever. Do you understand me?"

She was almost surprised at herself—at the near-feral protective nature that had been roused in her—but at the same time, she was glad it was, for Violet twitched slightly. Clearly Ivy's ferocity had had an effect on her.

"I ... I can't help the way I feel," Violet stuttered out. "If I could, I would. I've tried not to love him, but I can't help it, Trifle. It's a simple fact."

"I don't care if it's a simple fact or not! He's my husband, and I need you to respect that relationship."

"But I—"

"Violet, just be quiet, for once in your life." She paced to the counter and braced her hands against it. "I won't believe it of you. I won't. If ... if this were true, surely you would have told me years ago. I don't know what madness has seized you to make you stab at me in the way that you know will hurt the most—to threaten the relationship I hold dearest—but I will not believe it. I love you, Vi." She bit out of the words, but she still said it, for no matter how sharp the sting of Violet's venom, Ivy's heart wouldn't release her friend, not yet. "Please, please don't hurt me in this way. Find another way. Stab at something else. That is too much."

"But, Ivy, I'm not making it up." Violet stood then, too, her chair scraping against the floor as she pushed it back. "Trifle, I've wanted him since almost the day I met him, since before I knew what it meant."

"Again, I will say, I don't believe you." Though a part of Ivy did believe her. That scared her more than the idea that Violet might simply lash out at her for no reason.

Granted, it wasn't unprecedented for Violet to suddenly decide to find a soft underbelly and take a knife to it. And that wasn't fun. Whenever Violet took to being particularly hurtful, Ivy either set a firm boundary or backed down. This felt a little like those times ...

A little.

But there was also honesty there, which was why Ivy had needed to turn her back to Violet. She couldn't bear to see the truth in her eyes, to know that Violet told her the truth.

That she loved Jordy. *Ivy's* Jordy. And that she had for some time and not told Ivy a word about it. Why hadn't she said anything before if it was true?

Ivy's mind wanted to begin the process of mulling over every interaction between Violet and Jordy, to seek truth, to try to see if there was anything to lend credence to Violet's claim.

No, she wouldn't let herself. At least not yet. She couldn't believe it. She couldn't.

"Look. I can prove what I'm saying is true. Do you remember All Hollow's Eve, that first year you came to Keefmore? When Jordy drank too much at the bonfire?"

Still grasping the counter, Ivy managed a nod.

"Men took him to a knoll not far from town and had him lie down. We stayed with him while he gained consciousness, but then you went to get water, and I kissed him. Ask Jordy. He remembers, for we had an argument about it the next morning, and he would tell you that it happened."

"But that was ..." A long time ago. Jordy had briefly, come to think of it, mentioned it to her at some point in the betrothal process, but he'd said it was just spite, and she'd assumed it was more of a 'peck on the cheek when they were children' situation.

Apparently she was never going to make any assumptions ever again, for even those closest could tell lies by omission.

"Ivy, I know it's hard to accept, but that's why I'm telling you. Because I want you to be forewarned. I know this isn't easy to hear, but—" Violet stopped suddenly, as if strangled by her own words.

Ivy turned to face her. "I do not accept this. I do not believe it of you. I believe that you are ... that you are hurting, as you often are. You ... you cannot help that, Vi. I understand you cannot help that. I don't blame you—not for a moment, dearest. But you must understand—and I hope this gets through to you—even if I know all those things, know you are not doing this because you want to, I ... It still hurts. So badly that I can scarcely think."

Violet straightened, her body stiff and her eyes seeming to catch on fire. "Perhaps I ought to leave."

"No, I ... I don't want you to leave. I love you." She stepped forward and stood next to Violet, close enough that she could feel the shivers quaking through her best friend, feel the way Violet's entire body was trembling as if from some great exertion, perhaps even from, in this moment, the mere effort of keeping on her feet.

"Aren't you just saying, 'I don't love you'? Perhaps that's it, after all. Perhaps my feelings for Jordy have outweighed our affection. Perhaps even now I'm thinking of ways to seduce him away from you. I suppose he might be weak, now that your body has changed, now that you can't—"

Ivy slapped Violet across the face.

Then she gasped and covered her mouth. "Vi! I ... I didn't mean that. I mean, I meant ... I meant to slap you, but it just ... came over me. I should never have struck you! But—"

Violet held up her hand. "No. I'm leaving."

"Vi!"

"I understand perfectly what I've done." She stepped forward and grasped the door handle.

Ivy felt she ought to dash forward, stop Violet, tell her not to leave, tell her she loved her ... but she didn't. She wasn't sure why she didn't, only that she didn't. She just stood there in silence while Violet did the same.

Violet was shaking even harder now, and Ivy wondered if she hesitated because of the tremors or because she wanted Ivy to stop her.

Ivy wasn't going to stop her, though. She didn't feel like doing much of anything but clinging to the back of a chair and staring straight in front of her.

Then, with a deep breath, Violet turned the doorknob and opened the door. "Good-bye, my little Trifle." Her voice was half a laugh, half a sob. "It was such a sweet time while it lasted anyway."

And with that, she stepped out of the house and left Ivy by herself, to collapse on the floor of the kitchen and weep.

# CHAPTER TWENTY-FIVE

iolet tossed open her trunk and began throwing her clothes in helter-skelter, regardless of how they might fit. She knew she'd have to repack later, though perhaps by sheer force of will she could fit all of her things in the trunk.

Regardless, time was of the essence. She must be on the coach in the morning. Thank goodness it was arriving tomorrow and not a later day, or even a later hour, for Violet could not wait. She must leave. She must run. Far, far away, and never come back.

At least, never come back soon.

She wasn't sure if this was forever, but for now, she had to hurry away.

"Violet?" Based on her voice, her aunt Daphne was standing in the doorway behind her. "What are you doing? Are you ... packing?" Her voice was full of confusion. "I thought you said you would stay through the end of the month."

She had said that, but that had been when she was sane, when the very idea of leaving filled her with dread. When she had wanted to remain more as the treasured friend and sister and aunt.

She scoffed now at those naïve thoughts. She'd been a fool, dealing with the truest sort of madness then. But now she was sane again, and now she would embrace reality.

In reality, Ivy wasn't Violet's sister, or even her friend. In reality, Violet could never make a good aunt to anyone, let alone Ivy's angels.

And in reality, Violet loved Jordy McAllen—more than that, wanted him, craved him, needed him—too much to stand by and just let him be with another. No, no. She must either stop it or leave.

So she was running, like the coward she was, afraid of the consequences, afraid of what it would do to both of them.

For though it would destroy her, would she otherwise have the restraint to resist him? No. She would not. She would not resist. And there she would be, lost, entirely lost, in a world that she didn't know of yet, couldn't understand yet. And at the same time, she felt she did understand and was willing to embrace the darkness of complete surrender.

Aunt Daphne came to her side. "Why are you leaving, Violet? Did something happen?" When Violet didn't respond, her aunt continued, "Something did happen. What was it?"

Violet didn't reply. Couldn't reply. She needed no feedback, least of all negative; it would only slow her down. She needed to move, to run, to hurry. She needed to find a way to escape the confines of her own body and soar away ... and yet she also needed to be near and of the earth.

For she could not give up this last bit of reality, this lust that tied her to real life. It was the only reality, or at least the only one she was interested in.

"Violet, are you running because of your feelings for Jordy? Is that it?" Aunt Daphne stood in the middle of the room, feet planted, glaring. "If so, you're more of a coward than I thought. I love you, but you need to face this, barefaced before God and your church. Admit your sin—this lust—and then allow yourself to move past it."

Violet rolled her eyes. As if it were that easy. "Leave me be."

"I cannot, for I love you. Don't you understand that, Violet? Has no one ever loved you? I thought Ivy would've taught you to understand about the love of God and man and how it can comfort you ... but also admonish you."

"I don't wish to be admonished."

"None of us do." Aunt Daphne sat on the edge of Violet's bed, but since she didn't attempt to stop the packing, Violet continued, emptying her drawers. She would empty this entire room into this trunk and run away with everything full, including her soul.

For if she emptied her soul, then ... well, the word "empty" was enough of an explanation, wasn't it? There was already precious little there.

Or maybe she had no soul. She didn't have a heart, at least, did she now? Yes, yes, maybe there was nothing left. Nothing at all.

All the more reason to fill herself with darkness. At least it was something to cling to.

"Violet, let me offer you grace and love if no one else will. I can love you; I do love you. I understand that all your life no one has, and you are seeking for love even now, but this is not the type of love you want." Aunt Daphne's pleading tone was unusual, and Violet paused, staring at her hands and waiting for her aunt's next words. "Let me take you to the Continent. Travel with me. See the world and let me show you that you are valued. There is so much I could tell you, could show you."

"You're settled here," Violet gritted out. "You're too old to travel. You told me so yourself."

"I did say that, but let me say this now: You mean more to me than that. I would give up a lot for you. I'm not ashamed to say you're my favorite niece—almost my favorite person—even with your bitterness. I don't care. I've loved far bitterer people than you, and I will love bitterer still."

Violet shook her head and turned to the wardrobe. She ripped out dresses, wrinkling and crumpling them in her haste.

"I see you do not believe me," Aunt Daphne said softly. "Violet, let's go even if you don't believe me! Please. Trust me when I say, speaking from a great deal of life experience, that clinging to bitterness over those who have mistreated you only lends to more bitterness. It doesn't fix anything. And furthermore, this lust—"

"It is love!" Violet snapped. "It's love, all right? I don't care what you or anyone says. It's love. And though I may call it lust, for it certainly contains that element, love is a part of it. I want what's best for him. That's all I want! He isn't happy with her. He never has been. She has ... she has no passion. She's holding him back. He had so much ambition, so much potential, and she's smothered him, turning him into this ... this small-town doctor who will never go anywhere or do anything. He's stifled away—he will live and die here, never rising to the future he could claim!"

"So there it is." Aunt Daphne sighed. "I wondered when you would admit it."

"It's true!" Violet's hands fisted, and her fingernails dug into her palms. "In his heart, he has always wanted more. He used to dream of castles in the sky, and look at him now, in that tiny cottage. He'll never go any further with her, and now the babies, weighing him down. She. Is. Smothering. Him!"

"But, Violet, if you would only listen to—"

"No! I will not listen, for I am right. He has lost everything that would make him great."

"Or he has found where his greatness truly lies."

Violet shook her head. "He could've been a grand doctor in London or taken over McCale House or started his own sanitarium. Or spoken, or traveled ... Made real, great changes in the world."

"But, Violet, have you considered that if a woman at times can find greatness in a calling as a wife and mother, a man can find greatness in a calling as a husband and father? What do we know but that he will raise the person who will do those great things you refer to? Or perhaps—"

"No. I was raised with him, and I know." She understood Jordy inside and out, and he could never be content where he was now.

Violet had seen Jordy grow, heard him dream, talked to him as he worked through one problem in life after another. She'd heard him speak of his deepest fears and struggles.

She'd loved him in spite of his faults and, more than that,

respected him. Seen what he was capable of. He could help people. He could make a name for himself in this world. He could become truly wonderful. And yet, Ivy was holding him back from that very goal.

Honestly, if Ivy weren't her Trifle, she would have to hate her.

But she didn't hate Ivy. That was the thing. If she hated Ivy, she would have to be a little more cautious, for no sane person would hate Ivy. Once her goals were accomplished, she could return again and make up, but until then, she just had to bear through and get things done.

Then she would come back to Ivy. And Ivy would forgive her. She always did. That said, it wasn't entirely necessary that Ivy know the full truth, or any of the truth, for it was clear she wasn't able to handle it.

Yes, it was better to leave Ivy out of it ...

There was nothing inherently wrong with Ivy. She was just different. A different kind of love, a different kind of salvation.

And, perhaps, if Violet kept these two worlds separate, she could have them both.

Aunt Daphne continued on, pleading with Violet, but her words were too much, and Violet didn't want to hear it.

She finished packing, managed to get the trunk's lid closed, and put a few small, necessary items in her carpetbag. She'd see in the morning that these things got onto the coach.

For now, she was simply glad to have finally succeeded in ejecting Aunt Daphne from her room, and lying on the bed.

For the first time in many years, she let herself dream, really dream.

Violet was gone, and Ivy wasn't quite sure how she felt about it.

On one hand, she was relieved. Violet's proclamation the night before her departure had shaken Ivy to the bone. She didn't believe her, no. At least, she didn't *think* she believed her.

Though a part of her did, certainly. She had seen truth in Violet's eyes. But one thing she'd learned from being friends with Violet for so long was that Violet could believe something and yet it might not be the absolute truth. Or even if she didn't believe it, she could put her fears or worries forward as an absolute.

On the other hand, watching Violet leave was never easy. It was like watching a part of her heart disappear, only to be brought back again at a random whim. For it was random. Or at least it felt random to Ivy.

She prayed for Violet, but for the first time, she felt a restraint on her heart. She didn't write. She didn't send letters to McCale House or to Felix begging for someone to check in on her.

And she didn't tell Jordy. For she couldn't. She didn't have the words to describe to him what Violet had told her, or perhaps she didn't want to find the words.

Perhaps she was a little afraid, in her deepest heart of hearts, that his desire equaled what Violet herself claimed to feel.

But Ivy didn't let herself think about that. She went on with her life, went on with caring for her babies and spending time with her family and doing all she could to not think about Violet.

The days slipped by, into weeks, into months. Alice and Peter went home, and people came and went from the cottage, helping Ivy ... and sometimes not helping.

The winter was long and hard, but her purpose in life was different. Different wasn't always better. However, in this case, the love Ivy felt for her daughters brought a different feel to the entire season which in the past had been such a difficult one for her.

This winter was still difficult in its own ways. In some ways, surviving this season was the hardest thing she had ever done. All right—in *all* ways. But she didn't care. Being a mother was ... indescribable.

Molly and Letty were her entire world now. In some ways, that was easier than before. Everything came down to them, from every slight movement to the bigger decisions of life. They simplified and complicated things all at once.

Winter turned again to spring, and that June, as the world turned to summer, Jordy took her up onto the hill overlooking their cottage. They brought the girls along and laid out a blanket and set them free, much to their mother's anxiety.

Letty was the venturesome one, already wanting to crawl away, while Molly was content to snuggle in Ivy or Jordy's arms—primarily Ivy's, as that was where the feedings came from.

Jordy and Ivy chatted about this and that, dreamt for the babies, and just caught up. There was a never-ending battle to play the same tune, or at least the melody and the harmony, in a marriage, and Ivy felt they'd only just started to understand how to maintain that.

"Ye never told me wha' became o' Vi. Is she no' comin' this summer? I'd an idea ye had a fallin' oot when th' twins were newly born, but at th' time, it seemed unimportant next tae all th' busyness."

"Oh ... well. We did have a falling out. Not a dramatic one. We just ... She needs some time to collect herself again."

Jordy nodded his approval to that. Thank God for Jordy, always siding with her even when she didn't explain herself very well. "Aye. Tha's good. Give Vi some time tae stew an' she'll come back tae ye, as she always does."

Ivy hoped so. For she couldn't live a life entirely devoid of her dear friend Violet. It just wouldn't seem right.

But for now, at least, she must trust the Lord to tend to Violet's soul. "I think she needs to find herself away from me. Not herself, really, I suppose. I mean God."

"O' course. We all fight tha' battle one time or another in life, an' Vi has relied on ye for so long. Give her time tae come tae God on her own terms."

*But what if she doesn't?* Ivy frowned and pulled Little Molly onto her lap, pressing kisses amongst the growing blonde curls.

"I ken wha' ye're thinkin'." Ivy looked up to find her husband's eyes on her, his smile affectionate. "God has Vi in His hands as sure as He has us. Trust Him tae care for her, a'right? He has her soul, I suppose, an' He will reach her. Dinna fear, Vee. Trust."

Ivy took a deep breath and breathed it out slowly. "Thank you for that, Jordy. You're right. I needn't fear, for Vi is safe with our God."

"Besides." He held a hand out to her, and she slid over a few inches to lean against him, her head resting perfectly against his chest and his arm cradling both their elder child and her. "We have enough tae focus on ourselves, dinna we? Raisin' these two ... an' any others tha' come along."

She glanced up at his face, but he didn't seem at all bothered by that pronouncement. His heart had changed, hadn't it, then? But to see him with the girls, that wasn't any surprise.

"You're right that it is a full-time job."

"Aye, raisin' our wee princesses an' all." He winked. "They'll be mobile soon, Vee, an' then we'd best be diggin' moats an' buildin' drawbridges around th' castle tae keep them still."

She laughed. "You're not half wrong. Ena said in a few months, I'll be wishing I didn't own anything but the biggest pieces of furniture, and even that will cause problems. But I'm sure we'll manage."

"Ach, aye, I'm sure we will." He leaned forward then and caught Letty by the hem of her skirt. "Ye wee monster. Tryin' tae escape again? Ye're far tae wee for tha'. Vee, dinna ye think she's ahead o' th' other bairns? I think she is. I dinna think any born tha' same month have really begun tae crawl yet as she has ..."

Ivy smiled at this. She thought Letty was right on time with her crawling, but Jordy liked to make everything about the girls into a competition, both between them and against every other child in Keefmore.

It didn't help, of course, that Tris was playing the same game with his newest baby, Keith, even though he was a few months older than the girls. *Men.* Ivy couldn't help but find it at least a little amusing.

Jordy lay on his back and held Letty up in the air, and Ivy demanded he put her down, but even her grasp on the girls' safety was slipping.

They were growing up before her eyes. Why, it was only a matter of months until she might be able to expect them to begin to walk, or at least stand, according to Ena. And especially according to Jordy, who thought Keith wouldn't walk before the girls.

An empty dream, of course, but it showed his adoration for them.

"Jordy," Ivy murmured.

"Aye, love?"

"We haven't left the dreamland yet. We're still in it."

He grinned. "Whoever told ye otherwise?"

"You did."

"Ach, weel, I was an idiot before I became a father. 'Tis taught me some new definitions for dreams in a hurry." He winked and returned to Letty, who was now exploring his face with her hands and tugging at his hair with both fists.

Ivy allowed Molly to leave her lap to join in torturing 'Da,' and plucked a daisy from the hillside.

*He loves me, he loves me, he loves me ...*

# A Note to the Reader

Dear Reader,

Thank you for being a participant in this continuing story! I can't believe we're already all the way to book 6, and yet here we are. A few years ago, I honestly wouldn't have believed we'd get this far, but thankfully, God had other plans.

I actually didn't intend to write this novel until 2021. I thought I would skip straight from book 5 to a different book entirely which would be set a full eight years later, in 1890 (with some novellas which would summarize events in-between).

However, that just wasn't working. There were too many plot points in-between ...

And I also realized I had a lot to say about Jordy and Ivy's early marriage, and the way Violet played into that.

So I outlined it and set it aside to get married myself. A few months after, when the wedding rush had calmed down and my husband and I were settled into our new apartment, I wrote the novel.

The jury's still out on whether this was a good idea or not. Though my marriage is absolutely nothing like Jordy and Ivy's, I still found myself relating with Ivy more than I ever had before. I was also dealing with my own journey toward motherhood, and as I worked on the book over the next year, I found a lot of my experiences sneaking in, for better or for worse.

This made writing Ivy's emotions easy. It also made it a tough book for me to re-structure and edit. However, with the help of my alpha readers, my editors Grace Johnson and Andrea Cox, and of course my brainstorming partners, I was able to create the book you just finished reading.

However, the series isn't over! I'm looking forward to returning to Ivy, Jordy, and Violet in book 8, *Love Once Lost.* In the meantime, be on the lookout for book 7, *Time of Grief.*

Until then, you can follow along by joining my newsletter or checking me out at social media.

You can find the information about all of that on my website:

https://kellynrothauthor.com/

Can't wait to meet you!
Until next time,

Kellyn Roth
October 2022
White Salmon, WA